D1364144

For ANNE PARRISH

"There are many choices and none is absolute;
and over the mountains there are people also."

By **LAVINIA R. DAVIS**

Come
Be My Love

Illustrated by Artur Marokvia

SCHOLASTIC  BOOK SERVICES

Published by Scholastic Book Services, a division
of Scholastic Magazines, Inc., New York, N.Y.

CONTENTS

CHAPTER	PAGE
To-morrow and To-morrow	1
The Blue Remembered Hills	7
Happily I Think on Thee	19
Walk Proudly Friended	28
Green and Pleasant Land	38
A Small House and Large Garden	47
Patterns	59
Home County	73
Nothing Unobserved!	82
Past with a Future	93
Land of Lost Content	105
In Gardens, when the Eve Is Cool	115
In Shadow of a Green Oak Tree	122
Hive of Glass	131
Seesaw	143
Beautiful for Patriot's Dreams	155
Listen, the Wind!	168
Pinkie!	178
The Storm Is Up	189
Come Be My Love	197
New-Minted World	209
Give My Love Good Morrow	216
Judgment Rock	225
This Bubble, Reputation	232
The Big Wheel Turns by Faith	244

1. TO-MORROW AND TO-MORROW

THE BOLTONS were moving. For weeks the comfortably shabby apartment where for four years they had eaten and slept, quarreled and made up, been unhappy and more often very happy indeed, had held out against change. Even after the trunks were up and the curtains came down the old place had continued to be home, but that was all over now. The few pieces of absolutely essential furniture and the irremovable landmarks like the roller-skate marks in the hall and the maps pasted up in the kitchen only underlined the emptiness. On the first day of June the Boltons would be gone for good, and now, on the twenty-eighth of May, apartment 5B, reeking of moth balls and echoing with the tramp of the moving men's feet, was no more homelike than a packing box.

In the living room Mrs. Bolton directed the movers, answered the telephone, and tried to pour tea out of a cracked teapot for her old school friend, Fay Clarkson. The twins hammered away on a traveling cage for their white mice, and Mr. Bolton carefully crated the banjo clock which had always hung in the hall.

Only Jib, standing alone in the temporary privacy of the bathroom, was no part of the maelstrom. Jib, officially listed at Foyle's Junior College as Jessica Infield Bolton, had so much on her mind that not even the most strenuous sounds and smells of moving could reach her. She stood very still and looked out of the window with tear-glazed eyes. She did not notice the dusty yards and the dreary tenement roofs below her, but if she had, the view would have seemed gay and cheerful compared to her own thoughts. The coming summer, which was what was bothering her, spread out in her mind's eye like a battle-wasted landscape. The prospect was hopeless, and the fact that it was nobody's fault but her own only added to her misery.

She turned numbly and picked up the letter which a few moments earlier she had flung from her in a spasm of disgust. The letter had fallen into the bathtub and one end of it looked tear-blistered from the dripping tap, but every word of it was still regrettably clear. The writer of the letter was Miss Martha Brandon, head of Pine Point Camp, where last summer Jib had served as councilor; its purpose was to inform Jib that since her application for a similar position for the coming summer had not been received until the previous Tuesday, Miss Brandon had been forced to assume that Jib had made other plans and so had filled her place some weeks earlier.

No one, so Miss Brandon wrote, could regret this decision more than she did, but it was a disagreeable necessity which she was certain both Jib and her parents would understand. As Jib reread those last words she fumbled blindly for the remaining bath towel, buried her face in it, and sobbed.

Jib had written to Miss Brandon late in March instead

2

of February, but the rub was that she had mailed the letter in the pocket of a seldom-used coat and found it again only when she had taken the coat to the cleaners a week ago. She had written a second letter at once and, since her family's plans were all based on her going to Pine Point, had said nothing, hoping superstitiously that if she never mentioned what had happened doom might be averted.

But doom, in the form of this very letter, had caught up with Jib a half hour ago when she had returned to the denuded apartment after a farewell visit to friends. Here it was, in impersonal and unfeeling typescript that no amount of rereading could change. Miss Brandon was friendly, even cordial, but also blunt. The reason for the delayed application seemed to her an indication of Jib's vagueness and immaturity, and, as Jib must understand, all Pine Point councilors were in positions of responsibility and *trust*.

T R U S T. Each underlined letter was a separate grain of salt on an open wound. It wasn't so much that Jib had broken faith with Miss Brandon, who was more than able to take care of herself, but what about the family? Months ago, just when Jib had been absorbed in her class play, both Mum and Dad had asked if she had heard from Miss Brandon. She had not lied to them, neither directly nor unintentionally, but the result was falsehood. With her mind, her whole soul at that time concentrated on the sophomore production of *Macbeth*, she had simply by-passed their questions. She was going to Pine Point—it was all months off, of course, but she was definitely going. In the meantime would either Mum or Dad help her to rehearse her part?

Just then Dickie, who was one of the eleven-year-old twins, stamped into the bathroom. "The mice need water," he said, and then, seeing Jib's blotchy face, looked up at her critically. "What's the matter with you?" he demanded. "Been reading another tear-jerker?"

3

"Don't be ridiculous!" Jib hung away the towel as though the idea of crying over a book were an absurd impossibility. "Are Mum and Dad alone?"

"Nope." Dickie filled a sardine can with water. "And it doesn't look as though they were going to be. Mrs. Clarkson's sure to stay for supper. I bet she'd spend the night if we had enough beds. She often used to at Cobble Top. Jeepers, I wish we were going there instead of to California."

With that he slammed the door behind him, and Jib groped for the towel again. Cobble Top was the name of the cottage in the hills outside of the Berkshire village of Quentin Oldtown where Mr. Bolton had been born. Always before, no matter where his work took them in the winter, Mrs. Bolton and the children had gone back to Cobble Top for the summer. They all loved the place, and the children had looked forward to going there even more than they looked forward to Christmas and birthdays.

If I could only go to Cobble Top by myself, Jib thought, I'd earn my living somehow. Instantly a complete panorama passed through Jib's mind. She could see the remote little house and herself as its solitary and romantic chatelaine. But it was no use pretending. Cobble Top was rented to strangers and, as a loud knock sounded on the bathroom door, Jib's vision faded.

"Jib. Hey, Jib, are you still in there?" This time it was John, the other twin. "Mum wants to know if you want some tea. There's crumb cake and crullers."

"Yes. No. No, I don't want anything," Jib said and searched around for powder. There was none left out, and she compromised with running a comb through her curly red-brown hair. The effect, since she had not dried her face and her eyes were red-rimmed, was of a half-drowned Ophelia, but Jib's mind was on *Macbeth*.

"There would have been a time for such a word. To-morrow, and to-morrow, and to-morrow, creeps in this

4

petty pace from day to day, to the last syllable of recorded time." Jib was engrossed with the gloomiest of all Macbeth's speeches from the bathroom to the threshold of the living room.

"Jib. You look a sight!" Mrs. Fay Clarkson's voice cut through Jib's thoughts like a knife cutting cheesecake. "For goodness sake, what happened? Did your best beau jilt you?"

Jib shook her head, stiffening, and then caught her mother's eye. "What is it, darling?" Mrs. Bolton gestured silently to the seat beside her on the sofa. "Was it saying good-by to the girls at Foyle's?"

"No. No, it isn't that," Jib said, and then, avoiding her mother's eyes, blurted out exactly what had happened. "It's all my fault, Mum," she finished. "But I'll get another job somehow. I know I will."

For a long-drawn-out moment nobody said anything at all, and then Mrs. Bolton spoke and her soft voice was gentler than ever. "Why, Jib," she said, "you poor lamb. You've known this might happen since last Tuesday when you found your first letter and you kept it all to yourself?"

"Yes," Jib said, and for an instant she felt proud, stoical, and almost pleased with herself, and then Mrs. Clarkson spoke.

"Well, all of us are fools sometimes. But now, Mary, the point is what are you going to do with her? It's too late to apply for another camp job, and since you haven't got money to throw away I don't suppose you'll want to take her to California until you're decently settled?"

"We'll manage some——"

"I'm not a child——"

Both Mrs. Bolton and Jib were talking at the same time when Mr. Bolton came into the room. He said nothing until he had heard the whole story, and then he moved over to the window. "Perhaps Honey and Oliver Stirling could take her," he said. "They moved back to

5

Oldtown during the war when Oliver had that break-down."

Oldtown was near Cobble Top! For an instant Jib's spirits soared, and then the next second, as she realized she hardly knew her Stirling cousins, who were her father's generation, they drooped again. Mrs. Bolton moved over to her husband, looking distressed and uncertain, and then Mrs. Clarkson made a suggestion. "I have a better scheme," she said and tapped a cigarette on a manicured thumbnail. "Tricksie Appersley—you remember John Appersley, Jack—who lives in that big house with the portico on Quentin Ridge is looking for some young thing to help her as a sort of social secretary during the summer. I ran into her last Friday at Bergdorf's sale and she told me she hadn't found the right girl. I'm almost sure she'd take Jib on my recommendation."

"I can't type, at least not much," Jib said, but Mrs. Clarkson waved away the interruption.

"Any baby could type enough for this job," she said, "and at least you have a decently sophisticated handwriting. What Tricksie really wants is someone young and energetic to help with parties. A flea brain could handle it. She doesn't pay much more than pocket money, but there's the board and lodging, and Jib would be in on all her entertainments. Personally, if I was nineteen or twenty I'd snap it up, but of course if Jib hasn't enough spunk to try it she'd better go to Honey."

"I hardly know the Appersleys, or any of the Ridge people, for that matter," Mrs. Bolton murmured, but Jib was so caught by the challenge imbedded in Mrs. Clarkson's last sentence that she hardly heard her.

"I'll take the job," she said and looked straight at Mrs. Clarkson. "If Mrs. Appersley will have me, I'd like to go."

2. THE BLUE REMEMBERED HILLS

JIB HAD no sooner spoken than Mrs. Clarkson stood up. "I'll telephone Tricksie at once, then," she said. "I happen to know she's spending the night in town." And the three Boltons, feeling like puppets in the hands of a master, watched her go to the hall telephone without saying a word.

"It's all arranged!" she said when she came back into the room a few minutes later. "I must say, Jib, I think I've done a good job for you."

"Th-thanks a million," Jib said breathlessly, and then her mother spoke.

"I think it's wonderful of you, Fay," she said, "and of course I'm grateful to Mrs. Appersley too, but before Jib goes I want to speak to Honey Stirling and be absolutely certain that Jib can stay with them if she isn't happy at the Appersleys'."

"Fiddlesticks!" Mrs. Clarkson snuffed out her cigarette.

"Honey means well, of course, but think of what the Appersleys have to offer. No girl who isn't an absolute washout would turn that down."

So it had been settled. As Mrs. Clarkson was going to the Appersleys' for a visit she and Jib went up on the train together, and a few days later, when Jib went to Cobble Top to make sure that the cottage was ready for the new tenants, Mrs. Clarkson drove her over.

Right now, as Jib stood on the familiar porch, she tried to pretend that this was like any one of a thousand other June afternoons when she had stood on this same spot to enjoy the view. It was no use. Even the unnatural neatness of the porch itself was a giveaway. Always before it had been littered with the twins' toys and Mum's painting equipment. The family's bathing suits, never entirely dry, had flapped congenially from the porch railing. Now there wasn't so much as a book of Dad's or a newspaper on one of the worn chairs or the old hammock.

Jib turned away from the house and looked out over the three Quentins. On the east was the Ridge, where the country club and a row of palatial summer houses stood out from the surrounding green like the raised pictures in a scrapbook. Westward, at Quentin Mills, the sunlight glinted on the tall smokestacks of the factories and outlined the squares of workmen's houses. Straight ahead, a few miles beyond the mountain known as Quentin's Cobble, was the smaller village of Quentin Oldtown and beyond that the Oldtown Hills rose up and up and then fell away into purple space and infinity.

Jib's eyes lingered on the hills, and the words of a poem she had learned years ago slowly fused in her mind. "What are those blue remembered hills, what spires, what farms are those? That is the land of lost content, I see it shining plain——"

The sharp blast of a motor horn sounded from the other side of the cottage! Jib jumped and hurried across the porch to lock the door. For a moment the key, which

Mum had given her the day she had left New York, refused to turn in the rusty lock. The horn sounded again, louder and more obviously annoyed. Jib gave a desperate twist, turned the key, and fled toward the road where Mrs. Clarkson was waiting for her.

"I thought you were lost or had fallen through those old floor boards or something," Mrs. Clarkson said, and although her words were light enough, her voice, like her French horn, held sharp overtones.

"I'm terribly sorry," Jib apologized. "I was looking at the view, and then when I tried the key it was frightfully stiff."

Mrs. Clarkson let in the clutch and drove the Appersleys' smart sports roadster down the mountain road. "It's a miracle to me your mother got the right one. But then she always does land on her feet. Nobody else would have been able to rent that shack in a million years."

Jib turned away from the smartly dressed, ultrasophisticated woman beside her and looked at the side of the road. It's for the last time, her heart said; you don't know when you'll be at Cobble Top again. They passed a mossy hillock where the six-year-old Jib had played Indians, and the tears stung in the nineteen-year-old Jib's eyes. She blinked them away. "I wonder who rented Cobble Top?" she said. "All the family heard was that it was two young men who've just moved here to work."

Mrs. Clarkson managed to shrug and turn the car skillfully around a treacherous corner in what seemed like one gesture. "Mill hands, I expect, or small-time shopkeepers."

"It'd be fun if they turned out to be friendly," Jib said. "I'd like to be able to go back there once in a while and write to Mum and Dad and the twins that everything's all right."

"First wait and see what sort they are," Mrs. Clarkson cautioned. "More freaks moving in here every day, if you ask me. And of course in your circumstances at the Appersleys' you can't be too careful."

Jib said nothing, but her eyes looked worried. She had been at the Appersleys' for three days now, and she didn't have the faintest idea of what her job, let alone her "circumstances," were. She had typed out two letters to New York shops and written out a longhand acceptance to a dinner invitation. When she had asked Mrs. Appersley about further work that lady had either fluttered on about one of her many enthusiasms or told Jib that she simply wanted her to enjoy herself. Once Jib had screwed up her nerve to ask what pay she was to receive over and above her board and lodging, but Mrs. Appersley had looked miffed and Jib hadn't dared to bring up the subject again.

"I think we'll stop in at the club," Mrs. Clarkson said. "All the young crowd will be out by the pool, and I could use a nice quiet cocktail in the bar."

Still Jib said nothing. She had always been so happy at Cobble Top that it was only within the last few days that she had realized that during all the vacations which her family had spent there they had never mingled with the community around them. Her parents had not belonged to the country club, and during the afternoons she had spent there since coming to the Appersleys' she had felt like a cat in a strange garret. The very fact that whichever way she looked she saw the Cobble, or any one of a dozen other familiar landmarks, only increased the strangeness.

As they drove up the bluestone driveway Mrs. Clarkson looked over at Jib. "At the pool you should go out of your way to make friends," she said. "Tricksie simply adores young people if they're the right kind."

Jib swallowed and hated herself because she couldn't think of a word to say. She had known for ages that Mrs. Clarkson and Mum were as different in their enjoyments, their standards, and their outlook on life as two very old friends could be, but right now that knowledge was cold comfort. Mum was on her way to California, and Mrs. Clarkson, who was most emphatically here, obviously expected her to be popular with people who were hardly aware of her existence.

Jib walked slowly toward the pool and one or two of the gang looked up and nodded or waved languidly and then, the next moment, went right on talking to one another. Jib had been introduced to them all only a few days ago. She had said at once that she had always spent her summers in the district, only to realize a second later that she had made a mistake. "Oh?" Mibsie Tarrant had said. "How funny you never came over to the club." From then on nobody had bothered about her enough to be actually rude, but they had somehow, and perhaps unconsciously, closed ranks and left her on the outside.

This afternoon Jib tried again to join in the conversation, but it was like playing a card game without knowing the rules. She asked Bill Hopper if he were spending the summer at the Ridge and he shook his head. "I've a job on a ranch starting next month," he said and then turned to talk to Mibsie Tarrant. Jib tried the same question on Jake Swann, but he told her he was going to work on somebody's yacht and another conversation died still-born.

The girls were even more difficult. None of them seemed to have jobs, nor had she learned about anything else in which they were deeply interested. Quentin Ridge, the country club, and the pool from which so much of their social life seemed to stem was nothing to them, it appeared. They simply took it for granted, and the very apathy of their acceptance made Jib feel more of an outsider than ever.

She was just wondering if she could find Mrs. Clarkson when a girl whom she hadn't seen before appeared at the edge of the pool.

11

"Stella!" "Hi, Stella!" "Stella Drelincourt, where have you been?" "Come on over, you stranger."

Jib turned to see who had excited such a sudden and universal response and saw a tall young woman with black wavy hair and light eyes. "Hello, everybody," she said, and her voice was low and throbbing like a torch singer's. "Oh, thanks for the chair, Jake." That was all, but the effect on the gang around the pool was electric. Jake looked smug, and Bill Hopper and Stew Harris, who had been slower than he had, looked irritated. Bracket Baits, who had been stretched out half asleep on the grass, sat up now at Stella's feet, as posed and erect as an after-shave ad. Fatsy Hammond, who was younger than most of the rest of the gang, and who had been eating peanuts ever since Jib had arrived, offered some to Stella and then, when she shook her head, tossed his bag out of sight as though he were ashamed of it.

The girls were equally affected. Two of them powered their noses, and Bet Barnes welcomed Stella as though they had met in the heart of the jungle. Mibsie Tarrant, who had a reputation for wisecracks, tried so hard to be funny that her voice sounded edgy.

"Stella darling, this is Jib Bolton." Bet Barnes was the one who finally remembered an introduction. "She's staying with the Appersleys for the summer."

Stella's hazel-green eyes glowed on Jib. "You're in luck," she said. "I think Mrs. App is a lamb, and they give the best parties."

"Are you going to be staying here too?" Jib asked. "I hope you are."

"Why, you sweet little thing, you," Stella said, and her smile shut out everyone but Jib and herself. "I wish I were, but I work at Powers' in New York. I only come up here when Cousin Annie Sage crashes through with an invitation. It's definitely, but definitely, not like staying with the Appersleys, but anything's better than town over the week ends."

12

"Oh, have pity, have pity on the Poor Woiking Goil," Mibsie croaked, but nobody paid the slightest attention. The boys were all concentrated on Stella and the girls were all concentrated on the boys. All of them, that is, except Jib, who now that she had encountered this fascinating stranger was suddenly delighted that she was staying at the Appersleys'. The very fact that Stella was older and more sophisticated than any of her friends at college only made her the more entrancing, and by the time Mrs. Clarkson called to her from the club veranda she actually hated to leave.

"It was wonderful of you to arrange for me to stay at the Appersleys'," she said as she climbed into the car. "And terribly good of them to take me."

Mrs. Clarkson smiled, and Jib saw how ages ago she really might have been as pretty as Mum said. "I knew you'd have fun," she said. "The minute I thought of it I knew it was better than anything else you could possibly do. I've only met your father's cousin Honey once, but I must confess she struck me as a bit on the worthy side. As for that iceberg husband of hers!"

"I've never met Cousin Oliver." Jib floundered between loyalty and politeness. "And I haven't seen Cousin Honey since I was a kid, but I know Mother always thought she was wonderful."

Mrs. Clarkson gave a high, fluty laugh. "Of course," she said. "Your mother loves everybody. She's always been so beautiful and talented herself that she doesn't understand that the rest of us who have to live by our wits must train ourselves to be choosy."

It was so transparently clear that she did not include Jib in the beautiful and talented class that Jib felt decidedly uncomfortable, and their arrival at the Appersleys' great white house was not reassuring. A smartly uniformed maid who had come in for the evening opened the door, and Mrs. Appersley, who looked like a heavily upholstered counterpart of Mrs. Clarkson, stood

13

right behind her. "I thought you two were never going to come," she said. "Dinner's at quarter of seven, which is a perfectly ungodly hour, but we're going to the Berksbridge Players. I've asked every attractive young thing for miles around to go with us."

"Tricksie's certainly starting off your social career with a bang!" Mrs. Clarkson said and turned to Jib with a look that so plainly expected the right answer that Jib felt as though she were about ten years old and expected to dive off the high board in public.

"It's terribly good of you, Mrs. Appersley," she began. "I honestly don't know how to thank you."

"It's all right, my dear, but for goodness sake call me Tricksie. All the rest of the young crowd do, you know. After all, I am years younger than your mother or Fay."

Fay Clarkson's carefully plucked eyebrows arched upward. She opened her mouth to speak and then, changing her mind, lit a cigarette. Jib, who had caught the look and guessed what was going on in Mrs. Clarkson's mind, managed not to laugh. "Yes. Thanks ever so much Mrs. Ap—I mean Tricksie," she said, and with that Mrs. Appersley shooed both Mrs. Clarkson and herself upstairs to dress.

"Your prettiest dress, now," Mrs Clarkson said as they parted in the hall. "The one I heckled your mother into buying for you early this spring. There's nothing more important that a first impression."

"Yes, of course," Jib said, but the high-board feeling was stronger than ever. She and her mother had never bought that dress. Mum, who had just sold a painting, had taken her to see it, but when they had learned the price Mother had turned white. "Fay didn't say what it cost," she murmured. "I feel terribly, Jib darling, but I simply can't afford it."

They had ended up with a dress that Jib had liked quite as well at a fraction of the price. There had been money left for shirts for the twins and twelve dollars beside. Jib had urged Mum to buy herself a new hand-bag, but Mum had insisted on getting balcony theater tickets for the whole family. "I do like my family," Mum had said late that night when the twins were in bed and she and Jib were telling Dad all about their shopping trip. "Fay Clarkson picked out an entrancing dress for Jib, but when we found out how much it cost she acted just as pleased over one for a tenth of the price."

"Which I am," Jib had said. "It's the dreamiest dress in the world." She had meant it at the time, but right now, as she took it out of the closet, she was not so sure.

It was carefully pressed, but the tear which she had gotten in it at the sophomore party still showed after being mended, and once she put it on, the neckline wasn't as becoming as it had been before she had collected her season's crop of little freckles. It'll have to do, she thought and began brushing her hair, hoping desperately that Mrs. Clarkson would have forgotten exactly what the dress which she had picked out had looked like.

Jib need not have worried. By the time she reached the bottom of the stairs Mrs. Clarkson was talking to two strange young men, and Mrs. Appersley swarmed over to Jib and began to introduce her to the various people whom she had not already met. Just as that was done someone else arrived and Mrs. Appersley puffed off like a tugboat in satin.

Jib found herself standing next to Jake Swann and asked him if he knew whether Stella Drelincourt was coming. "Yes, and with Stew Harris, the lucky bum," he said. "God, she's beautiful."

For the first time Jib felt honestly drawn toward Jake Swann "Isn't she, though?" she said. "It's her color, I think You know, like the woman in 'She walks with Beauty like the night, and all that's best of dark and light, meet——' "

Jake looked actually terrified and walked off to join a group of other boys before Jib had even finished. She tried her luck with Mouse Duncan, and this time, although she was careful not to quote poetry, she was hardly more successful, and she was glad when they went in to dinner.

She found herself between Mr. Appersley and Stew Harris, who had Stella on his other side. Stew was polite and friendly enough when Jib tried one or two remarks, but his mind was clearly on Stella, and Jib, who couldn't blame him, soon gave up trying to attract his attention. At that point she noticed that the roses in the center-piece were of an unusual, curiously deep shade of scarlet which she had always associated with Cobble Top. How Mum would love those, she thought. If we'd had them at home she'd have started sketching them while the rest of us were all still eating. The idea brought back Cobble Top so vividly that for a moment Jib was trans-ported, and then she caught Mrs. Clarkson signaling to her across the table and realized that she was expected to talk to Mr. Appersley.

"Those are the most heavenly flowers," she said. "I've never seen anything lovelier."

"Tricksie seems to like them," Mr. Appersley said. "But I can't say as I can get awfully excited. But then I guess most men don't care about flowers. They only have to pay for 'em."

"My father loves flowers," Jib said, and then, worrying for fear she had been rude, added, "Mostly wild ones, of course, and the ones we grow ourselves. He used to take me off hunting for wild orchis when I was about six."

"O.K. if you have time for it," Mr. Appersley said. "Your father's Jack Bolton, isn't he?"

"Yes, he is. How nice you remember him. Dad was afraid you wouldn't, because he's only been here in the summer since he was a little boy."

"I know him." Mr. Appersley bent over his turtle soup so that the candlelight reflected on his bald spot. "Short, blond chap. I used to see him at the Niblick Club in New York."

16

Jib, whose father was tall and dark and who had never belonged to a New York club in his life, felt like a pricked balloon. "I'm afraid that's not my——" she began, but by that time the fish had appeared and Mr. Appersley had turned to the girl on his right.

It'll be better later on, Jib encouraged herself. I'll have a chance to talk to Stella, and the play is sure to be fun.

But as soon as the coffee had been served, Stella rustled off with the other girls to the unused guest room, leaving Jib to get ready alone. Later, when they reached the summer play-house, Stella was seated on the other side of the theater, and the play was the one Jib had seen from the peanut gallery with her family in New York. She still might have enjoyed it if the best lines had not been drowned by sibilant whispers from Mibsie Tarrant, whose seat was directly behind Jib's. Mibsie was trying hard to outsmart the playwright, and she was apparently successful, because at the end of the play, when the whole party clustered around Mrs. Appersley to say good night, Jake Swann stood right at her elbow ready to drive her off.

"Is little Cinderella going home with the old folks?" Mr. Appersley asked when Jib got in beside him in the front seat of his car after Mrs. Clarkson and Mrs. Appersley had gone into the rear. "I thought all you kids were going over to Duke's Mill to dance?"

"I'm not going," Jib said and didn't tell him that no one had asked her. Once they reached the house, Jib said good night and started for the stairs. She moved quickly, but even so she could not avoid hearing Mrs. Appersley's high, excited voice. "Now honestly, Fay, you swore to me that child was attractive, and after seeing the mother, who has got looks in a vague sort of way, I believed you."

Mrs. Clarkson's tinkling laughter set Jib's teeth on edge. "I must confess she was mousy tonight. Always has been the plain child of a beautiful mother, but I must say up to now I thought there were possibilities. Perhaps——"

Jib ran so that she would not hear another word and darted into her darkened room. Outside the moonlight shone down on Quentin's Cobble and lit the face of Judgment Rock, but Jib never noticed it. She wasn't on the high dive any more. She had dropped and taken such a belly flop that she didn't have enough breath left even to cry.

3. HAPPILY I THINK ON THEE

THE SOUND of the vacuum cleaner woke Jib at half-past eight. She dressed and looked out of the window to the westward, where the smokestacks of Quentin Mills were already sending out smutty streamers against the early sky. She could go to Cousin Honey's, of course. Mum had emphasized that, both in talking to herself and over the telephone to Mrs. Appersley. "She's a bit worthy, and as for that iceberg husband of hers!" Fay Clarkson's words echoed in Jib's mind. Those, and the crueler ones, spoken after the play, which she had not been intended to hear. I'll show them, Jib thought and unconsciously squared her shoulders. I'll prove to them I can cope. After all, I'm really here to do a job. This morning Mrs. Appersley's sure to have work for me to do.

Breakfast was not encouraging. Mr. and Mrs. Appersley were down ahead of her and arguing so fiercely that they hardly noticed when she came into the room. "Of course

I don't agree with the fella," Mr. Appersley was saying. "But gosh, Tricksie, he was born near here. Why, my father used to play euchre with his father."

Mrs. Appersley, her face haggard without its make-up, rolled her eyes to the ceiling. "Nobody, absolutely nobody, knows what I put up with. Here I work my fingers to the bone to lift us out of a life of unbearable provincialism and then you ask me to invite a renegade, a communist, to dinner because he was born in some hovel near Quentin and his father played euchre! Euchre!"

"Ah, Tricksie." Mr. Appersley's round face was redder than ever and his gruff voice was pleading, but his wife paid no attention.

"Why I ever left Cleveland to bury myself, yes, bury myself in this place——" she began, when for the first time Mr. Appersley became aware of Jib's embarrassed presence.

"Morning, girlie," he said, and then, turning to his wife, muttered that Jib might like some coffee.

Mrs. Appersley lifted the silver pot but before she poured it gestured with it toward her husband. "You ask Bennett Drayton to dinner!" she said. "Ask him for a week end. And then see what Millard Bean has to say about insurance! Heaven knows we're hard up enough already."

The names meant nothing to Jib, but the effect on Mr. Appersley was unmistakable. His round red face looked haunted, and when he spoke his voice was apologetic. "Ah, Tricksie, be reasonable," he said. "I haven't any intention of seeing the chap. Don't even know for sure if he's coming to Quentin. I just happened to mention him because it burned me up when Bean kept referring to him last night as an incendiary foreigner when I know he isn't."

He pushed his plate away and strode off to his car while Mrs. Appersley finished pouring Jib's coffee. "Did you sleep well, dear?" she asked, and Jib nodded, doubly grateful for her hostess's change of mood and change of subject.

"Oh yes, thank you," she said. "I hope you did."

"Wretchedly." Mrs. Appersley yawned and poured herself more black coffee. "But then I suppose no one, certainly not John Appersley, realizes the strain of trying to entertain decently without adequate servants."

Jib thought she saw an opening and plunged in. "If there's anything I could do to help," she began. "I'm used to helping Mum——"

Mrs. Appersley, who had begun to write out orders for the cook, only waved her away. A few moments later she looked up, and there was a worried frown between her small eyes. "What are your plans for today? I have some women coming in for bridge this afternoon, and I imagine you'll be meeting some of the young people at the club. But I wondered about this morning. It is difficult when people don't play golf. I have to go over to Pittsfield myself to have my hair done. The local people are utterly impossible."

Jib gulped her coffee so that it burned her throat. Not only was it transparently clear that Mrs. Appersley didn't want her help, but she also expected her to have engagements of her own, which was disconcerting when none of the swimming-pool crowd seemed likely to invite her to do anything. At that moment Mrs. Clarkson came into the room. "Jib can go down to the express office with me," she said. "That is, if you don't mind lending us the roadster. I really ought to get my trunk off to Newport. Then this afternoon, as you said, she'll be perfectly happy over at the pool."

Mrs. Appersley straightened her housecoat and sighed with relief. "Morning, Fay dear," she said. "I wish you could stay longer. How I'll ever manage without you I simply cannot imagine."

The remark might have been meant impersonally, but

it stung Jib like a whip and she found to her horror that she was blushing from her neck all the way up to her forehead. "Toast?" Mrs. Clarkson said, and Jib helped herself. She was usually as hungry as the twins when she came down to breakfast, but now, when she bit into her toast spread with marmalade, it tasted like ashes. She was a complete flop at the Appersleys', and the only alternative was going down to Cousin Honey's, who was dreary according to Mrs. Clarkson, and who would know, by the very fact of Jib's arrival, not only that she had failed on her camp application but that she had been miserably unsuccessful at the Ridge.

At that moment Mrs. Appersley rose from the end of the table. "That Juan!" she said. "There he is mooning about in the garden when he knows the whole house needs to be vacuumed. Honestly, these Filipinos."

"I'll get him!" Jib was on her feet, ready to do anything, go anyplace, simply to get out of the dining room.

The Filipino boy looked up as she came toward him and his white teeth flashed in his dark face. "Great day," he said. "Beautiful."

"Yes, it is," Jib said and then added apologetically that Mrs. Appersley wanted him indoors.

Juan straightened and grimaced. "Too bad," he said. "This garden need work."

It was all too true. The long formalized beds, once elaborately planted, were badly in need of weeding and trimming, but Jib was unconscious of details. The cool, moist smells, the early morning trilling of the birds, and the wide familiar outline of the distant hills had all taken her back to Cobble Top. On such a day Mum would hurry out of the house, leaving dishes, beds, even an unfinished painting, to get at the garden. Jib reached out and touched one of the Etoile de Hollande roses, and the familiar softness, the fragrance, brought on a wave of homesickness that left her trembling. " 'I am the master of my fate: I am the captain of my soul,' " Jib muttered

22

to herself, but the brave words were only a mockery, and she began to walk, stiff and unseeing and as fast as she could go, to keep from sobbing out loud.

By the time she felt under control enough to go back to the house Mrs. Clarkson was waiting for her and the roadster stood under the portico. "Well, we're off," Mrs. Clarkson said as she turned from the driveway onto the state road that ran down the Ridge and into Quentin Mills. "But we haven't any too much time. I simply have to get my trunk onto the morning train or I won't have a thing to wear next week end. Lord, how I wish I owned this car."

The train was just whistling around a curve to the south as they pulled up at the Victorian Gothic station. Somehow they managed to jerk it out of the rumble seat and Mrs. Clarkson checked it through on her ticket. "If you want it to go this morning you'll have to hurry," the man behind the wicket warned them. "The ten-thirty pulls out of here in three minutes."

They lugged the small trunk out on the platform where the baggageman was pushing a luggage cart ahead of him. "Oh, you, help us!" Mrs. Clarkson shrieked, but the baggageman moved on like a sleepwalker.

"I think we can make it!" Jib panted. "Look, they're still unloading all those trees." At that moment she caught a glimpse of an old truck and saw a young man in khaki catapult out of it and dash toward the trees.

"You. Oh, you!" Mrs. Clarkson was so out of breath that she sounded like a wailing buoy. "Young man, you must help us!"

The stranger glanced over his shoulder, and Jib had the impression that he had a crew haircut and a very sun-burned face. "Put it down," he yelled as he raced forward. "Got to stop 'em."

"Honestly, have you ever seen such manners?" Mrs. Clarkson gasped, and the perspiration began to cut ugly little lines through her make-up. "He ought to be shot!"

"I think he means to come back," Jib said. "I imagine he wants to help with those trees. They're just ruining them."

"I've got to stop!" Mrs. Clarkson said, and as they put down the steamer trunk Jib saw what was happening. The young man had reached the baggage car and he caught the trees and set them down carefully as the train man hurled them toward him. As soon as that was done he turned and helped the baggageman unload the hand truck.

"Yooo-hoo, help *us!*" Mrs. Clarkson called, but neither of the men turned from their work. "This is inexcusable!" Mrs. Clarkson fumed. "I'm certainly going to report it."

"We can do it ourselves," Jib urged. "We've still got time." She had hardly finished before the young man, the truck unloaded, turned and ran toward them.

"Let go ladies," he said, and his accent might have been Southern. "I'll be glad to put it on."

"About time!" Mrs. Clarkson snapped, but the man was already running for the train, the steamer trunk held in both arms like a giant football.

The baggageman moved out of his way with tantalizing slowness, and then, with a quick, athletic heave, the stranger pushed Mrs. Clarkson's trunk up onto the train just as it pulled out of the station. A moment later he came back down the platform and his smile was a pleasant mixture of friendliness and satisfaction. "Made it," he said. "Just!"

Mrs. Clarkson was seething with heat and anger. "It's perfectly outrageous," she stormed. "I don't see why you trainmen can't be around when two women——"

Jib, who had seen the man leave his car, started to explain, but he apparently needed no assistance. "I don't work for the railroad, ma'am," he said, and now Jib was sure he came from the South. "I just happened to be here to collect these trees and saw you all were havin' trouble. I called out for you all to stop 'til I could get back."

"Oh, I see," Mrs. Clarkson said, but as she fumbled in her purse her expression was not more friendly. "Well, then, thank you very much." She pulled out a coin and pressed it on the man, who looked as though she'd hit him.

"No, thank you, ma'am," he said, and amusement chased the shocked look from his face. "I was very glad to help you."

Mrs. Clarkson's eyes were following the baggageman as he pushed the hand truck to the far end of the platform, and she dropped the coin back into her purse without glancing at it. "So that's the man I want," she said. "I'm certainly going to give him a piece of my mind. He could have helped us perfectly well." She started forward and then, as though the length of the hot platform had discouraged her, stopped short. "On second thought, I'll report it," she said. "Millard Bean, who happens to be a friend of mine, is a director of this railroad."

The young man touched her arm impulsively. "Please don't," he said. "I happen to know the baggageman's deaf and pretty old, and there aren't so awfully many jobs he could get."

Mrs. Clarkson jerked herself free. "I don't see how this concerns you," she said. "I understand that you are not connected with the railroad."

"No, ma'am." The young man stiffened. "I work for the United States Soil Conservation Service. The name is Stanton Jefferson Carter."

"Well, then, I'll thank you to leave me alone, Mr. Carter," Mrs. Clarkson said and turned to leave. "Come on, Jib. We've wasted time enough."

Jib's mouth was open to thank Stanton Carter, to apologize, to try and reassure him about the baggageman, but Mrs. Clarkson had taken her arm and was actually pulling her toward the car. "Thanks awfully," she got out, but Stanton Carter gave no evidence of hearing. At Mrs. Clarkson's last words he had turned on his heel,

25

and the last Jib saw of him he was loading the fir trees onto his truck.

The drive back to the Ridge had a good effect on Mrs. Clarkson's temper. She parked the car with a flourish in front of the Appersleys' and began to repair the damage to her make-up before she stepped out. Finally, as she fluffed up her hair and made a little moue of satisfaction into the mirror, Jib thought she saw a chance. "You know, I honestly don't think that baggageman heard us when he went past," she said as she followed Mrs. Clarkson into the hall. "And I'm sure, with his truck all loaded and all, he didn't see us."

Mrs. Clarkson, who was going through the mail with eager, predatory fingers, tore open a letter. "Invitation from the Van Courtlands!" she purred, and then, aware of Jib, shrugged. "Possibly not. At any rate, I'm not going to trouble Millard Bean or anyone else about him."

Jib, who was not used to such lightning changes of mood, still felt breathless when the maid came down the hall and handed her a message on a silver tray. "Miss Drelincourt wanted you to call her before twelve," she said. "Sooner if possible."

Jib looked at the little note in her hand as though she did not believe it. "Miss Drelincourt wanted me to call her," she said. "You're sure?"

The maid's professional impersonality gave way to friendliness. "Yes, miss," she said. "Miss Drelincourt sounded most anxious to reach you at once."

Jib moved to the telephone in a trance and rang the number which had been given her. "Hello!" The voice at the other end of the telephone was unmistakably Stella's!

"Oh, hello. This is Jib Bolton. Did you want to speak to me?"

"Honey lamb, I certainly did." Stella's voice over the telephone was even more entrancing than Jib had expected. "I'm leaving tomorrow and I'm so anxious to see you again. I wonder if you could just manage to run down here this evening after supper. You're only about a mile from Cousin Annie's."

"Yes, I'm sure I could. Mrs. Appersley wouldn't mind. Oh, Stella, I'd love it."

"Good for you, darling!" The voice, the words, left Jib tingling. "Now don't forget I'm counting on you."

4. WALK PROUDLY FRIENDED

JIB DID walk over to the club pool that afternoon, and although her reception was no different from what it had been before, it no longer mattered. She, Jib Bolton, among all the dozen or so people around the pool, had been singled out to spend the evening with Stella Drelincourt, who was their undisputed queen. Stella herself did not appear, and once Fatsy Hammond stopped eating the crackers he had bought at the club buffet long enough to ask where she was. "I don't know," Jib said and tried to sound casual. "But she asked me over to her cousin's this evening because she's leaving for New York tomorrow. Any messages?"

At that moment the atmosphere around the pool was charged, but Jib was blissfully unaware of it. Mibsie Tarrant turned to Bet Barnes and one plucked eyebrow arched knowingly upward. Amory Holt, who was older than the rest of the gang and had just stopped in on his way home from work, looked at Jib as though he were going to speak and then, changing his mind, plunged into the pool. Only Stew Harris, who had taken Stella home the night before, spoke, and all he said was, "No messages."

The club pool seemed like a concrete bathtub after the natural pool deep in the woods behind Cobble Top, and Jib decided against a swim. It was only half-past six when she started back for the Appersleys', but as she went up the porch steps Mrs. Appersley called out to her to hurry. Jib, glancing into the dining room, saw that only one extra guest was expected, but even so there was more excitement than there had been last night over twenty. Mrs. Appersley looked up from the flowers she was frantically changing and demanded another bowl; Mr. Appersley shouted up from belowstairs that he couldn't find the keys to the wine cellar; and in the upstairs hall Mrs. Clarkson, who was already dressed for dinner, waylaid Jib and followed her into her bedroom. "Mr. Bean is coming for dinner," she said. "Mr. Millard Bean. You'd better put on an evening dress."

Jib, who had thought of changing into a clean print, looked surprised, and Mrs. Clarkson went on. "You know who he is, don't you?" she said. "Surely your family must have told you?"

"I don't think they know him," Jib said. "Should they?"

Mrs. Clarkson looked annoyed. "He happens to be the richest and most influential man in this community," she said. "He bought up all the Titanic Paper Factories in Quentin Mills during the depression and made a killing. He's more or less retired now, but he still owns a number of smaller mills, an enormous farm, and heaven knows what all. The point is that he owns the mill that used to belong to John Appersley's family, and sometimes John isn't very tactful, although he's more directly dependent on Bean than most people. I promised Tricksie I'd warn you to help keep the wheels greased."

"But I don't understand," Jib said. "I thought Mr. Appersley was in the insurance business."

"So he is," Mrs. Clarkson said, and she sighed as she turned toward the door. "When they had to sell the mill he took over the local agency for Mutual Indemnity. His biggest account is Millard Bean's holdings. Now do you understand?"

"I—I think so," Jib said, but the conversation was so different from anything she was used to at home that she was completely bewildered, and it was only by concentrating on her coming visit to Stella that she kept from feeling miserably naïve and inadequate.

By the time Jib was ready to go downstairs, Mr. Bean, who was a tall, sallow bachelor of about sixty with sharp eyes and a sardonic smile, had already arrived. His appearance was not encouraging, but as he sat on the sofa between Mrs. Appersley and Mrs. Clarkson, while the older people had cocktails, Jib did not have to speak to him. By the time they were in the dining room he was launched on a comparison of his own hard-working boyhood with what he described as the pampered luxury of present-day youth. "Nobody works nowadays," he said. "At least not in my mills. They all expect a living handed out to them. Now when I was a youngster we expected to hustle!"

The two older women purred agreement, but Mr. Appersley shook his head. "Perhaps each generation thinks that about the oncoming one," he muttered, and as he turned to Jib his red face was beetier than usual and his doglike eyes looked troubled. "What do you think, little one?"

As Jib turned to him it occurred to her that he was distressed on her account because her own generation was being run into the ground, and she felt so grateful that all shyness left her. "I'm afraid I don't know much about it," she began. "But Dad always used to tell us how my great-grandfather, who was the doctor in Quentin

Oldtown, walked all the way to Boston to get his medical training. I'm afraid I wouldn't be ready to do that!"

Her remark was an unexpected success. The two women laughed, Mr. Appersley began to eat again, and Bean patted her shoulder approvingly. "When I first moved here people were still talking about Old Doc Bolton," he said. "A fine specimen of the horse-and-buggy doctor. They bred men in those days."

The good old days, when limited to country physicians and separated from paper mills, was apparently a safe subject, and from then on the conversation buzzed until Mrs. Appersley led the way back to the drawing room where a bridge table and cards were already set out.

"I'd like this little lady for my partner," Mr. Bean said and once more reached out toward Jib with a dry, scaly hand. Jib managed to escape and say that she had an engagement with Stella Drelincourt for the evening.

"Oh, you gay young people are impossible," Mrs. Appersley said, but her coyness was well laced with relief and approval. "Help yourself to the Chevvie, dear. It's still at the door."

Mrs. Clarkson gave Jib a quick nod of applause and both ladies called out to her to have a good time as the men escorted her to the car. Jib, feeling that she was undeservedly riding a perfumed wave of approval, let the car into gear and started off.

A moment after she had turned out of the driveway she forgot the Appersleys as though they did not exist. Her whole mind and heart were concentrated on Stella, and a phrase from Rupert Brooke echoed in her memory like soft music. "Walk proudly friended. Walk proudly friended." That was exactly what she was doing in going to see Stella Drelincourt.

She had no trouble with the car or in finding the house which Stella had described over the telephone. It was a Victorian building set back from the road among a planting of larches and yellow oak. "Looks as though with a good face lifting it'd make a nifty funeral parlor," Stella had said, and as Jib parked the car she giggled to herself at the accuracy of the description.

In another moment she was at the door and a hatchet-faced woman in a soiled apron answered her ring. "Is Stella, that is—Miss Drelincourt in?" The woman shut an inner door behind her before she let Jib into an entry that smelled of stale kerosene and must. "You the girl who's staying over to Appersleys?"

Jib nodded, smiling. "Yes, I'm Jib Bolton. Stella called me up this morning and asked me to come over."

The woman opened the door behind her and gestured for Jib to mount the carpeted stairs that rose precipitously upward from the entry. "Stella's room is the second on the left by the back stairs," she said. "You can't miss it. She's left the radio goin'."

Jib caught sight of a cluttered Victorian parlor to the left of the stairs and saw that an elderly lady with her back to the door was crocheting beside a radio turned on full blast. This must be Stella's cousin, Miss Annie Sage, she realized, and wondered if she should go in to greet the old lady before she went upstairs. Her quandary was written on her face, and the woman in the apron shrugged her shoulders. "You kin go in if you like," she said. "But Miss Annie's deaf as a post, so there ain't much future to it. Stella built it up with her you was comin' and going straight up to her room."

"Oh, thanks. Thanks a lot." Jib was relieved that she did not have to introduce herself to the old lady, who from the rear view looked incredibly formidable. "I'll run right up, then."

The woman disappeared into the dark back regions of the house and Jib made the trip up the unlighted stairs by herself. The upstairs hall was almost as dark and close as the entry, but Jib heard the strains of "Nature Boy" from behind the second door and knocked. There was no answer and she knocked again, and then, deciding that

Stella could not hear above the wail of the radio, let herself in. "Stella. Stella, where are you? It's me, Jib Bolton."

An old-fashioned ceiling light made the room blindingly bright after the hall, and Jib blinked owlishly. "Oh, Stella," she began again, and when her eyes focused on the untidy room it was obvious that her friend was not there. Everything about the room, from the rumpled bedspread to the shoes and stockings dropped on the imitation Brussels carpet, gave evidence that Stella had come in, changed her clothes, and dashed out again.

Jib's heart began to thump uncomfortably. She had come the right night, that much the woman downstairs had made clear, but where was Stella? She turned, hoping against hope that Stella might appear from another room, and then she saw the note, addressed to herself, that was propped up on the old-fashioned dresser between a bottle of nail polish and a bottle of perfume. She picked it up, her eyes eagerly devouring the bold, flourishing hand. "Honey chile!" Stella began. "Sorry not to be here to welcome you, but I had an errand I had to do. I'll be back just as soon as I possibly can. If you see Cousin Annie before she goes to bed, you might tell her I'm getting a book out of the library before it closes. But if you wait in my room you won't see her, which would be easier. She knows, of course, that you're coming, and it's just my running out for a minute that might upset her. You know how old people fuss. See you soon, honey. Your loving friend, Stella."

For a moment a puzzled look lined Jib's forehead and then it cleared as she reread the signature. "Your loving friend, Stella." Jib folded the letter carefully and put it in her pocket. If Stella signed herself that way, it was true, the beautiful winged hoped that had grown in Jib's heart since her morning telephone call. Your loving friend, Stella. Yes, it was true. Stella had felt drawn to Jib from that first moment at the pool just as Jib herself had felt drawn to Stella.

"Walk proudly friended. Walk proudly friended." The three words grew into a joyful chorus in Jib's heart. She turned off the radio and looked around for something to read. There wasn't anything but a couple of old movie magazines and a soiled copy of *Glamour*. We Boltons are just a lot of bookworms, Jib told herself and fought down the recollection of the bookshelves that emerged in every crack and cranny at Cobble Top. Besides, wasn't Stella even now at the library probably getting out a book for her train trip back tomorrow?"

She looked around the room, which, with its ugly heavy furniture and spidery wallpaper, was exactly what she would have expected from the hallway. She dismissed it with a grimace and walked over to the window. No wonder poor Stella had envied her staying at the Appersleys'. This room no more represented Stella's own taste or background than a wooden crate represented an orange.

Jib pulled up the shade and found that by leaning down she could see through the drooping branches of the larches onto the hill road. A car passed slowly and Jib crouched on the floor to watch for another. She would count eight cars, not using trucks, and by that time Stella would be back. The cars were few and far between, and the minutes ticked drearily from an ugly brass clock. Jib counted eight, fourteen, then twenty cars before she pulled herself to her feet again. She switched on the radio and then, startled by the noise, switched it off again. She was suddenly frightened, and her strong young fingers clenched and unclenched themselves as an entire tragic drama unreeled itself in her mind. Stella had been hurt leaving the library. She was undoubtedly walking and some brute of a hit-and-run driver had knocked her down in the twilight and roared away. Stella lay on the curb still breathing, still beautiful, but dying. "Tell Jib Bolton," her last words came with a pitiful effort. "Tell Jib Bolton!"

34

Jib knew she was being a fool and flung open the door and hurried down the back stairs. It was after nine now and the house was pitch dark, but she had to find someone, even if it was only the hard-faced servant woman or the equally terrifying cousin. The woman, who apparently slept out, was just hanging up her apron.

"I'm awfully sorry to bother you," Jib burst out. "But do you know where she, that is, Stella, went? Did she take a car or did she walk to the library? I'm so afraid something has happened."

The woman didn't even turn around. "I don't know a thing," she said. "Not one thing. But if I was you and fixin' to wait up for Stella, I'd settle down for a real good nap!"

Then, before Jib could say another word, she pushed a garbage pail under the kitchen sink and stalked out of the back door. Jib stood still for a moment and heard the rattle of the woman's car as she drove away. She turned and went back upstairs, and the sound of her own footsteps was terrifying as it echoed and re-echoed through the silent, unfamiliar house. She forced herself to go back to the parlor, but the radio was turned off and the room was black. So Miss Annie Sage was already in bed. Jib's throat felt dry and her hands were icy as she slipped back up the stairs like a frightened ghost.

Once back in Stella's room, she sat upright under the glaring light and waited and waited, and all the time the knowledge that Stella was not going to come grew in her heart like a fungus in a Disney film.

Finally an owl hooted in the distance. Jib's skin shriveled at the sound, and the next minute she picked up her wrap and crept out of the house like a thief in the darkness.

She had parked the car in a little lane for safety, and as she hurried toward it she saw that another car had just pulled up ahead of hers. She herself was in shadow, but the moonlight slanting through the open window of the car showed her Stella in the arms of a man she didn't know as plainly as though they were actors on a stage.

The man said something Jib couldn't hear, and Stella pushed him away, laughing. "You just relax and I'll be back in five minutes," she said, and her deep, vibrant voice carried perfectly. "Now that Cousin Annie has gone sleepy-bye I've got to get rid of my baby sitter."

The man protested, and Stella's voice rang out more loudly. "Don't you worry. I can get rid of her just as fast as I want to. One minute of my fatal charm and little Jib Bolton will float home in a happy haze. I have her simply pinned down."

Jib did not wait to hear another syllable. Her eyes stung and her cheeks flamed as she fled down the dark side of the road. If they see me I'll die, she thought. If they see me I'll die. But she reached the car unnoticed and, after a moment of frantic fumbling, heard the strong, reassuring sputter of the engine.

She drove back recklessly and, leaving the car in the driveway, went up the broad steps to the Appersleys' porch. Through the long French windows she could see that Mr. Bean had gone and that the others had left the bridge table. Oh, don't let them hear me, she prayed. Oh, don't let them hear me.

She was halfway across the hall before Mrs. Appersley caught a glimpse of her passing. "Oh, hello, dear," she called out. "Have a nice evening?"

"Yes, I did, thank you." Jib choked out the lie and ran upstairs, but there was no escaping Mrs. Clarkson.

"Hello, my dear," she said, and once more she followed Jib toward her bedroom. "I've been waiting up because I wanted to congratulate you. You really made the most colossal hit with Millard Bean."

Jib said nothing, but there was something in her face that made Mrs. Clarkson hurry on. "Now I know your mother's brought you up to be deliciously unworldly, but as I said the other day, I think it's time you faced facts. After all, it must be perfectly clear even to you that what Tricksie and John want you up here for is bait!"

At that instant Jib was beyond manners, beyond disappointment, even beyond pain. She was only conscious of the overwhelming wave of disgust, as concrete and inescapable as seasickness, that choked up inside her throat. She shut her door, bolted it, and then threw herself face down on the bed.

5. GREEN AND PLEASANT LAND

THE NEXT morning Jib put on her dungarees and a patched cotton shirt for the first time since she had arrived at the Appersleys'. She was not at all sure of what she was going to do, of what she could do, but was only dreadfully certain that she had to escape. If she was asked many questions about last night she'd cry, and she knew, as surely as though it had already happened, that the crowd around the swimming pool would ask a very great many questions. Then there was the more important and immediate matter of her staying on at the Appersleys'. She had not felt comfortable about her job since her first day, but last night, though Mrs. Clarkson had intended a compliment, she only convinced Jib that her visit could never work out on a businesslike plane.

"Bait!" Jib muttered the word as she brushed her tousled hair. "Bait!" The whole idea that she was to stay at the Appersleys' house simply to attract other young people to come there was loathsome and disgusting. How Mum would hate it, Jib thought. She wouldn't want me to stay.

She tried to powder her nose, which was shiny from crying, and at the same time to escape an unpleasantly candid voice in the back of her own mind. Neither attempt was successful. The powder would not stick, and as she turned toward the window the voice became inescapable. Jib winced as the daylight hurt her eyes, but she could no longer lie to herself. She was disgusted with Mrs. Appersley, with Mrs. Clarkson, certainly with Stella, but how did she, Jib Bolton, stand? The candid voice grew triumphant, cackling. "You're a prig and also a faker. The real reason why you resent being bait is because you're no good at it."

Jib moved back to the bureau, but the truth went with her. It was a fact that she had been shocked by Mrs. Clarkson's cynicism, but it was only partially honest indignation and partially another case of very sour grapes.

She went down to breakfast feeling whipped and raw. Mrs. Appersley and Mrs. Clarkson, who was leaving that day, were both ahead of her, and she crept into the dining room fearing the worst. "Good morning," she said, and her voice sounded tearful and reedy in her own ears. Apparently neither of the ladies noticed anything unusual.

Mrs. Appersley was busy with her ordering and Mrs. Clarkson was studying a complicated series of timetables.

"Morning, Jib. Yes, that's right, I could change at Pittsfield."

"Good morning, dear." Mrs. Appersley pushed her pad away from her as she spoke. "You look as though you were off for a picnic."

The idea had not occurred to Jib before, but instantly it presented itself as her one easy means of escape for a few hours at least, in which time she might be able to thrash out some kind of plan. "I don't know what you're going to do about a car," Mrs. Appersley fumed. "John insisted on taking the Buick, and I've absolutely got to have the Chevvie. Or maybe some of the others can call for you?"

"I'm going to walk," Jib said, and although that was true enough, she felt like a liar.

"Well, have a good time, but for heaven's sake get back in plenty of time for dinner. We're dining with Millard Bean and then going to the country-club dance." Mrs. Appersley disappeared into the kitchen and Mrs. Clarkson looked over at Jib and nodded.

"You see, they're counting on you," she said. "Now don't you dare let them down."

Jib bit her lips, and a few moments later she said good-by to Mrs. Clarkson and left the house. As she stepped off the porch she thought vaguely of going to Cobble Top, but even before she reached the road she knew that it would not be bearable, not this morning, anyway, to see that beloved spot in strange hands, and turned resolutely in the other direction.

She trudged along steadily over the winding country road, unconscious of the hard earth still damp with dew beneath her feet or of the cool greenness of the trees on either side of her. She stopped once when she came to a long driveway that led to what looked like the pictures she had seen of Norman villages. For an instant she was puzzled, and then when she saw the bold sign that read "HI ACRES. M. BEAN" she ran away like a witch from a hex mark. She was going there tonight. Unless she could blessedly die in the meantime, from that there was no escape. A long, ghastly evening in which dodging Mr. Bean's long fingers alternated with being snubbed by people of her own age unreeled itself in Jib's mind with the relentless clarity of a slow-motion movie.

And after this evening, what? She had thought last

night of going to Quentin Mills or Quentin Oldtown to try and get a job and find a boarding place, but she knew in her heart that there wasn't much chance of her getting anything that would pay for her keep. Of course there was still Cousin Honey. She was on the back road which, skirting Quentin Mills, ran on into Oldtown, and that was where Cousin Honey lived. Unconsciously Jib's steps quickened, and then a moment later she slowed down again, floundering in a quagmire of self-distrust and self-pity. Cousin Honey was too overworked to want her. Mrs. Clarkson had understood that, even if Mum hadn't or wouldn't.

She walked on and on, vaguely aware that she had gone down into a broad valley and now was climbing the hill on the other side. Her legs began to ache and her eyes stung after her wretched night. Perhaps if she got tired enough she would be able to sleep in some shady spot out of sight of the road. "To sleep: perchance to dream: ay, there's the rub." Once more Jib's memory came through with words that seemed exactly to express what she was feeling.

She left the road and, climbing onto a stone wall, looked out over a stony pasture to find a sheltered spot. She was halfway over before she saw the boy and the pony. At least they were together for the first half second of her looking, and then just as she found a better toe-hold on the wall the pony put down his head and the boy shot out of the saddle. He sat up instantly, picked up some papers which he had been carrying, and considered the pony while he ruefully polished his glasses. "Are you all right?" Jib called out. "Did you hurt yourself?"

"Only my pride," the boy said, but his voice sounded completely unembarrassed. "Billy Baines, who's only ten, rides that nag all over the place, but he pitched me off in no time. I wonder how come?"

Jib, who had ridden a good deal, was interested in

spite of herself. "Maybe it was your papers flapping or maybe you had the curb too tight," she said and walked slowly toward the pony. He looked up at her with nothing more than idle curiosity, and she caught him without any trouble.

"Good for you." The boy sprawled out comfortably on the grass. "I tried to do that for twenty minutes before I saddled him, and then I had to get Billy to do it for me. Was my face red."

Jib grinned back at him. He was probably a little older than the twins but as pleasantly direct, and she liked his intelligent scrubbed-looking face and the shock of corn-colored hair that sprouted away from it. "Mind if I try him?" she asked. "I'm used to horses."

"Jeepers, I'd be grateful," the boy said. "I only borrowed him while my bike is being fixed because I have to get out my papers."

"Do you have a paper route?" Jib asked as she changed the stirrups. "My kid brothers always wanted to do that."

"You can skip that kid-brother connection." The boy brushed himself off as he spoke. "I happen to be fifteen and I'm running the paper. Collect the news, write the copy, print it on the church mimeograph, and sell it. It's some job."

"Oh, I know," Jib said. "I ran the Lit at school."

"A Lit!" The boy was scathing. "Out once a month at the most. I get my *Chronicle* out on the streets twice every week."

Jib, who was already in the saddle, didn't hear him. The pony, as though trying her out, fumbled for the bit and began to back ominously toward the gate at the far end of the pasture. Jib gave him a sharp, expert clap with her heels. The pony's ears pricked forward with surprise, and then the next moment, as she continued to urge him forward, he trotted obediently around the pasture. She made him go around twice and then brought him up

42

beside the boy. "You're pretty good," he admitted. "D'you suppose Jinx'll go that way for me?"

"If you make him," Jib said. "Which way are you going? I might go along with you a way to make sure he behaves."

"That'd be neat," the boy said. "I'm going to Oldtown. And by the way, I don't know your name." Jib told him and asked him his own.

"Buzz Winslow," he said. "Real first name's Brewster, but only my great-aunts use it. You don't live here, do you?"

"I used to," Jib said. "In the summer, anyway, in the woods on the far side of Quentin Cobble. Right now I'm staying on the Ridge."

"Snob Hill," the boy said, and Jib liked him better than ever. "I live in Oldtown myself."

"My cousin, Mrs. Stirling, lives there. D'you know her?"

"Know her? You bet!" Buzz Winslow's alive young face was good to look at. "She's a knockout, and so's her husband. He's the guy that got the church people to lend me their mimeograph for my paper."

Jib held the pony as Buzz mounted, and then she handed him the rucksack of papers. Once more Jinx put down his head, but Jib pulled him up as Buzz fumbled for his reins. "Keep his head up and keep him going," she ordered. "If you do that, you won't have any trouble."

"I hope you're right," Buzz said. "If it wasn't for these papers, I'd sure enough wait for my bike. One spill a day is enough."

He was inexperienced, but completely fearless, and quick to carry out Jib's instruction. She helped him get the pony onto the road and then walked along with him on the way toward Oldtown. She had no trouble as long as they were going downhill, but once they reached another of the long upgrades the pony easily outdistanced her.

"See you again," Buzz Winslow called back. "And thanks a million."

Jib waved and watched him move out of sight around a curve in the road. A nice kid, and managing the pony had been fun. Nothing was changed, of course. She was still in the same mess she had been in before, but somehow life did not seem quite so hopeless, and for the first time all morning she was keenly aware of the curving mountain road ahead.

It was probably a road very like this one which Great-grandfather Bolton had taken years ago when he had set out on foot for Boston. She wondered what he had thought about as he had walked along and where he had spent the nights. She was nearly at the top of the hill, and on her left was a small saltbox cottage with a pretty old-fashioned garden. She thought of stopping at the cottage to ask how far it was to Oldtown, and then, catching sight of some children in a field beyond the cottage, she went on to ask them.

She crawled under the wooden barway and was within a few feet of the children before she saw what they were doing. The biggest of them, a boy of about eight, stood in front of a newly dug hole while three little girls and a boy of three or four rolled a toy wagon, on which was mounted a shoe box covered with flowers, toward him. "Are you having a funeral?" Jib asked, but the biggest boy, who was playing the part of the minister, was too absorbed to answer. The little girls looked curiously at Jib and then, reassured that she had not come out to stop them, went on rolling their wagon toward the grave. Only the smallest boy of all was interested in a spectator. "We're having a funeral," he said. "A really truly one for Fwedwick."

"Frederick?" Jib looked uncertainly at the shoe box.

"He was a wobin," the little boy explained. "He fell out of his nest and we tried to bring him up on a milk out of a dwopper, but it deaded him."

44

"What a shame!" Jib said, and now the older children rolled the wagon slowly round and round the grave in some silent prearranged ritual of their own. The smallest boy glanced after them and then decided to give out some more information. "His whole name was Fwedwick Augustus Kimberley," he said. "After my grandfather. You know him."

"I'm afraid I don't," Jib said and then asked how far it was to Oldtown.

The boy put his hands in small pockets and gazed up at her scornfully. "Don't you know anything?" he asked. "This is Oldtown. This and down over there."

At that moment one of the girls called back to the smallest boy and he scampered off. Jib straightened up, and then, as she looked down in the direction in which the child had pointed, her breath caught in sheer admiration of the view ahead of her. She was standing on a mountain meadow that looked down into a wide green valley. To her left was the sweeping arc of a bare mountaintop that on this clear day looked as though it had been pasted directly onto the sky. Jib realized that this was simply an unfamiliar view of Old Baldy and, turning, picked out Quentin's Cobble and Mount Blashfield. Then her eyes traveled downward, and as she saw the steeple and cluster of houses directly below her realized what the child had meant and that she was already in Oldtown township.

She went back to the road, and for the first time all morning she began to hum a song: "And Did Those Feet in Ancient Time Walk upon England's Pleasant Green."

She stopped when she came to a fork where the country lane joined the main road and took her last lingering look at the view below. She had driven over the main road plenty of times and knew that from here on it ran through small farms and second-growth woods that obstructed the view. The tar smelled hot and stuffy after the cool dampness of the dirt road and there was a good

45

deal of traffic. She was really tired now, and she was delighted when an old man with a battered station wagon filled with fruit stopped to give her a lift. "You goin' to Oldtown?" he asked, and when Jib said she was he asked her where.

"Why, to Mrs. Oliver Stirling's, I guess. She's my cousin, but I'm not at all sure where she lives. I was taken there once when I was about six, but I don't remember much about it."

The man put back his head and laughed. "Go to Mees Honey's?" he said, and his accent was richly Italian. "You staya aboard and I take you right to the door."

"Oh, you know where she lives," Jib said, and once more the old man laughed, and the sound was neither mocking nor superior but only delightfully friendly.

"Yes, mees. You betta my life. Everybody in Oldtown knowa Mees Honey."

6. A SMALL HOUSE AND LARGE GARDEN

THE FRUIT DEALER, whose name was Tommy Genovese, drove Jib through the outskirts of Quentin Oldtown and on into the foothills that rose up behind the village. About a mile out of town he stopped in front of a square, serene-looking house set well back from the road. The house's shingles had weathered to a soft pewter and the white-shuttered windows looked out over the mountains like friendly eyes. To one side lay a sloping mountain meadow, and on the other there was a fence of white palings that shut out everything except the tops of a few apple trees and the pointed spire of a pear tree. "Meester Stirling's garden." Old Genovese nodded toward the fence. "Best in Oldtown. Best in all three Quentins."

Jib said nothing, suddenly and uncomfortably aware of how little she knew about her father's cousins. She could remember seeing Cousin Honey at Cobble Top ages ago, and she knew that the Stirlings had moved to

Washington during the mid-1930s. Cousin Oliver, who was an economist, had gone there to work for the government, but his health had given way during the war and they had moved back to Oldtown in 1944. Mum had seen Cousin Honey since the war, but it had been when Jib was away, and she had never met Cousin Oliver. "Mees Honey she'll still be atta da work," Tommy said. "But the Meester's at home. You find him easy."

"Yes, of course," Jib said. "And thanks a lot for the lift."

"Don't mench," Tommy Genovese said. "And give my love to the folks."

His car sputtered off, and Jib stood alone in front of the rose-covered doorway. She found the old-fashioned bell-pull, and when she saw the name BOLTON in beautiful engraved script on the silver plate beneath it she felt better. After all, Cousin Honey was Dad's first cousin and was living in the house that had belonged to her own great-grandfather, the doctor. She pulled the knob and the bell jingled in the distance. She waited for a moment but there was no answer, and then she was aware of footsteps behind her. She turned and saw a tall white-haired man in work clothes with a stack of books under one arm disappear through a gate into the walled garden. The sudden spurt of confidence that Jib had felt in seeing her own name on the plate went out like a match in a windstorm. If that was her Cousin Oliver, he was not very anxious to meet her. She stood irresolutely on the step, when a backfire made her turn and she saw an old-fashioned open Ford career crazily down the road and come to a stop in front of the house. A small, plump woman who looked like a modern-dress version of toy ark's Mrs. Noah popped out and trotted toward the garden gate. She was halfway toward it before Jib recognized her. Jib started down the steps, wondering how she should introduce herself. "Cousin Honey," she began. "Cousin Honey!"

The little lady paused and then, with a turn like a spinning top, hurried toward Jib. "How do you——" she began, and then the next moment her face glowed with recognition. "Why, Jessica!" she called out. "Jessica darling. All grown up and beautiful and exactly like your mother. My darling child, we were wondering when you'd come. Why, only last night I told Noll that if you didn't come down soon I'd go straight up to the Appersley's and kidnap you."

She put her arms around Jib and kissed her on both cheeks while her clear gray eyes looked into Jib's darker ones. "You're Bolton *and* Infield," she said, as though she had just reached an important decision. "Couldn't be a better combination, especially as the Lord spared you the Bolton nose and figure and gave you your mother's. But you look tired, child. Don't tell me you walked all the way down from the Ridge?"

"Yes—I mean no," Jib said. "A fruit dealer—I think he said his name was Genovese—gave me a lift from where the old road comes out on the highway."

"Good for Tommy. He's the best gardener around here, except for Noll, of course. Vegetables, mostly, and some fruit, but his geraniums are splendid. Still, that's a long pull. At least seven miles."

"I liked it," Jib said, and as she smiled her dimples made exclamation points in either cheek. "I guess I needed the exercise. I haven't done a thing since I arrived here except sit around the Quentin Ridge pool."

"Keeping up with the Joneses?" Mrs. Stirling said. "It would kill me in a week. I know, because I tried it years ago up at Bar Harbor, and at the end of three days I didn't have enough confidence left to say boo to a goose. But come inside, pet, while I find Noll. He'll be dying to meet you."

"I think I saw him," Jib began, and then, as her cousin laughed, she wondered if the older woman were possessed of second sight.

"Sneaking off to the garden, I'll bet, with a book or most likely an armload of books. He didn't know you were coming, you see, and he probably thought you were collecting for something. Noll'd give his last shirt if he knew anyone needed it, but he dodges collectors, especially if they come when he's busy. His health has been marvelously better for the last year and he's begun work on a book on co-operatives, you know. People can't seem to understand that he does some of his best work out in the garden."

"Oh, I see," Jib said and followed Mrs. Bolton through a small, light hall past a book-lined study into a surprisingly spacious living room filled with agreeably used-looking mahogany furniture.

Mrs. Stirling had already reached the window and, putting her head out, called to her husband. "Oh, Noll. Noll! Come on in. Mary and Jack's child has finally come to stay with us."

"Oh, I can't," Jib began. "You're awfully busy, and I'd just be a lot of bother."

"Don't be silly. You're a blessing. A lovely spring morning smelling-of-apple-blossoms blessing. I was cross at your mother for the first time in my life when she let that Clarkson woman talk her into sending you up to the Appersleys' even for a week end."

At that moment Oliver Stirling walked in, and Jib realized that in spite of his prematurely white hair he was probably around her father's age, which was fifty-two. "Jib, this is Oliver. Noll, you know her name's really Jessica but she's always called Jib."

Mr. Stirling shook hands without speaking. A moment later Mrs. Stirling went into the kitchen to start lunch and, after a moment of good-natured protest, let Jib help her. "Noll's very quiet," she said. "Probably comes from living with a chatterbox like me. But he enjoys people, the ones that don't try to change him, anyhow, just as much as I do."

50

"My, he's good-looking," Jib said, thinking of Mr. Bean's selfish, saturnine face and Mr. Appersley's bumbling redness. "If I ever get married, I hope that my husband will look like that when he gets old." She stopped short, thinking of Mrs. Appersley's emphasis on youth and wondering if she had been rude.

Mrs. Stirling only laughed and went on beating eggs. "You're like your mother," she said. "Honest and observant. We're going to have fun."

In a surprisingly short time she had their eggs and salad ready and they went into the cool, high-ceilinged dining room that overlooked the garden. Jib paused for a moment at one of the French windows, and for the second time that morning her breath caught in the face of dazzling, unexpected beauty. The garden fanned out from the back of the house in a series of beds and small meandering paths that seemed to lead on and on past masses of bloom until they melted into the remoter green of the Quentin Hills. "Tommy Genovese said you had the best garden in Oldtown," Jib said, and her eyes sparkled. "Even so, I didn't expect anything like this."

Oliver Stirling opened the door that led directly into the garden and beckoned to his wife and Jib to follow him. "This will be Noll's prize spot for the week," Mrs. Stirling said and took Jib's arm as they followed him down a small herb-lined path. "Every week at this time of year there's something that's at its peak. I don't know what this is, but I promise it'll be well worth eating cold eggs to see it."

Mr. Stirling turned a corner and pointed back to the sloping rear of the house, where bleeding heart, bordered by blue gilly-flowers, reached almost up to the eaves. "Do you like it, Honey?" he asked. "Do you think I was right in moving the pear tree?"

"Oh, Noll!" Mrs. Stirling said, and as she looked up at him her face was lit from inside like a happy child's. "It's just like Essex!"

51

At that moment words that had been stumbling like lost sheep through some corridor of Jib's mind suddenly arranged themselves in an orderly procession. She quoted:

"Ah yet, ere I descend to the grave,
    May I a small house and large garden have;
And a few friends, and many books, both true,
    Both wise, and both delightful too!"

Oliver Stirling's lean face looked years younger as he turned toward her. "Why, my dear girl," he said, "fancy your saying that. It was that very poem I had in mind all day yesterday when I was working here. I didn't know people read old Cowley nowadays."

"They don't," Jib said. "At least, I'm afraid I don't. I just happened to learn that one at school. I went to a Friends school during the war and they made us learn a lot of poetry."

"Bully for them," Oliver Stirling said and led the way back to the house. "And bully for you. Honey, why have you cheated me out of knowing this cousin of yours all these years?"

Cousin Honey laughed, and as Jib sat down between them at the dark polished table she felt happier than she had felt for days. By the time lunch was over it was settled that Mrs. Stirling would speak to Mrs. Appersley on the telephone that night and call for Jib and her bags during her lunch hour the next day. In the meantime she questioned Jib about every detail of her morning's walk from the trip down the Ridge, to her meeting with Buzz Winslow and her encounter with the children who were burying the bird. "You're a good reporter," Mrs. Stirling said as Jib finished. "And so's Buzzie. I think it's wonderful you two got together right away."

"Oh, he's just a kid not much older than the twins," Jib said.

"I wouldn't discount him on that account," Oliver

Stirling said slowly. "He has an excellent mind and, what's even more, rare persistence in using it. He's one of the most interesting people around here."

Just then Mrs. Stirling pushed back her chair. "I hate to leave you," she said. "But I have to go back to work. I'm the executive secretary at the town hall, Jib. Would you like me to give you a lift as far as the bridge at Old-town?"

"I think I'll walk, thanks a lot," Jib said. "I've the whole afternoon." She did not add that now her summer's plans had so suddenly and delightfully changed she actually looked forward to being by herself.

"It's only half-past one, Honey," Oliver Stirling said. "Let's sit out in the garden and have some coffee."

Mrs. Stirling shook her head. "You know how I'd love it," she said. "But I can't. Kurt Cramer's back in town, Noll. He's coming in this afternoon to see me about getting a job."

"Louisa, he isn't!" For the first time since Jib had been in the house Oliver Stirling used his wife's real name

"Came back yesterday," Mrs. Stirling said. "Nobody knows why or for how long. But every time he comes it stirs up trouble for somebody, and always for himself, poor boy. You remember the time he worked for Millard Bean."

"You're not to get involved." Stirling moved possessively toward his wife. "I don't mind you being father-and-mother-confessor to the entire village, but I draw the line at Cramer. He's a grade-A rotter, that lad."

"I won't get involved," Louisa Stirling said. "And now I hope I can trust you two to leave the dishes alone. I'll see you tomorrow, Jib darling, and don't worry about the Appersleys. I'll tell her tonight that we browbeat you into coming."

A moment later she was gone and the house seemed suddenly empty without her. "It'd be all right if I washed the dishes, wouldn't it?" Jib asked. "I'd really like to."

Oliver Stirling lit his pipe and nodded. "It would be very nice," he said. "I hate it, because I always drop things, and Louisa's far more tired than she's willing to admit when she gets home, and she'll be especially so tonight if she has Cramer on her hands. Sure you don't mind?"

"Of course not," Jib said, and it ended up that she washed the dishes while Oliver Stirling smoked his pipe and talked to her through the open door.

"Who is Kurt Cramer?" she asked and found that now she was working with her hands Oliver Stirling was as easy to talk to as Cousin Honey. "Does he live here in Oldtown?"

"Used to," Oliver Stirling said. "He had an unfortunate childhood, and as a result he's always looking for something stronger than he is to cling to. When he was a lad he toadied to the school bully, and now that he's a man he's a hanger-on of the Communist party. Honey says it's not his fault, but I'm less charitable. Buzz Winslow's parents died when he was a baby, and he's been brought up by two maiden great-aunts, which is less than perfect, and still he's turning into a fine citizen."

Shortly afterward Jib finished the dishes and Oliver Stirling started for the garden. At the threshold he stopped. "I'm glad you're coming here to stay," he said. "Very glad."

Jib left the house feeling as pleased as though she had received a delightful and completely unexpected present. As she started down the hill she remembered Mrs. Clarkson's remark about her cousins. "She's worthy, and as for that iceberg!" Jib laughed out loud at how completely mistaken her mother's suave, sophisticated friend had been. Cousin Honey might be overworked, but she was the exact opposite of dreary, and certainly Oliver Stirling was no iceberg. Jib searched her mind for the right words to describe him. He was a gentleman and a scholar, that much was plain, but what was the special thing that set him apart from the other older men she had known? Challenging, that was the nearest she could come to it, challenging because of his reserve and his honesty, which were as obvious characteristics as his white hair and thin, thoughtful face.

Jib had not mentioned either Stella Drelincourt or her distress over her job at the Appersleys' to the Stirlings, and she did not think of them now as she swung down the hill. She still had to tell Mrs. Appersley that she was leaving, but that interview was no more than a vague cloud on the horizon. For the present she was so busy thinking about the Stirlings that her earlier worries were blotted out as though an eraser had rubbed out a sentence on the blackboard.

She walked steadily through the shady streets of Quentin Oldtown past Victorian and colonial houses out onto a small village common. At her left was a sprinkling of shops and two gas stations, and on her right a covered bridge that led to the dirt road to the Ridge. She crossed the echoing planks of the bridge and, as she came out on the road, saw a small boy in blue jeans leading the pony which both she and Buzz Winslow had ridden that morning. "Hi," she said. "Are you Billy Baines?"

The boy looked up. "Yep. How'd you know?"

Jib told him about meeting Buzz and the pony and asked if Buzz had reached home safely. The boy shrugged his shoulders. "Don't know and don't care," he said. "All I know is Buzz rode in here a little while ago and left Jinxie boiling hot. All Buzz thinks about is that old paper of his, and today he was so excited about old man Kimberley he didn't even let Jinx cool off."

"Kimberley?" Jib said vaguely and suddenly remembered the funeral. "You mean the bird the children up the road were burying?"

"Don't know nuthin' about a funeral," the boy said and began to rub the pony's flanks. "All I know is Buzz left

Jinx in terrible shape because he had to get out a 'bituary,' whatever that is."

Jib laughed and started up the hill, and then on an impulse turned around and went back to Billy Baines. "Could I use your family's telephone?" she said. "I'd like to call Buzz."

"You can't," Bill said grimly. "I been tryin' for the last hour. Line's out of order."

"Where does he live?" she asked. "Is it far from here?"

"'Bout a quarter of a mile. First yellow house after you pass the library. If you see him, tell him for me I hope he chokes."

Jib grinned and started back the way she had just come. It would add another half mile to her walk, but she wanted to know for certain whether Buzz Winslow had mistaken the death of a robin for the death of the children's grandfather.

She had no trouble finding the house, and as she started up the walk Buzz himself greeted her. "Hi!" he called out. "Come in and see my office. I'm getting out a special memorial edition. I'm going to have it on the street tomorrow if it kills me."

Jib walked into what had once been a corncrib and was now furnished with a battered typewriter, a filing case, a homemade desk, and several excellent maps. "Is it about a bird?" she asked, and then as Buzz looked at her she wondered for the first time if she had gone on a wild-goose chase.

"Bird? What are you talking about? It's an old gent named Frederick Augustus Kimberley. Been a leading citizen around here for sixty years."

"Do you know much about him?" Jib asked. "What he did, how he died, and so on?"

Buzz waved with a lordly gesture toward his filing cabinet. "Best obit material in the county. I collected it from old man Kinberley himself last week down at the drugstore. Didn't know I'd be using it so soon, of course."

"But when did he die?"

"This morning, so his granson said. I didn't dare go up to the house and ask any more right then. You can't be too tactful when you're just starting out. Say, what are you laughing about?"

"You!" Jib said when she could speak. "It wasn't Mr. Kimberley. It was a bird the children had named after him. I went to the funeral."

For a minute Buzz Winslow only glared at her through his glasses. Then the next minute he was on his feet. "You stay right there!" he ordered. "I'm going over to the Pollards' to telephone. If you're being funny I'll—I'll——"

What he planned to do Jib was never to know, because his blue-jeaned legs had already carried him out of earshot across the lawn toward the next house. He was back in about five minutes, and even before he sidled slowly into the corncrib Jib knew she had been right.

"Well?" she said and suppressed the impulse to say I told you so.

Buzz gestured expressively. "I bit," he said, "and if it hadn't been for you, I'd have wasted five hundred sheets of paper, a long day's work, and given the *Chronicle* a bad name besides. Golly, I'm grateful to you."

Jib stood up from the orange crate on which she had been sitting and stretched. "It's all right," she said, "but now I have to start back for the Ridge. Six more miles, and boy, am I going to be stiff."

"Sit down," Buzz said. "I've had an idea. I think I'd like to take you on as a reporter. Are you going to be staying on at the Ridge?"

"No, I'm moving to the Stirlings'——" Jib began, but Buzz, who was completely carried away by his newest idea, interrupted her.

"Well, then, it's a natural," he said. "You won't make much, but you'll make something. I cleared ten bucks last week, and I haven't even begun on advertisers."

"I don't know," Jib said, but the recollection of Oliver Stirling kept her from saying she was after a real job and couldn't be bothered with playing at journalism.

"You wait and see," Buzz said firmly. "And before you move down to the Stirlings' you can pick up all the country club dope. They're having a dance tonight. Will you be going?"

"Yes," Jib said and realized that it was hours since she had thought of it. "And now I've got to tear. If I don't get a lift back I'll be so late I'll be murdered."

As she left the corncrib Buzz picked up a few issues of his mimeographed paper and thrust them at her. "Read these," he said, "and that'll give you some idea of what I'm after. If you could take care of most of the personals, it would give me that much more time to go after main features and advertising——" He was still talking excitedly as she left him at the side of the road, and the last thing she heard was his voice calling out after her, "Don't forget to get a story tonight," he called. "I'll-be-up-after-it!"

7. PATTERNS

JIB WAS lucky enough to get a lift all the way up to the
Ridge, but even so she was late. Mrs. Appersley, coifed,
powdered, and in an evening dress which Jib thought
made her look like a circus horse, was at the telephone
in the hall. She put down the receiver as Jib came in.
"Wherever have you been?" she asked. "I've called the
Swanns, the Hammonds, the Duncans, and everyone else
I could think of with young people, and nobody'd even
heard of a picnic!"

"I've been down at Oldtown," Jib began. "I had
lunch——"

"Oldtown! Whom in heaven's name did you pick up
there?" But before Jib could answer the phone rang, and
Mrs. Appersley interrupted herself to answer it.

Jib stood still, hoping that this might be Cousin Honey,
but the next moment Mrs. Appersley turned from the
telephone and called up to her husband. "John. John,

what do you think! The Televerius Quartet is coming to the Ridge next week and they're all going to lunch here."

Mr. Appersley, redder and plumper than ever in his tuxedo, muttered something Jib couldn't hear, and then once more Mrs. Appersley was aware of Jib. "Hurry, child," she said. "Millard Bean's frantic if people are late." And then she turned to answer the telephone again.

"I'm terribly sorry," Jib said and hurried for the stairs. "I'll be just as quick as I can."

In a matter of minutes she was dressed and seated between the Appersleys in the front seat of the car. Now I'll tell them about my moving, she thought, but between Mrs. Appersley's groans over early dinner parties and her ecstatic enthusiasms over the prospects of entertaining the Televerius Quartet, neither she nor Mr. Appersley could get in a word. It was only as they drove up to Mr. Bean's pseudo-Norman buildings and saw that there were only two cars ahead of them that Mrs. Appersley began to relax. "What a relief," she said. "It's such a bore trying to be punctual."

"It's all my fault," Jib said. "I'm frightfully sorry. You see, I was——"

Mrs. Appersley patted her knee with a plump, manicured hand. "It's all right, dearie. Millard Bean thinks you're cute as a bug, which is a help. And after dinner there'll be Twinkie Teale, and I know all you young people are crazy about him."

She meant to be kind, but Jib, who had never heard of Twinkie Teale and dreaded the country-club dance and Mr. Bean for different reasons, was not reassured. She followed Mrs. Appersley through the large, hideously ugly hall into a smaller room where they were to leave their wraps. "Too, too parvenu for words, isn't it?" Mrs. Appersley said as she powdered her nose. "But still, that's what you have to expect with rags to riches. And mark my words, he's a very important man."

Jib, who was wondering who would be the first to ask

her about her visit to Stella Drelincourt, did not answer, and a moment later Mrs. Appersley led the way past two suits of armor and an equally stiff butler on into an enormous oak-beamed drawing room. "Well, well, if it isn't the Apps and little Miss Jib Sheet," Mr. Bean called out and hurried toward them. "Glad to see you. Glad to see you. Like to have our young lady meet the Prescotts and the Simpsons."

Still holding Jib's hand, he led her around to meet the couples who had already arrived. Finally Jib got her hand to herself and sat down next to Mrs. Prescott. "Do you live here?" she asked, and the young woman nodded. "We've just come," she said. "Bill, that's my husband, worked in one of Mr. Bean's Southern plants before he was moved up to Titanic. Isn't this house too beautiful?"

For a second Jib thought she was being sarcastic, and then as Mr. Bean leaned over them she thought she understood. "This is the most heavenly room, Mr. Bean," Mrs. Prescott cooed. "I was just telling Miss—er—Belton how much I liked it. Bill's always told me that you had the most marvelous eye for interiors."

Mr. Bean took the flattery like a pike bolting a minnow. "I know what I like," he said. "So I just picked the best decorator in New York City and told him what I wanted. But now tell me what you young people have been doing all day. Fussing over your pretties for the party, I imagine."

Mrs. Prescott giggled, and Jib decided that she had come to dislike the phrase "young people" more than any other two words in the English language. At that moment the other guests arrived and Mr. Bean stood up, pulling Jib with him. "Now I want you to meet all these young people," he said. "Can't have a sweet young thing like you wasted on an old man."

Jib caught a glimpse of Mrs. Prescott's face, which was far from friendly, but there was nothing she could do but follow her host. Her heart beat faster as she saw

61

that the latecomers were mostly the familiar swimming-pool crowd. Now I'm for it, she thought. Now they'll ask what I did at Stella's——

But Stella Drelincourt's name was not even mentioned. "Hi, Jib," "Hello there," "Hi," they greeted her mono-syllabically and moved on into the room, laughing and chattering about today's joke, today's amusement.

Once when Jib found herself next to Amory Holt she screwed up her nerve to ask him if he had seen Stella before she had left. "Lord, no," he said. "She left on the early train. Won't be back for weeks. Say, Mibsie, have you heard——"

As he turned away Jib could have laughed out loud with relief, but Mr. Bean had reappeared by her side and once more he found a dozen reasons for taking her hand, touching her dress, or putting his arm around her waist.

It was a distinct relief when they went into the dining room, which was even more oppressively armorial than the hall, and she found herself seated between Mr. Appersley and Fatsy Hammond. Both of them were much more interested in their food than in conversation, but at least they were easy to talk at and they kept their hands to themselves. The soup course started fairly well, but she hadn't counted on Mr. Bean, who sat only a few places away from her at the head of the table. Every few moments he made some remark about how lucky the Appersleys were in their house guest or how he himself had fallen in love with Jib at sight. Jib felt more dis-gustingly conspicuous and false by the minute and wished with all her heart that Cousin Honey had reached Mrs. Appersley or that she herself had estab-lished the fact of her leaving before the dinner party. She thought of telling Mr. Appersley, but at that minute Mr. Bean cleared his throat for a story he plainly wanted the entire table to hear.

Jib missed the beginning, and only small, unintelligible snatches reached her ears. "Communism, pure and simple. I told him what I thought of it. Government interference! I said I wouldn't have my farm gone over by the Soil Conservation Office or any other darn New Deal agency either. I told him I believe in the American way of life and no nonsense."

"What did he say then?" Mrs. Appersley offered up the right cue. "Who was it, do you know?"

"Young chap by the name of Carter," Mr. Bean said, and Jib, remembering the good-looking stranger at the railroad station, was suddenly attentive. "Cyarter, he calls it. Had the cheek to tell me it wasn't communistic or he wouldn't have touched it with a ten-foot pole, as though that proved anything. Asked me to exert my influence in the community to have other people, particularly the dairy farmers, use his services. Got quite peppery when I said I'd do the exact opposite. For a minute I thought I'd have to have Scott—that's my farm superintendent, you know—throw him out on his ear."

A few minutes later dinner was over and the girls went into the drawing room while the men, moving their chairs closer to Mr. Bean, stayed on in the dining room for their coffee. "What was Mr. Bean saying about Stanton Carter?" Jib asked Mrs. Appersley. "What does he do?"

"Some kind of soil testing for the government, I think. John didn't think it was such a bad idea, but of course if Millard Bean's against it nobody around here will touch it with a ten-foot pole. In a small place you can't be too careful."

They were the same words that Mrs. Clarkson had used, only over a different occasion. Jib looked around at Mrs. Prescott and the other girls, who had broken up into little groups of two and three as they drank their coffee. They looked so smart and so at ease, but for the first time it dawned on Jib that perhaps they fitted the pattern of life at Quentin Ridge like the paper on the wall because, like wallpaper, they had been cut and flattened and fitted until the result had no connection with what they really were.

A few minutes later she heard the sound of men's voices in the hall, and as the women began to regroup themselves Mr. Bean and his guests came into the drawing room. "Time we started thinking about going to the club," Mr. Bean said. "A poor old bach can't expect to compete with Twinkie Teale."

Jib heard Mrs. Prescott eagerly protesting that she could simply stare at Mr. Bean's view forever, and then she started to follow the other girls toward the powder room. A few of the young men exchanged glances with the girls they had asked to go to the dance with them, while others followed their host into the hall. Only Fatsy Hammond was left behind. "Doesn't anybody love a fat man?" he asked. "Here I spent a whole morning arguing my way to having the family's car and nobody wants to go with me."

"I'd love to go with you," Jib said and then felt the hot embarrassed red creep up her neck as Fatsy cast a mournful glance after Mibsie Tarrant.

"That'd be swell," he said, but his round face was anything but cheerful. He waited for her, though, when she went to get her wraps and was only a few feet away as she thanked Mr. Bean for dinner.

"Ah, but you're going with me." The older man held both her hands in his as he spoke. "I've already arranged it with the Apps."

"Oh, thanks a lot." Jib fairly pulled herself free. "But I promised to go with Fatsy." Before he could say another word she had taken Fatsy's arm and started out of the door.

"Listen, you shouldn't have done that," Fatsy said when they were in his car. "Mr. Bean won't like it."

"So what!" Jib said and found that she was shivering. "He's—he's repulsive."

Fatsy's voice sounded frightened. "He may be, but his

64

bank roll isn't. When I get through school I want a good job in one of his plants. You gotta be careful."

Jib shrank back into her own corner of the seat. There it was again. So the men too, even the young ones like Fatsy, were steam-rollered into a pattern. "What are patterns for?" The last line of Amy Lowell's poem came into her mind. "Christ! What are patterns for?"

But it was easier to be philosophical in the front seat of Fatsy's car, or even in Mr. Bean's drawing room, than it was at the country club when a dance was going full swing.

When she came out of the dressing room all the people who had been at Mr. Bean's dinner, even the Appersleys, were already dancing and Fatsy was nowhere in sight. She felt cold and frightened, and then she saw him coming toward her and, at the same moment, saw Stanton Carter dancing with a girl she didn't know. "Hello there," he called out over his partner's shoulder, and as Jib smiled back at him her spirits soared.

"Dance?" Fatsy said, and as she nodded he began to pilot her around the room.

"Twinkie Teale's giving, all right," Fatsy said, but Jib never heard him. She had seen out of the corner of her eye that Stanton Carter had been cut in on, and felt, more than saw, that he was coming to her side of the room. Oh, Lord, let him see me, she thought. Let him cut in.

At that moment Fatsy dropped her hands and she saw that Mr. Bean had tapped his shoulder. "This is my dance," he said, and his voice carried above the wail of the orchestra. "I claim this dance with my little guest of honor."

For an instant Jib hesitated, but then she was aware that Mibsie Tarrant and Amory Holt were staring at her, and the sudden impulse to show them that she was sought after and popular was overpowering. "Oh, thank you," she said and beamed up at him. "What a wonderful party!"

As he moved her away she looked straight into Stanton Carter's face. He must have seen and heard both herself and Mr. Bean, and now his bronzed, good-looking face became stiff and expressionless as he turned away and melted into the stag line.

"I've been waiting for this," Mr. Bean said and held Jib close as they circled the room. "The first time I saw you I knew you'd be a good partner."

Jib said nothing and tried to follow Mr. Bean's lead, but he danced awkwardly and held her tight while his long fingers fumbled at her waist. I've got to get out, Jib thought. I'll have to pretend I'm sick and go home. And at that moment Stew Harris cut in on her.

"What's the matter?" he asked. "You didn't look very happy dancing with the big shot."

"I can't stand him," Jib said. "He's disgusting." And for a moment she was so relieved to be dancing with somebody healthy and scrubbed-looking and her own age that she felt almost happy.

A moment later Amory Holt cut in. "Say, what is this?" he asked. "You seem to be starting a local——" He did not finish his question before Mr. Bean cut in again. "I always like dancing with the belle of the ball," he said, and when Fatsy cut in again he waited until Mr. Prescott cut in and then claimed Jib again. He backed away almost instantly, and for a moment Jib thought they had been cut in on and then she saw that it was one of the club servants. "I beg your pardon, miss," he said, "but are you the Miss Bolton that's staying with the Appersleys?"

"Yes, I am," Jib said, and the man nodded toward the veranda. "There's a young man out there who's very anxious to speak to you."

"Here, you can't leave me like this," Millard Bean began, but at that moment one of the older members of the party came up to speak to him and Jib darted for the porch.

It's Stanton Carter, she thought. It's sure to be. But

when she had dashed down the carpeted stairs Stanton Carter was nowhere in sight and she nearly fell over Buzz Winslow, who was sitting on the bottom steps.

"You!" she gasped. "Did *you* send for me?"

"Sure thing," he said. "Did you get a story on the party?"

"No!" Jib said. "No, of course not——"

"It doesn't matter," Buzz said and he pulled her into the shadow of some big hydrangea bushes. "Listen, the story of the ages has just broken up at Millard Bean's farm, and it'll take two of us to cover it."

"What do you mean? What's happened? I can't go now!"

"Sure you can. It's only a mile, and I've got my bike all fixed and my new lamp's a knockout. Bean's cattle all got out when there wasn't anybody but an old watchman left on the place."

"I can't," Jib protested. "Not in these clothes!"

For answer Buzz pulled something long and dark out of his bicycle basket. "I know all about women!" he said and handed her a pair of blue jeans. "Comes from living with the great-aunts. I got these at home on my way up here."

For a second Jib hesitated. From where she stood she could hear the wail of Twinkie Teale's saxophone and see the couples still twirling inside. She saw the stooped, cadaverous figure of an older man emerge on the porch and look about as though he were searching for someone, and instantly her mind snapped to a decision. Rather than go back to dance with Mr. Bean, or boys who only rushed her because Bean did, she would go anywhere, do anything! "Give me those jeans!" she said and, stepping behind the hydrangea, stuffed the soft folds of her dress into them.

A moment later she stood beside Buzz Winslow. "Let's go," she said, and he thumped her back approvingly.

"Good girl! Now you get on the crossbar, and for Pete's sake sit still. I'm going to ride like fury."

The wind swept past Jib's face as they rolled over the empty road, and for the first time all evening her heart pounded with happy excitement. This was a crazy, a lunatic thing to do, but it was fun, and she would be back long before Mr. and Mrs. Appersley were ready to go home. "This is something," she said, and the words chattered out of her mouth as they passed over a bump in the road. "I feel as though I were flying!"

Buzz was an inexperienced horseman but he was a very expert cyclist, and a few minutes later they rolled up Millard Bean's driveway. The house was ablaze with lights, and from the barn they could hear men's voices shouting.

"They've probably gotten most of 'em!" Buzz panted. "I'll leave you at the house while I go to the barn. See if you can find out how it started. I'll be back as soon as I can."

Jib hurried up the steps and through the open front door into complete confusion. One of the suits of armor had crashed to the floor, the hall table was upset, and beyond her in the drawing room a white-haired maid struggled to capture two small Chester pigs and a Saanan goat!

The woman saw Jib, started as though she had seen a ghost and the next second rushed futilely after the goat. "Stand still!" Jib said. "You're scaring it to death. If we move slowly we can catch it."

"But the garden!" The woman sounded desperate. "If they go out through them windows they'll ruin the roses!"

Jib saw that she was right and began slowly, warily, to head off the little pigs. In the meantime the goat jumped up on the sofa and looked at her through suspicious, slot-shaped eyes. "We'll get the pigs into the powder room," Jib said. "They can't do so much harm in there."

The woman nodded, and they managed to shoo the

pigs toward the small room at the left of the hall. Once, as they approached the doorway, one of the pigs turned and fled squealing straight toward Jib. She plunged forward and caught its small, incredibly hard little body between her two hands. For a second she was afraid it would wriggle free, but a moment later she had it inside the powder room with the door shut.

She turned, panting, and followed the maid into the drawing room, where the goat still stood perched on the arm of the sofa. "We'll never get it," the woman said. "It's that wild!"

Jib tore open two cigarettes from one of the boxes on the nearest table and then held out the tobacco in the palm of her hand. The goat looked at it, sniffed, reached forward gingerly, and Jib's fingers closed tight on its collar. "There!" she said. "Now where shall we put it?"

"I'll get a rope," the woman said, and a moment later they had the goat fastened to a leg of the biggest sofa. "Sure the men must be coming from the barn. Do you hear them, miss?"

Jib shook her head and darted out of the front door. For an instant she was aware only of the small summer night noises, and then she heard the unmistakable sound of a human sneeze. She turned and caught sight of a young man, his body hidden behind some bushes, his thin face spotlighted by the light from the house. "We've got the goat and the pigs!" Jib shouted, but the man disappeared and at the same moment a truck drove up from the barn and two perspiring farm hands jumped out of it. Jib turned the animals over to them and then went back to help the waitress straighten up the drawing room. "How did it happen?" she asked. "How did it start?"

The waitress pushed the hair out of her eyes and lifted up the suit of armor. "The others went off to the Bingo as soon as the dishes were done," she said. "I was asleep, when I heard men shouting and I came downstairs and

69

nearly fell over the pigs. Glory be to God, but they gave me a turn!"

"I should think they would have," Jib said. "Have you any idea of how they got out?"

"That I have not, but it must have been let out they were, and nobody but old Tim Brady and meself left on the place." They had just finished getting the room into something like order when Buzz reappeared in the front hall.

"We ought to beat it," he said. "They've all the cattle back, and somebody's telephoned Mr. Bean at the club and he's on his way over!"

Jib dashed after him, but it was too late. A whole caravan of cars had already turned into the driveway, and although most of them went straight to the barn, Mr. and Mrs. Appersley stopped at the house. For a second Mrs. Appersley stared at Jib as though she were seeing things. "Jib!" she said. "Jib Bolton, what under the sun are you doing here in those clothes?"

"I just came——" Jib began, but now the Irish waitress had joined them.

"Mrs. Appersley, is it? Sure and the young lady was the greatest help imaginable. Faith now, without her I'd have gone clear out of my mind."

"I came over with Buzz Winslow," Jib tried again. "We were only going to be gone for a little while and I didn't think you'd mind. He lent me these blue jeans." She looked around for Buzz, but he was no longer in sight.

"Well, he was here," she went on desperately. "When you first came——"

Mrs. Appersley waved her still with the motions of someone fanning herself for air. "That little boy?" she asked. "The one in dungarees?"

Jib nodded. "I hope you don't mind. We really didn't mean any harm."

Mrs. Appersley stared at Jib with small, puzzled eyes.

"Oh, it isn't anything shocking," she said. "It's—it's just so ridiculous. A girl of nineteen leaving a perfectly beautiful party to go off on a bicycle with a village boy."

For the first time since they had met in the hallway Mr. Appersley turned away from the door. "They're coming up here," he said. "So they must have all the cattle in, and if you ask me, I think we'd better clear out. Bean's furious, of course, and I don't think it's exactly tactful for us to wait here to meet him."

Mrs. Appersley got into the car, and after Jib had said good night to the waitress she followed. "Jib, I don't understand you," Mrs. Appersley said. "I've always been sympathetic with young people, but to go off when you were having such a success——"

At that moment Jib blurted out that she was leaving the next day to go down to stay with the Stirlings. "It's been wonderful of you to have me." She fumbled over the words. "But there really isn't enough work to justify——" She hesitated, afraid that she had hurt Mrs. Appersley's feelings. But to her surprise that lady only put her hand to her mouth and yawned.

"Oh, of course," she said. "Honey Stirling did call up just before you came back, but everything was so hectic with arranging for the Televerius Recitals and all that, I forgot it. John, did I tell you that Millard Bean said he'd take twenty tickets?"

They had reached the Appersleys' house by this time, and Mrs. Appersley went straight to bed. Jib stayed behind to help Mr. Appersley put out the lights, and then as she started up the stairs he stopped her. "How come you and young Winslow went over to Bean's?" he said. "Haven't I heard something about his starting a paper?"

Jib told him everything she knew about Buzz Winslow, and for the first time since she had known Mr. Appersley he listened to her with intense interest. "Can you tie that!" he said when she had finished. "There isn't a newspaper for twenty miles around that would print a word

71

Millard Bean wouldn't like, and now a fifteen-year-old kid turns up who's going to say anything he wants."

"But he won't say anything that isn't true," Jib protested. "I really think he tries very hard to be accurate."

"That's just it," Mr. Appersley said, and he put back his head and bellowed with laughter. "That's what's so perfectly beautiful."

8. HOME COUNTY

THE NEXT morning, by the time Jib reached the dining room, Mr. Appersley had left for his office, and Mrs. Appersley, still in her dressing gown and with her peroxide hair unbrushed, was already at the telephone. Jib breakfasted alone and was just thinking about going out to the garden when she met Mrs. Appersley on the stairs. "Nobody knows what I have to contend with," that lady fumed. "Here I'm expected to entertain the Televerius Quartet, who have just been staying with the smartest families in Lenox, and John refuses to pay for extra help from the club and Juan hides in the garden when I need him in the house."

"Could I help?" Jib asked. "I haven't done anything useful since I arrived."

"No. Nobody can. Eventually I always have to do things myself," Mrs. Appersley said and then, turning on the stairs, looked down at Jib. "But I'm sure you don't expect to get paid for the few days you've been here? It isn't that I grudge anyone a cent, but John keeps me so frightfully close. He simply doesn't understand."

"I couldn't possibly take a penny," Jib said and found, to her own disgust, that she was blushing. "Not possibly."

"Well, I'm glad we understand one another," Mrs. Appersley said. "I was afraid Fay Clarkson might have given the wrong impression."

Jib said nothing and went into her own room. She finished packing, wrote a long letter to her family, and then settled down to read the papers which Buzz Winslow had given her.

She had, momentarily, been furious when Buzz had evaporated last night, leaving her to face the Appersleys alone, but that did not interfere with her reading his paper with interest and growing respect. Buzz's *Chronicle* was mimeographed on double sheets of cheap newsprint, but that was the only amateurish thing about it. It was livelier and better written than any of the school or college magazines she had read, and right from the first issue Buzz had kept to a formula which she could see made sense. On the first page he concentrated on the local news of the three Quentins: the sale of a big farm, a motor accident, a Parish Silver Tea at Quentin Oldtown, and an account of the graduating exercises at the high school in Quentin Mills. On the second and third pages he had a long list of personal items, advertisements, and accounts of local sports. On the fourth page he had an editorial and a longish article which in one issue was about the Oldtown Library and in another about the lunches served at the elementary schools.

Jib had just finished his latest issue when she heard the sound of a car and Juan came up to tell her that Mrs. Stirling was waiting for her. Jib started down and saw Cousin Honey, looking like a bantam hen in a turkey house, standing alone in the vast front hall. Jib had just reached the bottom step when Mrs. Appersley fluttered in from the drawing room. "I'm sure I don't know what John and I are going to do without Jib," she began. "We're never happy unless we're simply surrounded by young people."

Jib felt herself grow tongue-tied, and at that moment the sharp, imperious tinkle of the telephone sounded through the hall and Mrs. Appersley gestured to them not to wait. "I'll see you both soon," she called back over her shoulder. "We'll have a lovely long visit when once I'm through this wretched Televerius business. Right now I'm simply frantic. Yes. Hello. Oh, Brenda darling——"

Jib looked up at Cousin Honey and they carried her bag out to the car without a word. "'It may not be the greatest love but ah, it is the latest love,'" Mrs. Stirling hummed as she turned the car onto the Ridge road. "And last week the greatest love was the young set and this week it's music."

"How did you know?" Jib asked, and now that she was out of the Appersleys' house she no longer felt embarrassed and ill at ease, but only amused and infinitely relieved that she was leaving. "I didn't realize you knew her well."

"I don't," Mrs. Sterling said. "But in a small place you're bound to know something about everybody. As Noll is fond of saying, 'A village is a hive of glass, where nothing unobserved may pass.' It keeps it from ever being dull."

They had left the Ridge by this time and were driving through the crowded commercial streets of Quentin Mills. Mrs. Stirling, who unlike Mrs. Clarkson was an inexpert driver, clung tightly to her wheel and, except to point out the hospital and two or three late-Victorian public buildings, did not speak until they came out on the Oldtown Road. "There!" she said. "Now we're back in what Noll calls the home county and I can take a deep breath."

Jib looked over at her and laughed. "We used to use Quentin Mills for shopping," she said. "But we never really knew it, and I certainly didn't know the Ridge or Oldtown. Are they all so very different?"

"Night and day," Mrs. Stirling said. "And even though some people live in one place and work in another, I always think it's just the hills that keep the towns from sliding apart completely. Quentin Mills is straight business, the Ridge is the result for a prosperous few of what you might call Big Business, and Oldtown's what it always has been—an old-fashioned typical New England country town that holds a lot more life and more surprises than you'd think."

They were at the long hill going up toward the Stirlings' by this time, and after stalling the engine once and missing an oak tree by a matter of inches Mrs. Stirling pulled up at her own front door. "There," she said. "Welcome home, my darling. Buzz Winslow called up twice before I went to work this morning, to ask if you'd come down to his aunts' house this afternoon, and I told him I'd let you know and you can decide for yourself. If I know anything about the Ridge you've probably had enough unsociable sociability pushed at you for the past few days to last you a lifetime. And now come up and see your room."

Jib followed her up to a small dormer-window room papered with a light flowery paper and furnished with curly-maple furniture. "This is lovely," Jib said, and then as she turned toward the window she gave a little gasp of pleased surprise. "Why, there's Quentin's Cobble and Judgment Rock," she said. "It's sort of the reverse side of the view I always looked out at from the Cobble Top."

Mrs. Stirling beamed. "Oliver was right," she said. "I would have put you in the other room down the hall, because it's bigger and airier, but Noll said you'd like this. It's funny, you know, I was born here and Noll was born

76

and brought up in England, but I think he knows more about how attached people can get to this countryside than anybody living. He'll be delighted you're pleased."

Both the Stirlings had to work that afternoon, so Jib took the old bicycle, which Cousin Honey had told her was in the shed, and went down to the Winslows'. Buzz was not in the corncrib, and as she turned back toward the flagstone walk she was aware that she was being watched from the house. There seemed to be nothing else to do but go in to ask for Buzz, and she went up the steps to find an elderly lady waiting for her at the door. "I am Miss Winslow," the lady said and led the way to a small and immaculate parlor. "Sister, a young friend of Brewster's is here."

Another lady, who looked like the quintessence of all the old-maid schoolteachers Jib had ever known, rose and shook hands while her sister indicated that Jib was to sit down on the prim plush-covered chair beside her. For a moment after Jib had introduced herself she felt as though she had forgotten to scrub her neck and wished she had worn a dress instead of dungarees. "I think Buzz wanted to see me," she said. "I imagine it was about the excitement at Mr. Bean's last night. We went to find out about it together for his paper, you know."

"Oh, so you're the girl who was so helpful to him about the funeral," Miss Winslow said, and Miss Lucinda moved forward eagerly.

"What a joke on Brewster that was," she said, and at that moment Jib saw that Miss Winslow's neat gray-stockinged legs ended up in a pair of bright red ski socks. "He isn't often caught like that."

"He told us about the pony too," Miss Winslow went on. "And I must confess, since no one was hurt, Sister and I both wish we had been there to see it."

"Buzz was a wonderfully good sport," Jib said, and as the two old ladies beamed at her she was warmly aware of liking them and of being liked in return. At that moment the door opened and Buzz rushed in like a pint-sized tornado.

"I've got it!" he said and kissed Miss Harriet Winslow, patted Miss Lucinda's erect back, and waved at Jib in what seemed like one motion. "It's good for a whole column."

"Sister, I told thee so." Miss Winslow turned to Miss Lucinda, and Jib remembered that the Stirlings had told that the Winslow ladies were Quakers on their mother's side. "Thee was mad not to see there would be news in a Shriners' picnic."

Miss Lucinda shrugged. "A few personals, perhaps, but I think I have done better for thee, Brewster. I telephoned Mrs. O'Flaherty while you were gone, and her son Michael gave me the scores for the Knights of Columbus baseball game over in Quentin Mills. Each one of the players that thee lists, Brewster, is sure to buy a copy of the paper."

Buzz took up the paper that Miss Lucinda handed him. "Thanks a lot, Aunt Loopy," he said. "It certainly was worth while teaching you to keep a box score."

Miss Lucinda Winslow looked irritated, and for a moment Jib thought it was her nephew's use of the fantastically unsuitable nickname, but the next moment she understood. "*Thee* teach me, Brewster Winslow," Miss Lucinda said. "Why, of all the perfectly slanderous bits of nonsense, that is the most nonsensical. I kept a box score before thee—or thy father, for that matter—was even thought of."

Buzz grinned apologetically and a moment or two later led the way into the corncrib. "They're terrific!" Jib exploded. "Why, they're both of them as keen about the paper as you are."

"You bet," Buzz said and dropped his papers down on the desk by the typewriter. "Aunt Loopy worked on a Philadelphia paper for years, and although Auntie Bed Socks always taught English in the high school up here until she retired, she's always been interested in journalism too. Besides, they're both born gossips, and that's the essence of running a village paper. Now what did you find out last night?"

For the first time since she had entered the Winslows' house Jib remembered that she had come down with a chip on her shoulder. "You big bum," she began. "That was a nice piece of business, simply evaporating and letting me handle the Appersleys."

"Velly solly," Buzz said blandly. "But the paper comes first, and I thought maybe I'd get into a lot of unnecessary entanglements if I stayed. I hope you didn't have much trouble."

"None, no thanks to you," Jib said acidly, but if Buzz knew that she was, or rather had been, annoyed he didn't show it.

"I don't suppose you found out who did it?" he asked. "It was obviously done by somebody with a grudge, but that leaves an awfully wide field."

For the first time since last night Jib thought of the man she had seen disappear behind the bushes near the Bean house. "He might have done it," she finished. "Come to think of it, he certainly didn't want to be seen."

"No use," Buzz made an X mark with his pencil. "Bean'd be furious."

"So you cater to him too?" Jib asked. "I knew everyone did at the Ridge, but I thought down at Oldtown a few people might not kowtow to him."

Buzz let his pencil clatter to the floor. "Are you trying to be funny?" he said. "I don't cater to Bean, or the Appersleys, or my own great-aunts, if you want to know. But I have to have facts. Who was the man? Did he actually let the cattle out? If so, why and at what time? There were dozens of strange men up at Bean's place by the time we got there, and probably a good half dozen of them had reason to hate Bean. We can't blame any one person unless we can make it stick, don't you see

79

that? Now the best we can do is to say that it was not accidental and that the cattle, including the pigs and that goat, were let out by a person or persons unknown. I only don't want to make Bean furious over something I can't prove. Read this and you'll see what I'm after."

He pulled a piece of paper from a box and handed it to Jib. "Gentleman Farmer's Cattle Escape While He Attends Country Club Dance," she read. "On Friday, June 6th, the Guernsey cows belonging to Mr. Millard Bean of Hi Acres, Quentin Ridge, made their way up from their pasturage toward his 23-room Norman-type dwelling . . ."

Jib read on to the end and then looked up at Buzz. "It's good," she said. "But it'll make Bean livid. He prides himself on being old Mr. Earthbound."

"But it's all true," Buzz said. "There isn't a word or fact in it that I can't check or double-check, and that's what you don't seem to understand. If you think I'd shield anyone or flatter anyone, you've just plain missed the point."

Jib looked back at the typewritten sheet she held in her hand. "I do get it, as a matter of fact. And your piece is just right the way it is. How about calling it 'Pigs in the Powder Room'?"

"That's wonderful!" Buzz said. "Absolutely knockout. You see, you can make sense when you don't get excited. Look, I'm going to put your name down on the masthead right underneath my own. J. Bolton, Reporter at Large."

He was so earnest and enthusiastic that he looked almost the twins' age, and Jib resisted an impulse to push her hand through his crew-cut hair the way she did with Dickie's. "I'd like that," she said. "I've missed working for the Lit."

"Good." Buzz typed down her name with a flourish. "It'll go in Monday's edition, and I'll either come over or telephone on Tuesday to see what you've picked up that might be useful for Thursday."

At that moment Jib stood up. "I'll have to get a job

80

first," she said. "I can't just sponge on the Stirlings for the summer without working."

Buzz shrugged. "That won't be hard," he said. "With all your swell friends at the Ridge, and Mrs. Stirling knowing every man, woman, and dog in Oldtown, it'll be a cinch. Aunt Loopy says that Mrs. Stirling could get a job for a one-armed paper hanger or a legless mule."

"I'm getting this one on my own," Jib said stiffly, and Buzz roared.

"O.K., Joan of Arc, go on and carry your fleur-de-lis. I hope you land a lulu."

For an instant Jib wavered between irritation and laughter. Then as she glanced at Buzz, his corn-shock hair on end and the sun on his glasses, busily typing away on his latest story, laughter won. She was still chuckling to herself as she started the bicycle trip back to the Stirlings'. What was it that Cousin Honey had said about Oldtown? That it was an old-fashioned New England town with more life and more surprises in it than one might think? She was right and then some. Jib could understand why her parents, after long, hard-working winters in the city, had been content to withdraw into the green peace of Cobble Top. They had probably made the decision with their eyes open, but now, for the first time, it occurred to Jib that there was a choice, and the alternative, if this afternoon had been a fair sample, looked distinctly amusing.

9. NOTHING UNOBSERVED!

A WEEK after Jib had moved to the Stirlings' she woke up to the already familiar sound of Cousin Oliver whistling snatches from Brahms' Second Symphony in the shower across the hall from her bedroom. As she dressed she heard the sputter of the electric percolator in the kitchen below her, and then a moment later, just as she had expected, Cousin Honey's cheerful voice called up the stairs. "Breakfast's ready. Rise and shine!"

Jib smiled to herself as she hurried down the stairs. Every house had its own distinctive pattern of morning noises, and at the Stirlings' house they were deliciously friendly and reassuring after the Appersleys'. She stopped long enough to take a deep appreciative sniff of the mixed fragrance of roses and furniture polish which belonged especially to the living room and then went on to the sturdy breakfast smells of coffee and bacon and toast in the kitchen. As usual Cousin Honey was all dressed and ready for work, and equally as usual Cousin Oliver appeared only a moment or two before she bustled off. "I'm afraid I'll have to be out for lunch," she said. "Do you think you and Jib can manage without me?"

"I doubt if we starve," Cousin Oliver said. "But I warn you we'll be hard on your supplies if we get the north bed cleared up the way we've planned. That's very hungry-making work."

Jib drank her orange juice and looked out at the garden through the kitchen window. She'd never cared a great deal for housework, and Cousin Honey's voluble, seemingly carefree housekeeping was so effective that it was hard to find even shreds of unfinished business that needed to be done. She had always loved gardening, though, and in that department her help seemed more than welcome. At Cobble Top the garden had always been of common interest to the whole family, and now, to her surprise, the Stirlings' far more beautiful garden had turned out to be an equally congenial bond between Oliver and herself. The first morning after Cousin Honey had gone to work she had followed him hesitatingly. The enormous flower garden and the vegetable and cutting beds that were neatly shut off from the house by an evergreen hedge were so obviously his personal pride and joy, the way painting was her mother's, that she wondered if he would welcome outside help. He had gone to work in silence, and when she knelt down beside him and had begun to pull small, incessant weeds out from among a low row of carrots he did not even look up. It was only at noon, when Cousin Honey had come home for lunch and he had called out to her, "Honey, come and see what Jib and I've done," that Jib was sure not only that he was aware of her help but glad to accept it.

Once, a day later, when she had diffidently suggested that ageratum would grow better in a corner of the small bed around the well and last longer than the cornflowers which he had started to put there, he looked down at her with obvious approval. "You're an excellent gardener," he said. "It doesn't happen often when people are very young. I knew some boys once in Scotland who were real gardeners at sixteen, but I don't think I've ever encountered one before in this country. Louisa was born and brought up in this place, but when I first knew her she didn't know the difference between a trout and a tuber."

"Mum loves it," Jib said and found that now she could talk about her family and Cobble Top without feeling stiff at the back of her throat. "It was one of the things we all did every summer when we came up here."

From then on they had talked more often and more easily, with the comfortable, unstrained companionship of two people whose minds are free while their hands are occupied. In the afternoon Oliver Stirling always went to work on his book and Jib read or walked or joined Buzz Winslow in one of his reporting canvasses of Quentin Oldtown. It had been a good week, Jib thought, the best in a way that she had ever had away from Cobble Top, but now she knew that the time had come when she would have to start seriously looking for a job. She had telegraphed her mother about moving from the Ridge as well as written to ask what the family thought she ought to do next. Mrs. Bolton's answer had arrived yesterday, and although it was loving and affectionate and she was obviously relieved that Jib was with her cousins, she had made it plain that from so great a distance she could not give specific advice about what work Jib ought to try for. "You can't always help the people you love most," Mother had ended her letter. "Sometimes you can only go on loving them and believing in them and let them fight out their own conclusions. This is one of those times, darling, but I'm not worried. I know eventually you'll find the right solution."

The letter lay on the small maple desk in Jib's bedroom, but she thought of it as she began on the eggs and bacon Cousin Honey set before her. "I wish I didn't have to be away," Cousin Honey said as she moved toward the sink, "but I'm going to try and get Kurt Cramer a job. He has been foolish, but I'm sure he means to turn over a new leaf. And after that I'm going to see if Bee Perkins won't take on Mable Platt's niece in the Frock Shop."

"The Employment Expert for Lame Ducks," Oliver Stirling said, and then a few minutes later, when Cousin Honey left, he lit his pipe and turned to Jib. "She's absolutely astonishing. She really has found work for half the misfits in this town."

Jib said nothing, but her chin lifted in a way that her younger brothers would have recognized. After the failure of her so-called work at the Appersleys' she had had no desire to get another job on "pull," and now that vague distaste hardened into a definite resolve. She was not a misfit nor, in Buzz's phrase, a legless mule, and she was most assuredly not going to lean on Cousin Honey for help.

She worked with Cousin Oliver as usual in the morning, but in the afternoon, when he shut the door to his study, she headed for the telephone. If she could arrange for transportation to the Ridge she would undoubtedly be able to get at least part-time work taking care of children of some of the younger executives of the big factories in Quentin Mills, but there was nothing about the idea that appealed to her. There were only half a dozen stores in Oldtown, and when she had been to them with either Cousin Honey or Buzz they had apparently had all the employees they needed. It was clear from what Buzz had told her that the only real industry which was not six miles away in Quentin Mills was the Mahoras Paper Mill down by the river, near the

85

oldest part of Oldtown village. She looked it up in the directory and put through a call to the office.

A crisp New England voice answered, but Jib was ready for it. "I'm looking for a job," she began. "Is there anyone who could see me about it this afternoon?"

There was a pause that seemed endless, and then the voice—clear, concise, and more impersonal than air—said that Mr. Blaisdell, the manager, would see Miss Bolton at three. Jib, whose spirits were always mercurial, dashed upstairs in high fettle. As she dressed she mentally tasted the triumph of coming back that evening and telling the admiring Stirlings that she had found a job on her own initiative.

It was only when she paused for a final inspection in front of the mirror that the first smoke curl of doubt rose up in her heart. Her new crop of freckles was a blot, and her hair insisted on curling all over her head like a well-fed baby's instead of falling into neat, compact waves like the new hairdos in *Vogue*. Still, the dark plaid cotton which she and Mum had bought at a sale looked both mature and efficient, and when she put on nylons and slipped into her best shoes for the first time in a week, the sleek, dressy feel of them was decidedly reassuring.

Her confidence lasted until she had reached the village and crossed the common with the sagging little bandstand at one corner and followed Mahoras River to the low wood-and-gray-stone building that housed the Mahoras Paper Mill. Suddenly, as she stepped into the cool shadow of the old building, she felt as lonely and insecure as she had felt years ago when, at the age of five, she had lost her mother in the frenzied shuffle of a big department store in the Christmas rush.

You've got to go through with it, she told herself, and struggled to concentrate on the river and the old-fashioned building beside it. Compared to the vast, sprawling factories with their modern plexiglass additions in

Quentin Mills, the outside of the Mahoras plant was as staid and peaceful-looking as a college library, but once Jib walked up the shabby wooden steps and into a bare hall that smelled of steam and caustics the illusion of peacefulness vanished. The Mahoras mill, with forty employees, was only a minnow compared to the leviathans that flourished farther down the river, but on this particular June afternoon, when the Christmas orders were already on hand, it was a busy place.

Jib walked on into a square, high-ceilinged office, the back door of which opened out on a wide loft where a dozen different machines stamped and pounded so that the whole building shook. For a moment Jib hesitated, more unnerved than ever by the staggering barrage of sound and smell ahead of her. She managed to pull herself together and turned to the girl at the desk nearest the door. "My name's Bolton," she said. "I have an appointment with Mr. Blaisdell at three."

The girl gave her a bored look and then minced off on tricky, high-heeled shoes. "That way," she said and jerked a scarlet thumb toward a door on the left marked "Private."

Jib went in and found herself facing a man of about her father's age with a knotty, homespun face that reminded her of Abraham Lincoln. "Good afternoon," she said. "I'm Jessica Bolton. I've come to apply for a job."

Mr. Blaisdell started to get up, changed his mind, reddened and sat down again, and then nodded to the chair beside him. "Do you—that is—do you know anything about papermaking?" he said, and Jib realized that he was even more embarrassed and ill at ease than she was.

"No, I don't," she said. "But I'd like to learn."

Mr. Blaisdell fiddled nervously with the inkwell before him. "Do you want a permanent job or just one for the summer?"

"Summer," Jib said. "I hope to go back to college in the fall."

Mr. Blaisdell sighed and looked over at her with dark, unexpectedly young eyes that were as pleading as a hound's. "Summer help is one of our big problems," he said and turned away quickly as though he didn't have enough confidence to look her full in the face. "By the time summer people are trained enough to be useful they're off again."

"I'm ready to do anything," Jib said. "Any kind of work at all."

But when he asked her if she could do speed typing or take dictation she had to shake her head, and her last bit of confidence melted away, leaving her defenseless against the contagion of Guy Blaisdell's embarrassment.

"What can you do?" he asked, and although the question was nothing more than an apologetic mutter, it shook Jib more than if he had roared at her. For a moment she sat rigid, unable to summon one single thought, and then finally she forced herself to speak.

"I ran the Lit at school," she said. "And last year I majored in English."

"I'm afraid that won't help here," Mr. Blaisdell said, and as he stood up she was afraid that the interview was over and that she had lost her chance.

"I can do things with my hands," Jib said. "I was fair at athletics at school, and I'm a pretty good gardener." The moment the words were out she felt ridiculously foolish, as though she were a small child who had boasted about his skill at jackstraws because he doesn't know how to swim.

Mr. Blaisdell did not seem to have heard. "Let's go out," he said desperately. "Perhaps if you see the plant, the machines, the real things, you'll understand what I mean."

Jib followed him down the hall through the outer office into the high-ceilinged loft she had glimpsed before. She found the noise of the machines overpowering, but neither Mr. Blaisdell nor the girls who were operating them seemed to notice it. "This is one of our newest folding machines," Blaisdell said, and as he touched the frame of the machine he spoke with confidence for the first time. "It's a beautiful thing really. Does the job a hundred times more efficiently than the old ones."

Jib glanced at the machine and then, with greater interest, at the woman who was feeding it. She watched the deft, intricate motions of the woman's hands and wondered, with a growing feeling of hopelessness, if she could ever achieve such skill. She straightened up and watched the other operators down the long loft, and each of them seemed to be as efficient as the woman nearest her. A grizzled man in overalls came in with a younger man to whom he seemed to be explaining some of the processes, and Jib looked over at them, grateful for the sight of another neophyte, but they left almost immediately and she was alone in a world of experts.

Blaisdell had not moved, and his face, as he listened to the revolutions of the motor, had the rapt expression of a musician listening to a symphony. At that moment the secretary who had first announced Jib came over to him and, shouting to make herself heard, told him that Mr. Millard Bean wished to speak to him on the telephone. Blaisdell sighed as he pulled himself away from the machine, and when he had gone the operator looked up at Jib and snickered. "Old Blaisie's still a mechanic at heart. Best one we ever had. If you ask me, it's a pity Bean kicked him upstairs to management."

Jib hardly heard and followed the secretary back toward the office without speaking. Millard Bean! The significance of that name suddenly overpowered even the crash and roar of the machinery around her.

Tell Blaisdell you know Bean! The voice in her mind was shrill and commanding.

Don't do any such thing, a second voice countered. You loathe Bean and you know it.

Bean's the Boss! If he says a word for you, you're in. And he'll say that word if you ask him.

No, don't do it! The second voice, braced by all the pride in Jib's heart, was triumphant. Don't ask for help from anyone.

A moment later, when the girl at the desk told Jib that Mr. Blaisdell was once more ready to see her, her mind was made up. Win, lose, or draw, she was not going to mention Bean!

The rest of the interview was mercifully short. "I'm afraid I can't use you," Blaisdell said, and now he avoided even looking at Jib's side of the room. "I wish I could have shown you more of the plant, so you'd understand why, but I'm afraid I haven't the time. Perhaps when you're through college——"

A few minutes later Jib was outside again and, instinctively avoiding traffic, walked eastward through a backwater of the village which was unfamiliar to her. She felt let down and humiliated, but at least nobody knew about it. Up at the Ridge every false step or gesture laid her wide open to mockery, and she realized that the fact that nobody had teased her about Stella Drelincourt was a bit of good luck which would not happen again. Well, this time she had been more careful, and except for Mr. Blaisdell, whom she would not see again, and his secretary, who did not count, not a soul knew that she had applied for a job and been turned down.

She walked slowly up a gradual rise until she came to a sign saying that this place was Squaw's Hill where the first settlers had built their houses in 1638. The settlers' log cabins had gone, and the small clapboard houses which had replaced them in the eighteenth century looked dwarfed and wizened beneath their giant elms. A woman came out of the rear of one of the houses and called out across her unfenced yard to a neighbor whom Jib could not see.

Jib shrugged and moved on. She had read enough

about colonial village life to know that when these houses had been built the people who had lived in them had been completely dependent upon one another not only for mutual protection and security but for every aspect of sociability and companionship. Cars and radios have changed all that, she thought. People are too busy to bother about their neighbors, and besides, we're smarter about minding our own business. I'm glad I didn't tell Buzz or the Stirlings about the factory.

She skirted the rest of the village and walked due west to the long hill that led to the Stirlings'. She climbed steadily to the halfway mark, where a depression in the road was all that was left of an old ford across a brook. Here there was a wide view, but as Jib stared across the valley to where Quentin's Cobble stood out like a sentinel among the sleeping hills, her mind was so engrossed with plans for another job that she never noticed it.

It was after six when she reached the Stirlings', and Cousin Honey hurried out from the kitchen to meet her. "Jib darling," she called. "You poor blessed lamb. Why didn't you tell me you were going to ask Guy Blaisdell for work. I could have arranged it so easily. I was in there earlier today anyway, getting a job for Kurt Cramer."

For a moment Jib stood still while her stomach turned over in a doughy ball of outraged pride. "How did you know?" she asked finally. "I didn't tell anyone."

Cousin Honey had already gone back to the kitchen, and she stirred something on the stove with one hand while she pulled out a kitchen chair with the other. "Come and sit down, you poor baby," she said. "All that walk after working all morning with Oliver. You must be half dead, besides being terribly disappointed. Now if you'd only let me talk to Guy——"

"How did you know about it?" Jib asked, and her

voice sounded harsh and cold above the warm simmering sounds in the kitchen.

"Why, one of the girls who works at the Mahoras factory has a sister she calls for in my office, and they told me just as I was leaving. Things get around in a small town, you know. Not that it matters, except if I'd only known I'm sure I could have helped——"

"I didn't want any help from anyone!" Jib snapped and started for the stairs. It was only as she rounded the newel post that she caught sight of Cousin Honey's face and saw that she looked as hurt and bewildered as though Jib had stepped forward and slapped her.

10. PAST WITH A FUTURE

By SEVEN o'clock, when Cousin Honey called out that supper was ready, Jib still seethed with a frustrated desire for privacy. What was it that Robinson Jeffers had written? "Give you heart to the hawks and not to men to tear." Well, it wasn't as easy as that. Sometimes you did everything in your power to keep your problems to yourself and then other people walked in and scuffled up your troubles like a boy kicking up leaves. She started downstairs, intending to say she didn't want any supper, but Cousin Honey was waiting for her at the bottom of the steps and before Jib could speak she had thrown her arms around her neck. "I'm sorry I was so stupid about your job," she said, and Jib's stiffness melted in the face of such unaffected warmth and humility. "I'm just a meddlesome old fool that can't recognize independence when I meet it. You'll just have to forgive me."

"I was awful," Jib said huskily. "Just a louse."

At that moment Oliver Stirling, who invariably chose the most inopportune moments to bring in the spoils from his garden, arrived in the kitchen with an enormous bunch of peonies that he said had to be put in deep water at once. Between fixing the flowers and putting supper on the table before the soufflé fell, both Mrs. Stirling and Jib were completely occupied for the next few minutes and nothing more was said about jobs.

"It'll be heavenly out in the garden this evening," Mrs. Stirling said when they had reached dessert. "The smell of roses is so strong you could almost sit on it, and there's going to be a moon. If it wasn't for the Library Council Meeting I'd sit out there forever, Noll, just like Ferdinand the Bull, and not do a thing."

"When that day comes all pigs will fly and butterflies will start bank accounts," Oliver Stirling said, and Jib laughed and felt better than she had all evening.

Although Cousin Honey left the house still protesting, she did not get back until long after Jib was asleep, and the next morning she was both amusing and enthusiastic in describing her meeting. "We had some tense moments," she said. "Old Mrs. Oakley began rattling her family crest again, and for once Simon Planter talked back. We were meeting to decide about the new water cooler, but they began battling over the Revolution and they fought all the way down to the present. It was quite an evening, but I think we really accomplished something before it was over."

Jib, who had toyed with the idea of applying at the library for a job, had given it up last night when Cousin Honey had said that she was on the board of directors. Now, as she and Oliver Stirling took up their garden tools, her mind was more on her cousin than it was on a job. "Cousin Honey really eats up meetings, doesn't she?" she said. "Mum hates them, and I think Mrs. Appersley only felt she ought to enjoy them, but Cousin Honey really seems to have fun."

Oliver Stirling nodded as he set out his garden line and then knelt down to make sure it was straight before he answered. "She's marvelously good at it," he said. "She seems to be able to get people to try to understand one another and at the same time to enjoy themselves. As a result any committee she's on accomplishes five times more than the average."

"So in a way she's made something that didn't exist before," Jib said, "the way Mum does with her painting and you do in your book and garden."

Oliver Stirling looked pleased. "That's just it," he said. "And it's exactly what you do in a garden yourself. I've had boys work up here off and on who have worked almost as hard as you do, but you're the first person I've met in a long while who pictures what a bed is going to look like long before the plants are half grown. You are what I'd call a creative gardener."

"I love it," Jib said, and then an idea, full-blown and beautiful, sprang into her mind. "Cousin Oliver!" She turned to him instantly. "I've had an inspiration! Why can't I get a job around here for the rest of the summer in somebody's garden? Almost everyone around here does have a garden, or at least lawns and flower beds, and you hear all over the place that part-time gardeners are hard to get."

Cousin Honey, or Jib's own parents, would have met her enthusiasm with enthusiasm of their own, but Oliver Stirling went on working without saying a word.

"Don't you—don't you think I could do it? You've said twice I was a good gardener, and Cousin Honey says you practically never pay compliments."

Oliver Stirling stopped to wipe his face, and she saw he was grinning. "Honey ought to know," he said. "But I'll be willing to put those compliments and a few more in a letter of recommendation for you to take around with you to show to people who otherwise might be prejudiced against taking on a girl."

"Thanks a million, but——" Jib began, and then she realized that Oliver Stirling had not finished.

"Pride's a luxury," he said, and it dawned on Jib that perhaps he had not missed the short contretemps that had occured between Cousin Honey and herself the evening before. "And false pride's worse than that because it's stupid. You've earned my letter, and if you don't use it I'll think you're foolish. And Honey could also tell you that I don't suffer fools gladly."

"She won't have to," Jib said and she threw her arms around Oliver Stirling's neck and kissed his cheek. "I'll use it and love it."

But even armed with Oliver Stirling's letter, which he carefully typed on his best stationery, Jib's second afternoon of job hunting was no more successful than her first. At Oliver Stirling's suggestion, she began with the stately, withdrawn-looking houses by the Congregational church, but although she went from house to house until her legs ached and the opening speech she had arranged in her mind came off like a victrola record, she had nothing to show for it when she finally pushed the bicycle back up the hill to the Stirlings'.

Jib felt tired and let down, and her hopes had flattened like a cold omelet. The hill seemed steeper than ever, and as she pushed upward she amused herself by rehearsing exactly what she would tell the Stirlings when she reached the top. At first she thought of remote stoicism, more courteous than her approach last night, but definitely Spartan and reserved. Another moment her mind spun out the whole tale of her afternoon's failure, with every discouraging detail underlined in one long wail for sympathy.

But once she was over the threshold of the cool, beautifully plain old house both plans evaporated.

"No dice," she said, and went into the kitchen where Cousin Honey was once more cooking dinner. "I've decided to hire out as a gardener, but people seem to consider that a man's world. Granny Infield, Mum's mother, used to tell us about being a suffragette, and for the first time I begin to understand how they must have felt."

"My aunt Lacey was a suffragette," Mrs. Stirling said later on when they were seated at the dining-room table. "And so was Miss Jane Winslow, who was Buzz's great-aunts' cousin. Miss Jane taught at the Quentin Academy, and she lost her job because the school board disapproved of what she was doing. That was before my time, of course, but I've always understood that Grandfather Bolton—that's your great-grandfather, Jib—resigned as a protest."

"Was *he* for votes for women?" Jib looked up at the bearded, bespectacled, ultraconservative face in the portrait above the sideboard. "I should think he'd have been shocked."

Cousin Honey laughed. "I guess he was," she said. "I was only a girl when he died, but I can still remember his fuming against what he called petticoat government. But he felt passionately that a person had a right to their own opinions and that Miss Jane had been treated unjustly. I know Grandmother used to tell a story about a time shortly after he had started in practice here, when he got into a fight with Clay Peters over a visiting preacher who had stood up for the Haymarket Anarchists. Grandfather was always rather a slight, frail-looking man, and he was half killed when all three of the Peters brothers waylaid him one night when he was driving back here after seeing a patient. But he went right on defending the visiting parson, even though he thought the Anarchists were all wrong himself"

"He'd read his Voltaire," Oliver Stirling said as he helped Jib to more fried chicken and fresh asparagus. "Did I ever tell you, Honey, that when I took down those old books of his that we found in the attic I came across the old gentleman's notes and markings? I think Jib might like to see them after supper."

"I'd love it," Jib said, and for the first time she understood what it was, over and above the personalities of the two Stirlings, that made their house seem stronger and more satisfying than any in which she had ever lived. It was a very special feel of the past that owed nothing whatever to lavender and old lace or a weak clinging to faded glories. It was, rather, a challenging continuity, as useful and enduring as the four stout walls or the fine old furniture within. It was a past with a future, that was it, where the old mingled with and foreshadowed the new, just as Cousin Honey's little stories about her own or her neighbors' grandparents more often than not merged into breezy anecdotes about what she had just seen or heard on Main Street.

After supper Jib was too sleepy to get much out of the old books, with their faded, scholarly notations, which Oliver Stirling showed her. It was only as he put the books away that a chance remark of his splintered light through her mind like a falling star. "You had to have courage to be an individual in those days," he said. "Especially in a small town."

Jib's thoughts went back to the houses on Squaw's Hill and her return to the Stirlings' the evening before. "Do you suppose it really was so much harder?" she asked. "Around here people still know everything about everybody at the drop of a hat, don't they?"

Louisa Stirling looked puzzled, but Oliver caught her meaning immediately. "I think it was harder a hundred years ago," he said. "Both here and in England. I rather imagine that spiritually, just as much as physically, only the robust could survive to enjoy old age."

A few moments later Jib went upstairs and undressed for bed. She was exhausted and no nearer a job than she had been the day before, but at least she no longer felt divided within herself or angry at the two good people with whom she was living.

The next morning she tried the two houses on the road down into Oldtown, but in the first no one was at home and in the second the owner looked at her curiously while she offered her services and then told her that he always did his own weeding and transplanting. "Seems funny work for a girl," he said as Jib started to leave. "If I had a daughter your age I don't think I'd want her doing it."

Jib said nothing and went straight to call on Mrs. Oakley, who lived in a big yellow house set back from the village green. In front of the house was a rectangular plot of ground where damask roses, late-leafing hydrangea plants, and a dozen other Victorian favorites were already well on their way to turning what must once have been a magnificent formal garden into a small jungle. Boy, what possibilities! Jib thought and stood still for a moment, conjuring up what the place would look like once the vines that covered the old sundial were cleared away and the overgrown bushes were checked and pruned behind the perennial border.

She went up the steps and pulled the iron knocker, and a moment later a maid led her into a parlor that looked like a room from the American Wing in the Metropolitan Museum crossed with the meticulously preserved gleanings from a hundred scrap baskets. Jib had just found a chair that was free of old magazines when Mrs. Oakley came into the room, and she sprang to her feet. "I'm Jessica Bolton," she said. "My cousin, Mrs. Stirling, told me she thought you were looking for a gardener."

"Oh, my dear child!" Mrs. Oakley's beads and bracelets tingled as she moved forward. "Don't tell me that Louisa has found someone for me? I declare, I'd be willing to part with a king's ransom just to get that garden in shape again."

"Well, I'm it!" Jib was so excited that she forgot the

formal little speech she had used so often. "I can work as many days a week as you'd care to have me."

The eagerness left Mrs. Oakley's face and her straight old nose sniffed as though something smelled. "A girl, a young lady, hiring out as a gardener? Of course they have farmerettes during a war, but in peacetime, for a private family, I'm sure I don't know what Louisa Stirling's thinking of."

"She likes the idea," Jib said. "And so would my mother, and Cousin Oliver has written this letter."

Mrs. Oakley waved away the letter without even glancing at it. "I'm so sorry," she said, "but it's quite impossible. Louisa's so deliciously unconventional herself, and then she lives way out of town and perhaps doesn't realize that those of us who are right in the midst of things have to keep up appearances. What people would say if they thought I hired a girl to work in my garden I can't even imagine."

A few minutes later Jib tried Simon Planter, who turned her down for much the same reasons as Mrs. Oakley, though he was less frank in voicing them. She had just crossed the graveyard by the Episcopal church when she saw Buzz emerging from the church cellar with a bundle of newly mimeographed *Chronicles* under his arm. He asked what she was doing, and when she told him he jerked his thumb in the direction of his great-aunts' house. "Meet me up at my place in half an hour," he said. "Tommy Genovese'll be heading up there then and he'll give you a ride. I've got to stop to see that the kids who are distributing for me get their papers on time, and then I'll meet you."

Jib made one more unsuccessful call and then, catching sight of Tommy Genovese just as he was crossing the new concrete bridge which was half a mile downstream from the covered one, she put out her hand, and a moment later he stopped to let her in.

Buzz's bicycle was outside the corncrib when she ar-

100

rived, and Buzz himself was all business. "There's a want ad in today's paper," he said and threw her a mimeographed sheet.

Jib scanned the short list of classified ads and then her eyes settled on a little box that read: "Wanted. Part-time gardener for private residence. Experience necessary. Light work only."

"Why, they're practically asking for me," Jib said. "Experience and light work. If they only aren't stuffy about females, I ought to be in."

Buzz led the way across the lawn to the telephone in his aunts' house. "Better give 'em a whirl right away," he said, and a moment later Jib had put through her call.

A young voice with a Scottish accent answered, and Jib said that she was calling in connection with the want ad for a part-time gardener. "Can you come right down?" the voice said. "It's the old reconverted stable across the river from the Mahoras Mill."

"I'll be there," Jib said, and then as she hung up she realized that she did not have the faintest idea whom she was going to see.

"Guy Blaisdell bought that old place," Buzz said when Jib told him where she was going. "About the same time that Bean bought the mill. The big house that belonged to the first millowner burned down years ago, and the stable was empty for ages. Then this spring Blaisdell bought it, and he and a guy called Kelly fixed it over, and now Blaisdell lives there with Kelly and Kelly's wife and kid. Kelly's the man who took over Blaisdell's old job as chief machinist at the mill. Say, what's the matter with you? You look funny."

"I'm fine," Jib said and swallowed. "It's just that Mr. Blaisdell's the man who turned me down a couple of days ago when I tried to get a job at the mill."

"So what?" Buzz said. "You didn't have any experience at that, and summer people are a headache in any factory. But in gardening the fact that you only want to work

101

until the middle of September's an asset. Besides, part-time gardeners who know anything are scarce as New Deal gold pieces. Aunt Loopy has an old man Greenough once a week who's practically a hundred and usually tight, but she's so glad to get him she'd serve him hot toddies in bed if he asked for it."

Jib grinned, and a few minutes later she started down toward the mill. She no longer felt as optimistic as when she had first read Buzz's want ad, but at least his unvarnished honesty about her attempt at getting a job in the mill had taken the last sting out of that episode as neither Cousin Honey's tenderness nor Oliver's philosophy had been able to do.

Guy Blaisdell and a young couple, whom Jib guessed must be the Kellys, were at lunch when Jib arrived. "I'm sorry to bother you," Jib said, "but I called in answer to your want ad for a gardener."

"A girl?" Kelly said, and his broad, freckled face broke up in a grin.

"And why not?" said his wife. "We have ever so many girls on the land in Scotland."

Blaisdell, who seemed less ill at ease than he had in his office, beckoned to Jib to follow him into a back room which had once been a harness room and was now a combination tool shed and storage closet. "You're Miss Bolton, aren't you?" he asked, and Jib nodded.

"The girl you couldn't use in the mill," she said and pulled out Oliver Stirling's letter. "But I really do know something about gardening, and I could spend as much time as you'd like."

Guy Blaisdell read the letter without comment and then opened the door out onto the land that lay between the stable and the river. It was wild and unkempt-looking, and the few patchy places that might once have been garden beds were engulfed with weeds. At one side was a narrow footbridge that led across to the mill property, and on the other side was the crumbling remains of a summerhouse. "It is a mess," Jib said, and Blaisdell smiled as though he approved of her frankness. "But those pines would grow beautifully if they were thinned out, and they do shut out the mill. The stretch between here and the river could be beautiful."

"That's just what Mrs. Kelly says," Blaisdell told her. "But she's got one little boy now and she's expecting another baby this winter, so she can't do anything, and neither John Kelly nor I are gardeners."

"I'd love to try it," Jib said, and her voice was alive with eagerness. "I'd come regularly and keep very careful track of the time I spent, so that you wouldn't be cheated."

"I'm not worried about that," Blaisdell said. "Could you work five mornings a week?"

Jib nodded and her heart jumped with hope. "Yes," she said, and with that Guy Blaisdell looked at his watch.

"Well, let's call it settled, then," he said. "Could you begin day after tomorrow?"

A few minutes later, when Jib started to walk home, she was so absorbed in plans for the land behind the old stable that she hardly heard the horn and started with surprise when Cousin Honey rattled to a stop beside her. "I've got a job!" Jib said, and instantly her own delight was reflected in the face of the woman in the car.

"I think it's wonderful," Cousin Honey said when Jib had jumped in and she had started the car uphill again. "Of course that place between the stable and the river will need a lot of work, but I'm sure you can do it."

"How *did* you find out about it?" Jib asked, but this time she was only amused and not in the least annoyed. "Mr. Blaisdell only hired me ten minutes ago by the clock."

Mrs. Stirling chuckled. "I saw Buzz when he came over to the office to leave some copies of his *Chronicle* and he told me you'd gone down to apply."

103

"But how did you know I'd been taken?" Jib persisted. "Did you hear that from somebody else?"

"That was guesswork," Cousin Honey said placidly. "Backed up by the knowledge that Guy Blaisdell's a very sensible man when he isn't trying to do a job for which God never intended him or when he's not so eaten up with shyness he can't speak. But I didn't tell a soul, and I'm sure no one else knows. When do you start?"

"Day after tomorrow," Jib said. "Which is just right, because it'll give me the whole day off to go over to see Cobble Top."

"Good," Cousin Honey said, "and I'm going to see to it that you get some rest and don't as much as hand Oliver his hoe. Then in the evening we'll think up something special to celebrate."

11. LAND OF LOST CONTENT

THE NEXT morning both the Stirlings left home early but Jib slept until nearly eleven. When she went downstairs the house was cool and very still, and out of doors the green hills stretched out tranquilly under cloudless skies. Jib took deep, satisfying breaths of the sweet June air. Now that her job was assured and she had had a long night's sleep, she felt so made over that the tired, discouraged person she had been two nights ago seemed as unfamiliar as the plump baby girl whose snapshot Mother still kept on her bureau.

She went into the kitchen where Cousin Honey had left out the choicest of Oliver's strawberries and a little note. The Stirlings had gone over to Pittsfield for the day, Jib read, but they looked forward to seeing Jib at supper. There was plenty of cream in the refrigerator.

Jib ate her breakfast with relish and then, as she made her bed, laid her plans for the day. She was beginning to know some of the tides and currents of Oldtown village and realized that if she stopped in to tell Buzz Winslow about her job she would just have time to be at the Four Corners to beg a ride from Tommy Genovese when he drove up the Ridge to make his late deliveries.

Miss Winslow had just gone out to the postbox for her mail when Jib turned the corner, and she looked up over her glasses and smiled. "Congratulations, my dear," she said. "Brewster was so pleased when Sister and I told him you were to start work tomorrow."

"How on earth did you know?" Jib asked, and the old lady looked amused at her bewilderment.

"The First Congregational Church gave an organ recital last night," she said, "and when I saw Mrs. Kelly I made it a point to sit next to her. I—er—deprecate any kind of meddlesomeness, but in a small town one becomes interested in one's neighbors and I knew she was well informed about music. Of course both Sister and I try and acquire any little facts we feel might be useful to Brewster."

A moment later, when Jib went into the corncrib, Buzz was typing busily, with his hair standing up all over his head like so much saber grass. "Sit down," he said and went right on typing. "It's swell about your job. You'll be able to pick up a lot for the *Chronicle.*"

"What is this?" Jib demanded. "Does everybody in Oldtown know what I've done as soon as I do myself?"

"Sooner," Buzz said and, pulling his paper out of the typewriter, handed it to Jib. "And of course both the aunts have ears like elephants. Almost all of this came from their going to the concert last night."

Jib glanced at the page he had given her: "Miss Sylvia Sawyer is leaving on Thursday for a motor trip in Canada. Mr. and Mrs. John Thurston entertained Mrs. Thurston's mother, Mrs. Henry Milkowski, for the week end." The lines of chitchat went on for two typewritten pages.

"They can't have heard much of the concert," she said

106

grimly, but Buzz only tapped another page at his left and shook his head. "Here's a play-by-play account," he said. "But thank heaven they both know it's the personals that sell a paper. Still, what I want now is to have a lead-off article in each issue stressing controversial local news, and that's where you can help me at the mill."

"But I'm not working there. I'm hired to fix up the garden on the other side of the river, where you can't even see the smokestacks."

"It's only two shakes of a lamb's tail away," Buzz said. "And since you're hired by both Blaisdell and Kelly it'll be a pipe to arrange to go through the mill and write a good human-interest story with a background of the whole process. You'd be surprised at how many people who've lived here or in Quentin Mills all their lives haven't the faintest idea about papermaking."

"I might try——" Jib began, but Buzz, riding his hobby-horse, took no notice of her.

"And gossip!" Buzz's eyes gleamed. "Local, personal, and industrial. In summertime the girls who work the finishing machines eat out of doors, and you'll be able to pick up scads of stuff about Millard Bean and everyone else. The girls won't even know you're around."

"I won't do it," Jib said. "If I get any news, whoever I get it from is going to know what I've done. I hate anything sneaky."

As usual Buzz was completely impervious to suggested insult. "Do it your own way, then," he said blandly. "As I've told you before, all I care about is getting out a crackerjack paper."

It was nearly time for Jib to leave if she wanted to catch Tommy Genovese, and she stood up when Buzz, grinning like a gargoyle, dug into the wooden box at his left which served him for an extra drawer. "Wait just a sec," he said. "I haven't told you my news yet."

He found what he had been looking for and handed Jib a folded piece of typewriter paper to which were attached five crisp five-dollar bills. She unfolded it and saw that "Compliments of A Friend" had been neatly typed across the center and that there was not another word.

"Mailed from Pittsfield the day after we published 'Pigs in the Powder Room,'" Buzz said. "So it's a snap it comes from someone who doesn't love Bean. And yesterday afternoon I got a good-sized ad from Carley's drugstore and three smaller one. I'm really beginning to make money, and twenty per cent of it goes to you."

"I don't need——" Jib began and then checked herself. In the first place, she did need it, since her pay from Blaisdell would never total a great deal; and in the second place, she knew Buzz well enough to guess that he would not take a cent away from his precious paper unless he thought it was earned and then some. "That'd be wonderful," she said. "And I'm terribly glad about your windfall."

A few minutes later she was on the road again and reached Four Corners just as Tommy Genovese rattled toward the bridge. "Theese good luck," he called out as he opened the door. "First I meet a friend of Kurt Cramer's, now, I meeta Mees Honey's cousin. You goin' to Reedge?"

"All the way," Jib said and nodded to an inconspicuous-looking man on the front seat who had moved over to let her in.

"I'm afraid I don't know your name. No can introduce——" Tommy spoke to the man beside him. "You are Meester . . . ?"

"Name's Parker. Michael Parker," the man said, and his deep, resonant voice was as unexpected as if a mouse had roared like a lion. "My car's over in the garage in Pittsfield and I'm hitchhiking to get it. Cramer was supposed to take me over, but he's started work at the Mahoras Mill."

"So?" Tommy said, while the name Cramer registered

on Jib. "That good. Very good. Cramer have bad luck with jobs."

"Some fool woman who likes to play the Lady Bountiful got it for him," Parker said. "Pull with the boss and all that stuff."

Jib stiffened with resentment. The fact that two days ago she herself had been unjustly irritated at Cousin Honey only seemed to underline her annoyance that this stranger, who didn't even know Cousin Honey's name, should speak of her so disparagingly. She would have said something, but by this time they had reached the top of the Ridge and Tommy announced that he would take them to where the Pittsfield Pike and the dirt lane that led up to Cobble Top all converged on the Ridge Road and then make his sales on the way back. "That save everybody a walk," he said, and his wrinkled old face was as pleased as a child's. "Old Tommy sell fruit and run taxi for his friends. Very good."

They were rolling across the top of the Ridge by this time, and as they passed one large well-kept house after another Tommy began to chatter about the buying habits of his various customers.

"Mees Pace buys plenty of banane. Mees Jones buys no banane but plums, peaches, vegetables, everything else. Is good customer." They were nearing the Appersleys' house by this time, and Tommy shrugged. "Ees one beeg house," he said, "but they only buy second-grade fruit. Very skimpy. Still, I remember when Mr. Appersley's father owned the Titanic Mill. Mr. Appersley very friendly gent and never proud."

Jib glanced at the familiar formal façade and grinned. "Queen Anne front and Mary Anne behind," she said, and old Genovese roared.

"Oh, thas good, thas reech," he said, but Michael Parker said nothing and the corners of his vaguely dissatisfied mouth curled contemptuously.

A few moments later they arrived at the crossroads

and Tommy stopped to let them out. "Thanks a lot," Jib said, and once more the old man's face grew beatific with pleasure.

"Don't mench," he said. "And regards to Mees Honey and Meester Stirling. You tell heem in two, tree week Tommy bring him a melon for present that make him sit up and wheestle." Then next moment he drove off.

"My, he's nice." Jib spoke her thoughts out loud. "He'd do anything to help anyone."

"Struck me as a reactionary old fool," Parker said, and this time Jib was struck as much by the cold inhumanity of his eyes as by the resonance of his voice or what he had said. "Well, I take this road."

"And I go this way. Good-by."

The man nodded without speaking, and a moment later they were separated by the hillock that divided the two roads. It was only a moment's walk from the highway onto the twisting dirt road that led directly to Cobble Top, but long before Jib had reached it she was too happily absorbed in the land around her to have time to think of either Michael Parker or old Tommy. She could anticipate every rock, every tree, even the thick clumps of early daisies, and as she hurried around one bend after another she was as thrilled as though she were meeting old friends.

The sandy hollow was next, and when she came to it she took off her shoes, reveling in the remembered feel of the dry, clean sand. She had written to Mum about her job last night, but now she began planning a letter to the whole family about Cobble Top. She would see the tenants too, of course, and write the family all about them, but first she wanted to sop up every familiar sight and sound and smell. I'll skirt the house, she thought, and go over to Hidden Pond and maybe have a swim and eat my lunch before I stop back to see the tenants.

She went around another bend and saw the orange day lilies which she and her mother had set out the summer Jib had been recovering from whooping cough. There are whole blending banks of them now, Mum, she wrote in her mind. She moved past them slowly and came to a mossy spot where first she and then the twins had made miniature gardens. She knelt down and saw a few snail shells and a circle of white stones where one of the little boys had left them.

She turned over one of the shells, paper dry and brittle in her fingers, and at that moment she would have given anything to be seven or eight again and playing in the moss with Mother working away a few feet farther down the road. If I only knew when we were coming back, she thought. If I only knew. But, as always, that question was followed by the darker thought that perhaps the little house would have to be sold and they would never return to it. The family all loved it, Mum and Dad and the twins, quite as much as she did, but what if Dad stayed on in California? She walked more quickly, as though she could escape her own thoughts.

She was breathless by the time she was halfway up the winding hill road and stopped by a bed of sweet ferns to rest. She reached out idly and picked a piece of fern, and as she pulled the green springy frond between her fingers an idea, as enchanting as her previous one had been depressing, flashed into her mind. There were only the coarser kinds of wood fern along the road, but in the woods she knew of a patch of osmundas which Oliver Stirling had mentioned as something of a rarity only a day or so ago.

I'll get him some, she decided and jumped the ditch and went into the woods, which she knew almost as intimately as the road she left behind her. She passed the old tree stump which she had helped the boys hollow out for a tunnel, saw the stand of white birches that Dickie always called the Canoe Trees, and, turning to the right, came to the depression where the rarer ferns grew. The next instant she stopped short. The beautiful, intricately cut fronds had never been profuse even here, but there had been at least several dozen plants, and now there were none! For a moment she thought she must have come to the wrong spot, and then as she plunged forward she saw the shovel cuts where the plants had been dug out and the broad, unmistakable prints of a man's boot. The vandals! she thought, and her eyes blazed. Coming in off the road and stealing our ferns.

She went straight back to the road and climbed doggedly up toward the house. Mother had moved a few of the osmundas around Hidden Pond, she knew, and perhaps she could take Cousin Oliver one or two of those. Still, that wouldn't be enough for the place Oliver wanted to cover, and the thought of all the ferns that had been taken made her so angry that she stamped up the worn path to the back door of Cobble Top hardly conscious of where she was. At that moment a young man in blue jeans flew out onto the porch with a saucepan in his hand. He caught sight of Jib and stopped short. "Why, hello," he said. "Where did you come from? Did you walk up here?"

"Yes, I did," Jib said. "My name's Jessica Bolton. My family——"

"Why, yeah, sure, of course. You're our landlord—I mean landlady. I'm Mike Gallagher, and here comes my roommate, who is your other tenant."

Jib turned and saw Stanton Carter, dressed in swimming shorts and with a towel over his shoulder, emerging from the woods in the direction of Hidden Pond. So he's found it, she thought bitterly, he's gone swimming in the place that no one but Dad and Mum and the twins and I knew about.

"Miss Bolton, this is Stanton Carter." Mike Gallagher waved his saucepan with mock formality. "Stant, this is Miss Bolton, our landlady."

Stanton Carter shook the damp hair out of his eyes

and hurried forward. "We've met twice," he said eagerly. "Do you remember down at the railroad station and then at the country-club dance?"

Where you couldn't be bothered to dance with me, Jib thought, and all her rage over the stolen ferns focused on the young man ahead of her. She said nothing and acknowledged the introduction with a nod, avoiding the hand that Stanton Carter held out to her. He stopped short and his face looked as surprised and much more hurt than when Fay Clarkson had tried to tip him. Only Mike Gallagher was unperturbed. "Well, it's nice you know each other," he said and shifted his frying pan to the other hand. "As a matter of fact, Miss Bolton, Stant and I have to get back to work, but we were going to have a quick lunch first, and if you don't mind canned beans we'd love to have you join us."

Stanton Carter, who was still looking at Jib, said nothing at all, and Jib turned away impulsively. "Thank you so much," she said to Mike, and the word *you* resounded. "You're awfully kind, but I'm afraid I'll have to start back. I—I just wanted to make sure that everything was all right."

"Everything's swell." Mike took her up with enthusiasm. "But you really ought to come inside and see how we've fixed things up."

Jib shook her head, not trusting herself to speak. She knew that if she had to go in to see the familiar shabby living room changed, moved around, and occupied by strangers, she'd cry. "No," she got out. "No, thanks." And she started down the road she had come up.

She walked quickly, her head down and her eyes unseeing, but she heard a surprised whistle and Mike Gallagher's heartfelt "Well, can you tie that?"

She started to run, caught her toe in a root, and sprawled flat on her face. For an instant she was stunned, but the next moment she scrambled up, embarrassed and furious, and wanting only to be out of sight. She

113

looked over her shoulder and saw that she was hidden from the two men by the sentinel firs that surrounded the rock garden, and started off again, so eager to be gone that she hardly felt the raw scrape on her knee. The next minute she heard laughter and then the sound of Stanton Carter's voice, drawling and deliberate, so that every syllable resounded above the green wall. "That's the Lady of Property come to visit the po' white trash, Mike. You won't catch her eating beans with the likes of us."

12. IN GARDENS, WHEN THE EVE IS COOL

BY THE time Jib reached the Stirlings', Cousin Honey
was in a cheerful frenzy over her cooking. She was already dressed for supper, but completely covered with
an enormous white apron, and she had a checkered bandanna on her head. She whirled around when she heard
Jib and, dropping saucepan, peelings, and knife, waved
to Jib to come in. "I think you were darling to stop in
and tell Buzz about your job," she said. "And isn't it
grand about his twenty-five dollars?"

"Wonderful," Jib said. "Did you see him?"

Cousin Honey shook her head so that the ends of her
bandanna nodded like rabbit ears. "No, but he's called
you up twice since I've been home. I heard it from
Cephus Drake, who came into the office, and I think he
said he'd heard it from Margaret Dunscombe, who had
it from Lucinda Winslow. They're both on the committee
to buy new dinner plates for the parish hall. I should

have gone myself, but I came home early because we're having company to dinner to celebrate your job. Some new young friends of Noll's we know you'll like."

"Can't I help?" Jib asked, but Cousin Honey, her small plump hands working even faster than her tongue, assured her there wasn't a thing to do, and Jib went upstairs feeling tired and a bit dazed by the intricacies of small-town gossip.

She washed and changed and then went out to the garden, which was heady at this time of day with the mixed fragrance of nicotiana and petunias. Oliver Stirling, immaculate in a white linen suit, was there ahead of her. "This time of the day is the reward," he said. "And after all the work you've done here you've earned every bit of your smelling and seeing!"

Jib took a deep, luxurious breath. "It's well worth it," she said, and at that moment they heard the tinkle of the bell and Honey's voice called out to them, "Noll—Jib. Come on in, darlings. Our friends are here."

With a caressing, all-inclusive backward glance, Oliver Stirling turned toward the house and Jib followed him. Even before they had crossed the terrace Jib was aware of familiar voices. The next instant she found herself face to face with Stanton Carter, while Mike Gallagher stood a few feet away. "Jib dear, this is Stanton Carter and this is Michael Gallagher. My cousin, Jessica Bolton."

Jib ignored Stanton Carter and smiled effusively at Mike. "We've already met," she said. "He was at Cobble Top when I went up there today."

For a second Cousin Honey's face fell, but the next instant it brightened. "And I did want to surprise you!" she said. "Still, that isn't very important, and it's fun you've all made friends. Jib, isn't it wonderful to have such nice tenants?"

"Yes, isn't it?" Jib spoke automatically, while all the time every inch of her was aware of Stanton Carter. He could not have missed her cut, even if Cousin Honey

116

had, that much seemed certain, but how was he going to take it? She managed to glance toward him while she answered some casual question of Mike Gallagher's and had to admit to herself that if he knew she hated him he wasn't going to show it. He had moved directly away from her and was discussing soil erosion with Oliver Stirling as though he hadn't another care in the world.

At supper Jib sat down beside Mike Gallagher on one side of the table, while Stanton Carter was by himself on the other side. A willow pattern soup tureen filled with lilies blocked his face from her view, and as the conversation was general she had no idea how he was feeling.

"I like the nickname 'Jib,' " Mike Gallagher said, and Cousin Honey beamed at him.

"We're both so proud of her!" she said. "Quite on her own she's gotten the job of doing the gardening at the old stable across from the mill. It has loads of possibilities, and Jib is just the person to bring them out."

"Is that right?" Mike looked down at her. "Are you thinking of being a landscape gardener?"

"No—that is, yes," Jib said. "I've always loved gardening, and I hope I'll be able to specialize somewhat next winter if my family stays out in California. I understand they have some marvelous courses at Leland Stanford." At that moment she caught the expression on Oliver Stirling's face, saw his raised, questioning eyebrow, and knew that he had guessed that the last part of her plan had popped fully blown out of her mind in response to Mike's question. She found herself blushing and was so piqued that the urge to make someone else uncomfortable was irresistible.

"I understand that all Southerners are very conservative," she said, and her voice sounded rude and aggressive in her own ears. "Probably Mr. Carter disapproves of careers for women."

"Not at all," he said quietly. "I think every human being has the right to make the most of his or her abilities. If that includes a career, so much the better. How do you feel about it, Mrs. Stirling?"

Even before Cousin Honey could answer there was a sound at the front door, and an instant later Buzz Winslow's bespectacled face appeared at the dining room. "Jeepers, I'm sorry!" he began. "I didn't know you were having a party, Mrs. Stirling."

"But it's wonderful. We'd all love to see you. We've just finished, and I'll bring you some éclairs out in the garden while we have coffee."

"That'd be neat," Buzz said. "Yours are the only ones in Oldtown that are better than Aunt Loopy's."

Jib giggled wildly at the absurd nickname, and Buzz looked at her through his glasses. "What's bitten you since this morning?" he asked. "Getting cold feet about your job or have you fallen in love or what's happened? Even your hair looks excited."

Instinctively Jib pushed her fingers up through her short curly hair so that it stood up more like a halo than ever. She wanted to tell him to shut up, but she was aware that both of the Stirlings and the two men were looking at her, and she could only pull self-consciously at the ends of her hair and mutter something unintelligible. Meanwhile Buzz had dispatched his éclair and was turning the full force of his considerable curiosity on Stanton Carter.

Jib tried to listen to the Stirlings and Mike Gallagher, but with Buzz's uneven voice, first gruff and then squeaky with interest, firing personal questions at Carter it was hard to concentrate. It doesn't mean a thing to me, she scolded herself, and then leaned back to hear Stanton Carter say that he had been in the army two years after he had graduated from agricultural school and then had begun to work for the government.

Jib jerked her chair around to force herself to keep

from listening, but even when she could no longer hear any individual word she was immensely conscious of the clatter of Buzz's questions and the deeper, more deliberate sound of Stanton Carter's answers.

She was glad when a few minutes later Buzz stood up to leave and Cousin Honey suggested that the guests might like to see the rest of the garden before it grew too dark. She went with Buzz to the gate, and as he picked up his bicycle he nodded approvingly toward the house. "Carter's a neat guy," he said, "and there's a whale of a story in the job he's doing. Next week one of us ought to go out with him and write a really detailed report on what he and his side-kick do when they chart a farm. They've only been here a short time and nobody knows anything about it."

"I'm afraid I'll be too busy," Jib said stiffly. "You forget I'm starting work tomorrow."

"That's right, the big businesswoman," Buzz mocked, but the next moment his controlling interest overcame his momentary desire to tease. "Well, be sure you get as much as you can from the mill, and remember any detail about Bossy Bean is red-hot news. What I really came over to tell you this evening was that he came over to our house this afternoon and tried to raise cain about the 'Pigs in the Powder Room' story."

"He didn't!" Jib was interested in spite of herself. "What did you say?"

"I missed it, worse luck. I was down in the church cellar setting up tomorrow's paper, but Aunt Loopy handled him. He started in saying it was libelous, and she said politely, but very firmly, that she believed there wasn't a word or implication which wasn't demonstrably true. Then Aunt Hat came out of her shell long enough to say that you could sue the Bishop of Boston for larceny but you couldn't make it stick, and he left. They were both still purring when I got home. Boy, do I wish I'd been there!"

"So do I," Jib said, and then as Buzz rolled away she turned back to the house, still smiling to herself over what he had told her. She had only taken a few steps when she saw that Stanton Carter had left the others and was waiting for her in the shadow of the apple tree that grew by the doorway. She started to by-pass him and take the path to the garden, but he blocked her way. "Wait a minute, Jessica Infield Bolton," he said, and she looked up, startled at his use of her full name. "Haven't you and I jumped to a lot of silly conclusions?"

Jib hesitated. She could not see his face in the half-light, but she was more than ever aware of the set of his broad shoulders and the timbre of his deep voice. For a fraction of a second she stood rigid, and it flashed through her mind that Mibsie Tarrant, certainly Stella, would use this occasion for archness or flattery, anything to pin him down, as Stella would say, to make a conquest. He moved a step nearer, and all of Jib's instinctive honesty rose to the surface. "Perhaps we have," she said. "But I don't think you've gone out of your way to be exactly friendly or polite."

"What do you mean?" Stanton Carter asked. "You started us off."

"*I* started it!" Jib exploded, and suddenly she was so angry that she no longer had the slightest thought of making an effect. "*I* started it off when you went out of your way to be snobby at that country-club party and then acted as though you owned the earth at Cobble Top. You meant me to hear that crack about the high-and-mighty lady this morning, and the other night you meant me to see you and then you just walked away!"

"Jib, please don't." Stanton Carter touched her dress and she jerked free. "Please stop. I thought you *liked* old Bean. You were his guest. He made that all too clear just as I came up, and the way you played up to him I thought you enjoyed it."

"I didn't, as a matter of fact," Jib snapped, "but I still don't see why it was any concern of yours."

120

"You don't understand," Stanton Carter said. "I'd had a serious quarrel with him only that afternoon. Bean practically kicked me off his place, and so I couldn't horn in on his party. We may be stuffed shirts in Virginia, but manners, courtesy anyway, do matter to us. Once I knew Bean had brought you, I didn't think I had the right to dance with you. I was just licked."

"I was licked, you mean," Jib said and began to laugh. "I think he's the most completely repulsive old man I've ever seen, but as I'd been taken to his house, I had to dance with him. Then when you came along I didn't want you or anyone else to think I was just a pill, so I tried to look as though I'd been having a whirl. And all the while I was simply praying for you to cut in. Can you understand that?"

For a long moment Stanton Carter said absolutely nothing, and Jib's excitement blew out, leaving her cold and depressed. Now I've done it, she thought. He's either going to think I'm a kid or a lemon no man on earth has ever wanted to look at. She would have turned away, but for the second time he stopped her. "I do understand," he said gravely. "And I apologize. And now I'd like to tell you about Cobble Top."

At that moment someone turned on the yard light from inside the house, and the next moment they heard the quick patter of Cousin Honey's voice and the voices of the two men behind her.

Stanton Carter turned instantly, and a moment later he was talking to Oliver Stirling about his lawn. It was only as he and Mike began to leave that he again spoke directly to Jib. "I'll see you tomorrow," he said, and once more Jib reacted against the quiet authority in his voice.

"I'm afraid not," she said. "I'll be working all day, and in the evening Cousin Honey and I are driving over to Pittsfield to a concert."

"My, what a spitfire!" Stanton Carter said, and then a moment later, just as Mike drove off, "Still, I'll be seeing you."

121

13. IN SHADOW OF A GREEN OAK TREE

THE NEXT morning Mrs. Stirling left Jib at the Mahoras Mill when she drove to her office. Jib crossed the footbridge and walked upstream to the old stable property, looking for Mr. Blaisdell. He was not in sight, and when she went to the door of the tool shed it was bolted from the inside. She stood still for a moment, uncomfortably aware that there was a tremendous difference between talking to the Stirlings about having a job and actually plunging into the beginning of it. She realized that she would have to go to the front of the house to find anyone, and had just moved in that direction when she saw Mrs. Kelly coming toward her.

"Is Mr. Blaisdell around?" Jib asked, and when Mrs. Kelly shook her head Jib's heart shrank with the sudden fear that he had changed his mind about needing her.

"Don't tell me he went off to the factory without leaving you a note, when both Red and I reminded him?"

Mrs. Kelly said, and Jib nodded, feeling more insecure by the moment.

Mrs. Kelly apparently guessed what was going on in her mind, and her smile as she put out her hand was both friendly and reassuring. "Please don't worry about it," she said. "He'll be back at noon and give you definite instructions, and I'm sure that in the meantime if you do anything you see fit to do it'll be perfectly satisfactory."

At that moment Mrs. Kelly's eighteen-month-old son called out to her from the house. She unbolted the tool shed and started back to him, pausing only to tell Jib that if she wanted to rest or to get a drink of water to be sure to come to the house.

"Thanks a million," Jib said and turned back to look at the land, which seemed even more junglelike than she had remembered it. She was still uncertain as to exactly what she was to do, but at least Blaisdell had not changed his mind about hiring her, and Claire Kelly was unexpectedly friendly.

She began by walking the boundaries of the place, with an eye to its ultimate possibilities. Although the factory was barely an eighth of a mile off, the wind, which was from the north, blew the sounds away, and the line of fir trees which she had noticed two days ago shut it out so completely that the small wedge-shaped plot of land seemed almost as separate and secure as a little island.

A robin flew off as she walked over the uneven grass, and when she reached the riverbank a small turtle who had been sunning himself on an old log plopped into the water. Jib nosed her way down through a wilderness of virgin's-bower and jewelweed. From here on, the river passed by the Mahoras Mill and all the bigger plants at Quentin Mills, but at this spot she was quite near the source and the stream had passed nothing but a few isolated farms on its way down from the mountains. Jib dribbled her hand in the cool water and a school of minute fish broke up like a spattered raindrop and then a moment later came together again. She drew out her wet hand and remembered that years ago someone had told her that all the Quentin Mills had originally been built by the river as much for the purity of the water, which was important for papermaking, as for the water power. Six miles downstream, below the Quentin Mills factories, she had seen the dirty, evil-smelling brew which this same river became, but here at least it looked as sparklingly clear as when the Indians had known it. When Dad comes up we'll explore the source, she thought, and in almost the same instant realized that for the first time in her life her father would not be spending his vacation at Cobble Top.

She straightened up, resolutely fixing her mind on her work, and saw the ugly remains of what had once been a summerhouse and was now nothing more than a caved-in litter of rotten wood. I ought to start by clearing that, she thought, remembering how they had begun the rock garden at Cobble Top by getting rid of an abandoned rubbish dump on the same site. Turn the eyesore into a feature, Mum had said, and the middle ground will take care of itself. She realized that if she could borrow a truck and induce either Buzz or Cousin Oliver to help her, the old wood would disappear like lightning, but that was impossible for the moment, and she compromised by working on the spot where the lamb's-quarters and dock grew rankest. It was heavy work pulling out the thick weeds, but once she had a small patch cleared, the ground was surprisingly soft and she guessed that it must have been spaded more recently than the rest of the land.

When she was tired of weeding she took out the garden line and a straight edge and began trimming the border of the driveway that led to the converted stable. It felt good to be working upright again, and as she cut through the moist sod she thought of the girls in the mill who worked endlessly at the same task, and it came to her all over again that she was lucky to have found a job in which she could have variety whenever she wanted it.

She had just finished the side of the drive nearest the house when she heard the sharp blast of the factory whistle, and a few moments later Mr. Blaisdell and John Kelly walked toward her from the footbridge. Guy Blaisdell murmured an apology for having forgotten her, but when she asked him exactly what he wanted her to do he turned to Kelly like a younger brother turning to an older and wiser one for explanations.

"You're part of a real-estate investment," Kelly said when he had answered Jib's specific questions. "If anything changes at the mill and Blaisdell has to sell, a prospective buyer would be put off by this wilderness. Isn't that right, Guy?"

Blaisdell nodded, his face reddening, but Jib had no way of knowing whether his embarrassment was due to Kelly's reference to the mill or at being asked a direct question. "You're your own boss," Kelly went on. "And right now we'd be glad of as much time as you can give us. Keep a record of the hours you work and turn it in to my wife on Fridays and we'll see that you get paid on Saturdays. Is there anything else?"

"Not a thing," Jib said, and Guy Blaisdell looked relieved.

"If there's any heavy work you want done, leave it until Sundays," he said, "and Kelly and I'll try and tackle it. I—that is, we are awfully glad you could work here."

A moment later the men left and Jib went back across the footbridge to meet Cousin Honey on her way home for lunch. She had only had an hour or so of work, but the results were stimulating. The neat edges she had cut made the land beyond the drive look rougher and more unkempt than ever, but it was also a definite achievement, a finished bit of work that was at one and the same time a good omen and a standard for future performance.

"You're your own boss," Kelly had said, and the words were enough to fill Jib's mind with the image of a fantastically beautiful garden that would be the admiration of the countryside.

How did she do it? Imagine a pretty young girl with so much ability. As Jib walked toward the road the fumes of imagined triumph, as heady and pervading as the smell of tuberoses, enveloped her.

By the time she had had lunch and had gone back to work the vision faded. The sun was hot and a small blister formed on her right hand. She began to weed again, but now that the morning dampness had dried out the earth the weeds were so hard to pull that she wondered if she could have even a blanket-sized patch done by evening. She worked on for a long time, not conscious of anything but another clump and always another just beyond her hand. Once the grass behind her stirred in a soft gust of wind and she stood up to stretch. For a moment she reveled in the welcome coolness that blew through her wet blouse. She started to kneel down again when an outline, almost a pattern, in the wind-blown grass beyond her caught her attention. She stared at it, frowning, and then hurried over to the remains of the summerhouse. From there the light green gracefully curved strip was even more clearly visible, and for the first time she saw that the tallest weeds arched forward in a definite arc to meet the curve of the thinner grass Her heart beat faster with the thrill of discovery, and she darted down to the river, following the curve For a moment she was uncertain, and then, hacking her way through nettles and cat brier, she came upon a half buried stone pier and a few pieces of blackened wood A bridge! It must have stood here years before the foot bridge had been built, and the lighter grass that had showed up in the wind was the last sign of a carriage

126

road that had connected the millowner's house, and the stable, and the mill.

She walked back slowly, and as she jerked up a clump of weeds in one spot and dug up a shovelful of earth in another, her guess became a certainty. This place had all been carefully and lovingly laid out and gardened years ago! As though in proof, she discovered a rose bush half throttled by weeds and pulled it free with eager, excited hands. This is it, this is perfect, she thought, as pleased as though she had found a Titian or a Da Vinci beneath a badly daubed canvas. This is just what I needed for an outline.

The impulse to tell someone of her discovery was almost overpowering, but the men were back at the mill and Claire Kelly had wheeled her baby away from the house over an hour ago. There was nothing for it but to go back to work, and now that she had a scheme and an over-all plan of attack even the most reluctant weeds seemed easier. There had once been four flower beds— she could see that from the four places where the weeds grew highest—and undoubtedly some special planting around the summerhouse. I'll open up the beds, she thought, and leave the grass on the old drive short for an opening, a sort of vista down to the river. Down there it'll be a job to get rid of the nettles, but once that's done the pickerelweed and the virgin's-bower'll make a perfect wild garden.

Jib hummed under her breath as she worked. The plan was simple, even tame, compared to her bright, forgotten picture of the morning, but completely satisfying. Now, while her eye traced the broad curve of the old drive, her mind was busy with the agreeable puzzle of what flowers she should put in which beds. Oliver Stirling could spare her plenty of annual seedlings, she knew, and perhaps she could beg a few clumps of August lilies from him if it wasn't too late to transplant them. She pulled and raked and then pulled some more. Since her discovery, and the plan that had sprung from it, she was so engrossed with the work at hand that there was no room in her mind or heart for the imaginary triumphs she had indulged in earlier.

It was nearly four o'clock when the sound of a motor made Jib look up, and then she saw that Stanton Carter had jumped out of his truck and was drawing himself up to a mock salute. "Lieutenant Carter reporting for duty," he said. "I started work at six this morning so I could come over. I thought you might need a truck and a strong——"

"Golly, I'm glad to see you!" Jib had dropped her tool and flew toward him. "I thought if I didn't see someone, anyone, pretty soon, to show them what I've found, that I'd bust!"

Stanton Carter's face fell at Jib's second sentence but she never noticed it, and when she showed him the old layout of the place he was quite as enthusiastic as she could have wished. "You really have found something," he said. "Using the old beds will make your work easier and the plants will grow better. Besides, it's all going to fit together, the old stable, those trees, flowers, and then your sweep down to the river."

"I've got to get rid of the summerhouse," Jib said. "You wouldn't want to help me and let me use the truck?"

Stanton Carter walked over and experimentally kicked the rotten lumber of the outbuilding before he answered. "It's as good as done," he said finally. "But only on one condition, and that is that you sit still while I throw my weight around. I've been drafting papers all day and I need to stretch."

For a moment Jib protested, but Stanton Carter was firm, and when she finally sat down on a shady bank overlooking the languid river every bone and muscle in her body welcomed the rest. "Do you know anyone who could use that old wood?" she asked once. "Kelly said they didn't need it here."

"I need it," Stanton said. "Mike and I hope to spend the winter at Cobble Top, and if we do we'll need all the firewood we can lay our hands on."

"Good," Jib said and fixed her eyes on a bright straw that was slowly eddying downstream. "I hope you do stay." It was less than twenty-four hours since she had resented the very idea of Stanton Carter's presence at Cobble Top, and she wondered if he would mention her change of heart. He said nothing, and a moment later, the straw forgotten, she sank back contentedly in the shade of an oak tree.

From then on Carter worked steadily, pulling up the crumbling wood and throwing it on the truck with easy, practiced motions. It was well after five by the time he had finished and came over to Jib. "You look better," he said and brushed the clinging particles of old wood from his work clothes. "Much better."

"I feel it." Jib smiled up at him lazily. "There's nothing as restful as watching someone else work."

Stanton Carter shook his head. "I didn't mean that. I meant that you look peaceful. Yesterday you were so busy hating me that I was afraid you'd end up by hating yourself."

"I did," Jib said and laughed because he hadn't missed anything after all. "But it's impossible to hate anyone when you're working in a garden. Mum said that ages ago, and it's absolutely true."

Stanton looked almost startled. "I know," he said. "I found that out in Germany during the war. There was an old man in a village where I was stationed, and when we first pulled in there I loathed the sight of him. Then one day I helped him with what was left of his garden, and although he was just the same and I was just the same, I couldn't hate him any more."

Jib might have asked him something more, but now he held out his hand and pulled her to her feet. "Come on," he said. "I'll drive you home, but first I'd like to ask you a favor. Will you come up and have supper at Cobble Top on Saturday? I know you love the place and hate seeing anyone else in it, but there's something up there I hope will make you feel better."

"I'll come," Jip said. "I'd really like it."

"Good. Wonderful!" Stanton Carter said and then whisked her unceremoniously to the front of his truck. "Right now we'll have to beat it. Here comes that Winslow kid, and unless I'm slipping, he's after you for help on his paper. He's a guy with one consuming purpose, and the fact that this is your first day at work and that you might be tired wouldn't faze him in the least."

He had just put the car into gear when Buzz bicycled up beside him. He waved at Stanton, but it was Jib he wanted to see. "Oh, there you are," he said. "Say, wait a minute, I want you to help——"

"Phone her tomorrow, son," Stanton Carter said as the truck roared forward. "She's had enough for today."

"Ah, heck——" Buzz burst out, but Stanton Carter kept on driving.

"Poor Buzz!" Jib said, but then, as she caught a glimpse of the surprise and irritation on Buzz's face, she had to laugh. "You have him taped, all right," she said as they rounded the corner. "He's the one-idea boy if ever there was one."

"I ought to know," Stanton Carter said grimly. "It happened to be land, and not a newspaper, with me, but I've always been one myself until very recently."

14. HIVE OF GLASS

Buzz Winslow reacted true to form, and for the next few days he haunted Jib with telephone calls and messages asking if she had heard any news at the mill. "I'll try at the end of the week," she put him off. "First I have to get my own work under way."

In the meantime her job grew more satisfactory with every day. Since Stanton Carter had removed the heavier timbers of the summerhouse there was nothing she could not do by herself, given time and patience. On Wednesday, when she finally had the first bed cleared and spaded, Oliver Stirling gave her a flat box full of annuals to set out in it. By the time she had the small sturdy zinnia plants and the lacier marigolds in place and watered, she felt her garden was really begun and called Claire Kelly out to see it. "By July these'll be a mass of color!" Jib waved at her seedlings. "And now I'm going to clean up and fertilize those old altheas and the hydrangeas so they'll really give in August."

"You've done wonders." Claire Kelly nodded at the neatly raked piles of rubbish and the careful edging. "But the best of it's still inside your head like a tune that's just being set down in notes."

Jib grinned and went back to work. For the last few days she had heard the sounds of first-rate piano music through the open windows of the converted stable and guessed that when Claire Kelly compared anything to music she was complimenting it highly. Jib had seen a good deal of Claire since she had started work. Although they never had time for long talks, she had learned to like and respect the quiet young Scotswoman who went serenely about her housework in the mornings and then, in the afternoons, when her little son played in his pen under the apple trees, filled the summer air with the strains of Brahms and Debussy and Beethoven.

On the Friday of Jib's first week at work she decided it was high time she kept her promise to Buzz, and at twelve o'clock she picked up her sandwich lunch and started for the mill. She had only crossed the footbridge and walked a few hundred yards before she felt as though she were in another world. Behind Blaisdell's converted stable the little river was sunny and peaceful, the property of visiting turtles and small frogs. Now, as she neared the factory, the banks were muddy and littered with old wagon rims, bottles, and an infinite variety of tin cans in various stages of rusty decay, and the water, although it was no longer used for industrial purposes, looked filthy.

"What a mess!" Jib spoke her thoughts and then, hearing a sound above her, looked up to see a dark, vaguely familiar young man staring down at her. "Awful, isn't it?" she said and nodded at the refuse.

"Oh? Yeah," the man said, and Jib realized that he

132

was more interested in what she was doing than in the condition of the river.

"My name's Jib Bolton," she said as she clambered up beside him. "I work back there. Do you work at the mill?"

"Yes," the man said, and his growing uneasiness manifested itself in his twitching hands and pale, unhealthy face. "What's it to you?"

"Nothing," Jib said and remembered where she had seen him before. "I just couldn't remember until this minute that I'd seen you in the mill the day I tried to get a job there and didn't, and I guess you did. Do you mind telling me your name?"

"Cramer," the man said. "Kurt Cramer."

For a moment Jib said nothing. So this was the man whom the Stirlings had been discussing her first day in Oldtown and for whom Cousin Honey had interceded at the mill. He was embarrassed, that was all, edgy perhaps because the man Parker, who had driven up to the Ridge with old Genovese and herself, had ribbed him about a Lady Bountiful getting him a job. "It must be a nice place to work." Jib nodded at the sunny yard and the plain stone building. "At least it's easy to get out of doors at noon."

Kurt Cramer murmured something unintelligible, but as he sauntered off he looked unaccountably relieved. Jib was in the mill yard by this time and, seeing some women eating their luncheons by a flight of stone steps, went over to join them. "Hello," she said. "My name's Jessica Bolton, and I'm the new gardener across the way. Do you mind if I join you for lunch?"

The women looked amused or embarrassed, but they were friendly enough, and one of them, who introduced herself as Ellen Perkins, made room for Jib on the first steps. "Hard work for young girl!" A foreign-looking woman who worked in the sorting room patted Jib's shoulder approvingly. "In America most young girls won't work outdoors."

"I like it," Jib said and bit into her sandwich. "Besides, I couldn't get any other job."

The atmosphere was instantly easier, and Mrs. Perkins introduced the other women and told Jib what they did in the mill. Jib smiled and nodded, and visions of a triumphal return to Buzz flashed through her mind. "I didn't know the town was clearing up that plot of land across the river," Mrs. Perkins said finally. "I thought they'd decided to let it go for a while."

"Oh, I didn't mean there," Jib said. "I meant farther upstream on Mr. Blaisdell's land. The piece he bought when Mr. Bean bought this factory."

The impact of her last sentence was astonishing. The foreign woman, who name was Mrs. Perisotti, and Ellen Perkins exchanged glances. Two of the younger women giggled, and a third, who had been chatting along busily, stood up and walked off without another word. For a moment Jib was too startled to speak. Around the club pool she had been simply ignored, but here, after the women's first friendliness, they seemed to exclude her purposely. "Do you know Millard Bean?" Mrs. Perkins asked, and Jib was uncomfortably aware that all the other women tensely awaited her answer.

"Why, yes," she said. "At least, I've met him a couple of times and had dinner at his house. Why?"

At that moment the factory whistle shrilled overhead and the women hurried away, leaving Jib alone. She picked up her sandwich papers and went back the way she had come. She had just reached the tool shed when she saw Claire Kelly hanging up some clothes. "Been over to the mill for lunch?" Claire asked, and Jib nodded gloomily.

"I went to get some news for Buzz Winslow," she said, "but a fat lot of good it did. Once they knew I worked here, they acted as though I had leprosy."

Claire put down her basket and came over to Jib. "I should have warned you," she said. "I suppose it's all part of the same old mess."

"What mess?" Jib looked her straight in the eye. "What is it all about?"

"It's Guy Blaisdell, mostly," Claire said, "and, behind him, Millard Bean. When Bean bought the plant Guy had the job Red has now, which is acting foreman in charge of machines. As you've seen yourself, Guy's hopeless with people, but he's a genius with machinery. He knew he wasn't fitted to run the show, but Bean put it up to him that if he didn't take on that job he, Bean, would close shop and start another, making a cheaper product, in Georgia. Guy's an idealist, and he felt it was his duty to keep work going here for these people, where they need it, and at the same time to see to it that the Mahoras Mill turned out the same grade of fine stationery they'd made in his father's time."

"But that's just what's happened," Jib said, "so I should think he and everybody else could relax."

"You don't know Guy!" Claire Kelly said. "He's always been reserved, and when he realized people thought he was a stooge for Bean, and hated him for it, he crawled into his shell more than ever. Red's tried to make people understand, but the fact that we both like Guy and share his house made us suspect from the beginning. It's been very hard on Red."

"And on you!" Jib said. "There's nothing worse than being frozen out by people when you want to make friends, and in a new country it must be simply ghastly."

Claire Kelly shook her head, and the love and serenity in her eyes made her thin face beautiful. "Oh, for me it's different," she said. "I have Red and Jamie, and then you know music is always a language. Even when Ellen Perkins wouldn't speak to me at all, we both sang in the same church choir. I could hear our voices and all the other voices floating out together, and I knew that what

135

we said or didn't say to each other made awfully little difference."

Jib said nothing more, but when she went back to transplanting some pachysandra that she had found half hidden under old leaves a day or so ago her mind was as busy as her fingers. Perhaps Claire was right and music was a language, and also great painting, and all the other arts and sciences. But what if you weren't a citizen of one of those worlds within worlds and people denied you their friendship, what happened to you then?

That evening she went down to help Buzz mimeograph his paper and told him what had happened and what Claire Kelly had said. "Sounds loony to me," Buzz said. "People understand each other and communicate through words or they don't communicate. Period. That's why newspapers are important. Well, if you can't get personal news you'll have to concentrate on machines. And whatever you do, get a complete list of the names of the people who work there."

Jib made no promises at the time, but a few days later, when Red Kelly stopped to talk to her about the garden, she asked him if she might go through the factory for the *Chronicle*. "Why not?" he said and gestured with a quick characteristic motion. "If you're really interested, come over this afternoon."

An hour later Jib met him in the entry to the mill, where she had waited to see Blaisdell, and they went from there to the sorting room, where a few of the women Jib had seen at lunch were busily picking over bales of rags. "We'll do it step by step," Kelly said, "and then once you get the flow of the thing, we can go back over any process that specially interests you."

Jib nodded and consciously focused every sense and nerve on the sights and sounds around her. When she had been in the factory before she had been too self-conscious and too concentrated on trying for a job to take in much of what was going on. Now, as she followed

Red Kelly through the sorting room to the giant boilers where the rags were cooked with chemicals, she felt she could absorb information like a sponge.

After cooking and bleaching, the rags were mechanically conveyed to big pressing machines which turned them into a sort of heavy blotting paper. "After this they're aged for ten days!" Kelly had to shout to make her hear above the pounding of the machines. "Then the stuff is mixed with sheets of wood pulp and put into the beaters. Actually the beaters are a series of shredding machines, and that process is so important that the old-timers used to say that half of papermaking is in the beating."

From there they moved on past long, ceiled conduits and giant vats up to another floor that was given over to the actual papermaking machines. The obvious, human hurly-burly of the sorting room did not exist here, Jib saw, and the three men who ran the papermaking machine looked insignificant beside the monster they tended. Jib watched the pulp pressed by heavy rollers over wire screens and emerge, for the first time in the form of paper, at the far end. From there the apparently endless sheets were mechanically propelled toward still further rollers and dryers.

The loft was hot and noisy and vibrated with the steady, rhythmic thud of the machines. Jib looked on, half hypnotized by the continuous flow before her, and when Kelly touched her arm to tell her that Blaisdell had joined them she jumped as though she had been wakened from a trance. Kelly had apparently explained to Blaisdell what she wanted, for now Blaisdell beckoned to her to join him at a spot farther along the conveyor belt. "This is a new type roller I worked out a couple of years ago and that we've just had patented," he told her. "It brings the pressure down more gradually on the paper and causes less strain with a greater effect than the older types. It's worked out nicely."

Even on his own land Blaisdell had struck Jib as cold as well as shy, but now he was enthusiastic and almost gay. Jib listened carefully to what he and Kelly told her and then asked questions about the points she had not completely understood. Always before, when she had seen the two men together, Blaisdell had hesitated, as though hoping that Kelly would answer for him, but now he was ready, even eager, to talk. He explained carefully and clearly how each machine worked and then, reaching out, took the small notebook Jib had been carrying and jotted down some quick, remarkably skillful diagrams.

It was only when they left the loft and went back into the hall near the front door that his confidence dropped away again. "Is any of this a secret process?" Jib asked. "Or can I write it all up?"

Blaisdell was silent for so long that Kelly spoke for him. "It'd be all right as long as she lets us check through her paper before it's mimeographed, wouldn't it, Guy?" Kelly said. Blaisdell nodded, and his long neck seemed to fold back into his collar like a startled turtle. He did not speak again and after a moment walked off toward his own office.

"You've seen everything now except the finishing and folding machines," Kelly said and led Jib into a big loft where Mrs. Perkins and the rest of the women she had seen out of doors were working. "There's only a short time until we close, but you can look around here by yourself. If you want to ask any questions, any of these women can answer them. I have to go downstairs again."

Jib thanked him and then stopped at an empty bench to scribble down a few quick notes beside Blaisdell's diagrams. She was so completely absorbed that it was only the sudden stillness, the lack of vibration, that made her look up. Then she realized that the two women nearest to her had switched off their machines and were looking at her with cold, unfriendly eyes. "Is it five

138

o'clock?" Jib asked, and at that moment Kurt Cramer came into sight carrying a huge stack of papers which he dropped on the bench beside Jib.

"Hello there," she said, but if Kurt Cramer had seemed nervous before, now he looked openly hostile. He jerked a thumb at Jib's notes, looked challengingly at the other women, and then marched off with the corners of his mouth turned down and his dark eyes sullen.

Jib's heart thudded faster as she realized that all of the women were looking at her and that there was hate and not simple curiosity in their faces. Why, this is crazy, she thought, and half seconds stretched out endlessly like time in a nightmare. They can't hate me like that. They haven't any reason.

The five o'clock whistle sounded and the operators filed silently out of the room. Jib caught sight of Mrs. Perkins and, remembering that Claire had said that she had finally made friends with her, ran after her. "Stop. I beg your pardon, but please stop," she began, but the older woman, her face hard and set, brushed ruthlessly past her toward the time clock and the coatroom.

For a moment Jib was nonplused and then, acting on impulse, darted down the long hall and into the street. For an instant she blinked owlishly in the sudden daylight and then, as she caught sight of a small, determined figure swinging toward the bus stop, plunged after it.

She had hardly reached Mrs. Perkins' elbow before she blurted out, "Look, what is this? What's happened? Please tell me——"

Mrs. Perkins kept right on walking, and Jib had to doublestep to keep up with her. "I was only taking notes for the *Chronicle*," she panted. "You know, the little mimeographed paper that comes out on Tuesdays and Thursdays?"

Mrs. Perkins stopped short. "The one that had the story about the 'Pigs in the Powder Room'?" she asked. "The one Lucinda Winslow's nephew runs?"

"Yes!" Jib said. "As a matter of fact, I helped write the 'Pigs' story——"

"*You did!*" Mrs. Perkins said, and amazement drove every other emotion from her face. "And we all thought you were working for Bean. You said you knew him, and young Cramer told us that you were working at Blaisdell's just so you could act as Bean's spy."

"Cramer doesn't know what he's talking about!" Jib said furiously. "And why Bean has to come into it at all I can't see. I help Buzz Winslow in my spare time, and he wants all the news and notes on the mill he can get. You all didn't seem to want to give me any personals the other day, so I was trying to do a story on the machines. There isn't any more to it than that!"

A round red spot appeared in each of Mrs. Perkins' cheeks and one hand fluttered toward Jib. "I'm sorry," she said. "I know that boy Cramer's a troublemaker. We —we shouldn't have listened to him. But we did think Bean had hired you."

"Of course he didn't," Jib snapped. "But even if he had, isn't it just possible that I might not be a heel? You people work for Bean without having sold out to him, don't you?"

A bus loomed up beside them, but Mrs. Perkins waved it on. "It won't happen any more," she said. "Bring over your lunch any day you can, and I'll guarantee the girls will help you for your paper. You see, we're all jumpy around here, and we have been ever since March when Bean bought the mill. There were rumors then that he meant to sell out, and we know as a fact he used spies and stooges over at the Titanic Mills. I guess it's gotten so that none of us even trust one another, let alone strangers."

Jib would have spoken, but Mrs. Perkins rushed on, her words held back for so long, tumbling over themselves like dammed-up water spilling through floodgates. "You're young!" she said. "And you have rich friends.

140

You were staying with the Appersleys, they said, and going to dinner at Bean's. You haven't an idea what it's like to know that if you lose your job your kids will go hungry. My husband was killed two years ago and I've got to work. You can't imagine what it's like never being sure from one day to the next whether your job is safe or not. You start listening and worrying until you're ready to believe anything!"

Jib's anger was all gone. As she looked at the older woman, nervously clutching her cheap handbag, she felt suddenly heavy with guilt which she could not explain. "I'm sorry——" she began. "I didn't know. I didn't understand——"

Another bus bore down on them, and Mrs. Perkins straightened her shoulders as though she were physically casting off the unusual indulgence of expressed emotion. "It's all right," she said, and her voice was at its most brusque New England. "Bring your lunch and you'll see. But now I have to go. This is the last bus."

Jib waved mechanically and turned toward Carley's drugstore, where she usually met Cousin Honey on her way home. "You can't know!" Mrs. Perkins had said. "You can't imagine." It was perfectly true. Neither Jib's family nor the Stirlings were rich, but in neither household was the daily bread a haunting problem.

She was so absorbed that she crossed the street without looking, and it was only the squeal of brakes and the yap of a motor horn that snapped her back to the immediate present. She saw that the driver in the car was waving frantically and in another instant registered that it was Mrs. Appersley. "Jib Bolton!" Mrs. Appersley began. "You're vaguer than ever. If you keep on mooning about like that, you're sure to be run over!"

"I'm sorry," Jib apologized. "I was thinking about something and I didn't look."

Mrs. Appersley waved away her apologies and rattled on about the country club, her servants, and a dozen other momentary concerns. "Well, do come up and see us sometime," she said as she let out her brake. "Oh, and, Jib, be sure and tell the Stirlings that the Blaines—the Cunningham Blaines, of course—are lending us their stable yard for a circus. It's going to be absolutely marvelous. Like the little intimate French circuses, you know. The tickets are only ten dollars apiece."

At that moment the combined tooting of the cars that had piled up behind her had an effect and she moved on, leaving Jib alone to walk the short distance to Carley's.

15. SEESAW

Ten-dollar circus tickets and the fear of hunger in the same community. The staggering contrast left Jib dazed, and it wasn't until she had stood in front of Carley's for five minutes that she remembered that earlier in the day Cousin Honey had said that she would not be driving home that evening.

Jib began to walk, and what Mrs. Perkins had said went with her like a smoke screen that blotted out the familiar world. Fear of hunger, fear of joblessness. The thought was an obscene cloud, a limitless, universal stain. "All the perfumes of Arabia will not sweeten . . ." Jib tried out the words in her mind, but Lady Macbeth was only embarrassingly improbable, while Mrs. Perkins' thin, driven face was so clear in her mind that it hurt.

She would have talked it over with Oliver, but both of the Stirlings were out that evening, and the recollection of "You don't know what it's like. You can't know," haunted her long after she went to bed. She still thought about it the next morning at breakfast, but once she had mounted the bicycle to ride down to Blais-dell's all gloomy thoughts blew away with the cool wind streaming through her curls. She had reached no con-clusions. Mrs. Perkins' problems were as unanswerable as they had been the night before, but now, flying down the hill on a perfect June morning, it was impossible to be aware of anything but sunshine, wind, and the breath-less thrill of motion.

Jib had only planned to work half a day on Saturday, and she had just finished the stint she had set out for herself the day before when Claire Kelly came to the tool-shed door with Jib's pay in an envelope. Cousin Honey's office was not open that day, and both the Stir-lings were out in the garden by the time Jib had bicycled home again. "I've been paid!" Jib danced out to them. "Seventeen dollars and seventy-five cents for my first week's work."

"Jib, how wonderful! It's the thrill that comes once in a lifetime." As usual, Louisa Stirling kindled in response to someone else's pleasure, and equally as usual, Jib burst out with the first thought in her mind.

"Now I can pay board!" she said. "I can't stay here and eat like a horse, like two horses, without paying for it."

Cousin Honey pushed the dark hair away from her forehead, and for the first time Jib saw her face. "I wanted you here," she said slowly. "Your mother knew that. I thought—I hoped you did."

At that moment Oliver Stirling came to the rescue. "I think if you took ten dollars a week it would be fair," he said and went on with his weeding.

"But, Oliver——" his wife began, and then as their eyes met she took the money without further protest. "Thank you, Jib darling," she said and went into the house to put the bill away.

"I hope she didn't mind. I didn't think. I wouldn't have hurt her feelings for the world!"

Oliver Stirling looked up at Jib with one of his rare, heartwarming smiles. "Independence is the best thing anyone could buy with their first earnings," he said. "Honey understands that. She's just so happy at having you here that she forgot. Now tell me, how are you coming along at Blaisdell's?"

Jib kneeled down to help him, and as she told him about her work her embarrassment lifted. It wasn't that Cousin Oliver had made a tremendous effort to be tactful, she realized. It was simply that his own mind was so free of false pride and imaginary insult that he could not imagine other people stumbling over such mental claptrap. The matter of board had been brought up, considered, and settled, and the idea of anyone's wasting time on embarrassment was beyond him.

They worked until lunch time, and then after lunch Jib read *A Burning Tree* until it was time to get dressed to go up to Cobble Top with Stanton Carter. She took her time bathing and dressing, and she had just finished when he pulled up at the postbox in a black sedan with a U. S. Soil Conservation Service emblem on the door. "I came early," he said. "It's such a knockout of a day I thought we might go the long way round behind the Ridge. We may not get another such day until September."

He drove up to the end of the motor road on Longman's Mountain, and then they walked to a cleared lookout from which there was an even better view than the one Jib had had on the day she had first walked from the Appersleys' to Oldtown. Now all three of the Quentins unfolded before her: the big houses of the Ridge, the squat confusion of the sprawling mills, and then to the west the more orderly divisions of Oldtown backing up into another range of hills. "It's divided against itself, all right." Jib spoke her thoughts out loud.

"You can actually see why the Mills, the Ridge, and Old-town don't mix. Fear of hunger in the valley and ten-dollar circus tickets on the hilltop."

Stanton Carter watched the five thirty-two chug past below them without speaking. Then, just as Jib had decided that he hadn't heard or wasn't especially interested, he pointed to the train, which had already dwindled to picture-book size in the distance. "I guess that and all the rest of the industrial revolution's the answer," he said. "We've become more and more expert on all the things that divide people physically, economically, and every other way, and we don't know any more about working together than a bunch of monkeys in a cage."

"Is that one of the headaches in your job?" Jib asked, and for the first time she was aware of Stanton Carter as another puzzled human being and not merely as a prospective "date," a young man in relationship to herself.

He took her arm and led her around to the other side of the lookout, which gave out onto a valley where the checkerboard fields of a dozen big farms sprawled out before them in the afternoon light. "That's all good land," Carter said. "Or it could be if people would only use their heads about the way they worked it. If they don't before very long, it's all going to look like that."

Jib followed his forefinger and saw the darker green fringe of second-growth woodland that encroached on the edges of the farmlands like an encircling fungus. "It's pretty," she said diffidently. "But I don't suppose it's useful."

"Sumac and swamp alder," he said bitterly. "Sheer waste coming over what could be first-rate dairy country, and that at a time when half the world is starving. The way people refuse to see it is incredible!"

"And Bean?" Jib hazarded. "Is he still being a nuisance?"

"You're awfully quick, Jib Bolton," he said, and as he

146

turned toward her his face was young and eager in the golden light. "Yes, he's still my personal Dracula. But what gets me is how I ever kidded myself into thinking that you liked him!"

"That was my fault," Jib said, and as she followed him back to the car she wondered how she had ever been tempted, even for an instant, to lie or pretend to this man whose own deliberate candor was as much a part of him as his springy walk or his crew-cut hair.

"You know, I really did snarl things up for a fare-you-well by fighting with Bean," Stanton said when he had headed the car toward Cobble Top. "But when he called me a communist because I believe in co-operative farm activities I saw red and only kept from hitting him because he's twice my age. I suppose I can't blame him for hating me, but it's infuriating that his personal spite should prevent just the people who need us most from letting us go over their land."

"Isn't there anyone on your side?" Jib asked. "People like Cousin Oliver, for instance, who couldn't be bought or sold by Bean or anyone else?"

"Mr. Stirling has been a help," Stanton said. "He was one of the people who petitioned to have us open an office here, because he's interested in co-operative work of every kind. There have to be five sponsoring petitioners, you see, but that's where Mike and I ran into bad luck. Two men died after the petition went through, and another sold his place and bought out in Ohio. That just leaves your cousin, who isn't really farming, and a man called Westerdahl, who has a good herd of Guernseys. Those two have fed us enough names of people who want their places gone over to keep us going so far, but the number's falling off, and every time we turn around we come up against a farmer who has a son or a daughter working for Titanic Mills or one of the other Bean interests and is scared even to speak to me."

"And if there aren't enough people you're out of a job?" Jib asked, but Stanton Carter shook his head.

"Mike and I are professionals," he said, and the very quietness of his voice was a measure of his justified pride. "If they can't use us here, they'll send us somewhere else. It isn't that; it's simply that I hate to be licked when I know what we can do. This is rich land, but I tell you it's criminal the way it's being bled."

They were already on the winding trail that led up to Cobble Top by that time, and a moment later Stanton Carter stopped the car at the house, where Mike Gallagher and a girl from the Greensfield Normal School were waiting for them.

Mike Gallagher, who apparently prided himself on his cooking, had started the outdoor grill some time ago, and a few minutes later he called them over to sample the skewered veal and the roast corn he had ready for them. The talk was general: about the food, the weather, and what they had all been doing for the past few weeks. Jib felt contented and happy, but even so it was a curiously lonely feeling to be back at Cobble Top with the family so far away and any return so remote and uncertain. She knew that sooner or later one of the two men would ask her to see the house, and she was glad when the other girl, whose name was Helen Benton, asked Mike Gallagher about his work and he plunged into an enthusiastic monologue digging up a little of the earth beside him to illuminate his points.

Both Mike and Helen Benton were absorbed, and it was a surprise when Stanton Carter, who had seemed equally engrossed in Mike's shoptalk, touched her shoulder. "Come and see what I've done while there's still enough light," he said. "You can't put it off forever, you know, even if it does make you feel like a rabbit running across its own grave."

Jib looked up at him guiltily, and he laughed as they left the others still sitting beside the fire. "I'd feel the

148

same way," he said. "In fact, I have. I was brought up on my great-grandfather's place along the James River. My family had been losing ground with it ever since the War between the States, but we held on until my father died in 1938, the year I went off to college. The people who bought it are said to be delightful, but I hate their guts and I'll never go back."

As he talked they followed the path to the hidden pool where Jib had learned to swim. For years her parents had planned to clear away the undergrowth around the sides, but with the small amount of time her father had been able to spend at Cobble Top and her mother's other interests, they had never attempted it. Now, as Stanton Carter stepped aside to let her see, she saw that all the work had been done! More than that, where there had been a tangle of cat brier and poison ivy only a few months ago, the land had been carefully graded, and the osmundas ferns which she had missed from the woods were flourishing as though they had never known any other home. "Stanton!" Jib choked out. "You moved those ferns up here the way Mum always planned and wanted, and I—I thought they were stolen."

He said nothing, but motioned for her to stand beside him, where he had arranged a shoulder-high opening, more peephole than vista, through the woods, so that, framed by green leaves, Jib could see the familiar, stirring outline of the Cobble. "Quentin's Cobble and the Judgment Rock," Stanton said slowly. "I sort of reckoned they meant something special to you all."

Jib said nothing but her face was a torch. "Now look at the springboard," he said anxiously. "Do you think the twins will like it? It's good and springy."

"The twins!" Jib sounded awe-struck. "So you knew about them, too, and the one thing they've always wanted!"

"There were a lot of pictures around," he said as he led the way back to the house. "And I asked questions from anyone who might know. You see, I knew quite a lot about you by the time we saw one another down at the railroad station and both felt badly about old man Coats, the baggageman."

"You knew who I was even then?" Jib asked.

Stanton nodded and opened the door of the bedroom that had been Jib's parents'. "I sleep in here," he said, "looking at you. I nearly dropped your friend's trunk that day because it's such a good likeness." He nodded toward a pastel of Jib that Mrs. Bolton had done during their last week at Cobble Top the previous autumn. "I wanted to ask you up here right away to—to sort of make things all right about our living here. Then there was that mess at the dance and I couldn't. The day you walked up here I'd just been working on the pool, wondering what you'd think of it. When I came through the woods and saw you, it was like a dream come true, and then—and then——"

"I acted like a skunk!" Jib blurted out and found that her heart was beating so fast that she could not say another word. They heard the sound of voices behind them, and Mike and Helen Benton crowded into the room.

"Stant fell in love with Jib's whole family," Mike said and pointed out the various pictures and photographs about the room. Jib managed to smile, but she wished that he and Helen had never left the fire. They did not return to it, however, and a short time later the party was over.

There was no moon that night, and the woodland roads were deeply silent as Stanton Carter drove Jib home. Neither of them spoke until they saw the lights of Oldtown twinkling up at them from the valley. "Let's stop at Carley's for a soda," Stanton suggested. "I hate to have this evening over."

"So do I," Jib agreed, and a few minutes later they were installed in one of the little cubbyholes at the back of the store. They had just been served when there was an explosion of voices, laughter, and jostling feet as the movie crowd swarmed over Carley's like a bright wave encircling a beachhead. "Mind if we sit here?" The familiar voice was right at Jib's elbow, and she looked up to see Stella Drelincourt, with a man she didn't know, standing above them.

Stanton Carter had already sprung to his feet, and there was nothing Jib could do but nod and introduce Stanton to Stella and have Stella's pallid escort, whose name was Foster Chubb, introduced in turn. If Stella had any feeling of guilt or even of embarrassment at the way she had used Jib she did not show it, and Jib found herself wondering if the older girl even remembered what had happened.

"Well, Jibbie pet," she said, and Jib stiffened at the diminutive, "I haven't seen you for ages. I heard you weren't staying at the Apps' any more but why don't you ever turn up at the club pool? I've been asking everybody about you."

"I'm living with my cousins, the Stirlings, and they don't belong," Jib said flatly. Stella reached for a cigarette, and as Jib saw her flashing fingertips she was aware that despite all her careful scrubbing her own hands, scratched and grass-stained from her gardening, looked ugly and unkempt in comparison.

"Oh, too bad. Dull for you," Stella said, and then she turned the floodlight of her personality on Stanton Carter. "We've met before, you know," she said and looked up at him through dark lacy eyelashes. "At the Beck Hall spread in 1941. You don't remember?"

"I'm afraid I don't." Stan Carter was polite and smiling, and Jib felt younger and more insignificant by the moment as she realized that in 1941 she had still been playing with dolls.

"I'm just the kind of a girl that men forget," Stella crooned, and although Foster Chubb grew apologetic

151

with denials, her smile and the lazy, completely assured gleam in her eyes were all for Stanton Carter's
benefit.

"Stella, what would like you like to have?" Chubb's
voice sounded desperate as he struggled to attract her
attention. "They're so busy at the fountain you'd better
let me go for you."

"Why, I think I'd like an orangeade." Stella brought
out each word slowly, as though her decision was a
revelation. "But you're such an old spilly-willy, Chubbie
darlin', I think I'll sponge on Mr. Carter here to get it
for me. He looks strong and efficient, and I'm simply
dyin' of thirst."

"What will you have, Chubb?" Stanton was already on
his feet, and Jib's heart felt as dry as pressed moss.
Stan's falling for her, she thought, he's ready to do anything she wants.

In miraculously short time Stanton was back and put
the soft drinks down on the table. "Oh, thank you, Mr.
Carter," Stella said, and now the husky voice that Jib
had once found so enchanting grated on her nerves like
a dentist's drill. "You all have saved my life."

"I'm delighted." Stan bowed, and then he beckoned
to Jib. "Sorry that we have to run along, but Jib's cousin,
Mrs. Stirling, is waiting for us."

Jib sprang up, nearly upsetting what was left in her
glass in her eagerness. Hope, fresh and unexpected as
rain in a heat wave, came down on her, and then Stella
spoke.

"Of course. I understand perfectly," she said, and her
voice was solicitous, almost maternal. "We can't have
them worrying about little Jibbie. But if you have time
later on, Mr. Carter, Chubbie and I would love to have
you join us at Zelletti's roadhouse. The music is quite
good there, and I do want to see if we can't get together
about some of the people we both must have known at
Harvard."

Jib held her breath as Stanton answered. "I'm afraid we wouldn't get very far," he said. "The nearest I ever got to Harvard was to go to the Arnold Arboretum when I was at Agricultural School. Beck Hall was a good guess, but something like a Grange picnic would have been closer."

His voice was still impeccably polite but his intention was beautifully apparent, and Stella Drelincourt flushed and then began to talk rapidly to Foster Chubb as Jib and Stanton picked their way out of the crowded drugstore.

"Lord, what a girl!" Stan Carter wiped his face when he had helped Jib into the car. "Is she always that obvious?"

Jib, who was breathless with a mixture of relief and joy, wanted to cry out, "Yes! Yes! Any fool would see through her." But she couldn't.

"I fell for her myself," she confessed, and then, having begun, twisted the knife in the wound. "For thirty-six hours I had a regular crush on her like an eighth-grade kid on teacher. I thought she was wonderful."

To her surprise, Stanton put back his head and roared with laughter as he started the motor. "And I bet she used you for a fall guy," he said. "Probably borrowed your last cent or stood you up on a date or did some other nasty little trick that happened to come handy. Miss Stella's just the type to prey on the young and innocent."

"Yes," Jib said, but her voice was so muffled he hardly heard her. He thinks I'm a kid and a fool, her heart said. He could handle Stella so smoothly even she didn't know until the last moment he'd seen through her bluff. For a minute Stanton Carter didn't say anything, then his right hand shot out and he squeezed Jib's left. "Don't you worry about that, Jib honey," he said. "Don't you understand that it's never foolish to love any man, or woman, or beast, or thing, as long as it's honest love? The only

153

disgusting and ultimately pitiful thing is to be exclusively in love with yourself, like that girl we just saw."

Jib's heart beat like a triphammer. "Stant. Oh, Stanton, yes!" she said, but he took back his hand, and as she turned toward him all she could see was his clean-cut profile as he concentrated on his driving.

16. BEAUTIFUL FOR PATRIOT'S DREAMS

FOR THE next few weeks Jib lived on two entirely separate planes of existence. There was the busy outward plane made up of her work at Guy Blaisdell's, the life she shared with the Stirlings, and the reporting she did for Buzz which took her into a dozen village activities she would otherwise have missed. All these were the things she wrote her family about, and whenever she found enough spare minutes for a letter she was startled at how much time had gone by since she had last written. The other plane, which she mentioned to no one, was infinitely more important, and it was exclusively concerned with Stanton Carter.

The moments of shared understanding, so sudden and so complete, which Jib had experienced in Stanton's company at Cobble Top and later in front of the drugstore still forked through her memory like lightning through a thundercloud. Both times she had thought he would say something more but he had not, and his speedy return to a matter-of-fact friendliness had challenged her into the same sort of attitude. Gradually, and quite unconsciously, as the summer weeks went by, Jib slid into accepting what Mike had said at Cobble Top as accurate. Stanton liked to be with her, the facts proved that, but as far as anything more was concerned he was simply, as Mike had put it, in love with the idea of her whole family. For the time being, while he came almost daily to help her out at Guy Blaisdell's or to drive her back to the Stirlings', that seemed enough, and she was startled when Claire Kelly came out one morning and asked if her "beau" was calling for her that afternoon.

"Who? Oh, you mean Stanton?" Jib, wholly hidden by a big syringa bush, was elaborately evasive.

"Of course!" Claire's rolling Scottish *r* was rounder than ever. "Even the village innocent could see he is daft over you."

Jib was pleased, but she had no desire to discuss Stanton with Claire the way she had talked over the other boys she had known with the girls at college, and she was glad when a whimper from Jamie Kelly recalled his mother to the house. Claire came out again during the afternoon but she disappeared when Stanton came over to help Jib with some scything, and neither of them saw her until they caught sight of her wheeling Jamie toward the Oldtown shopping district about a half hour later. "She's a dear," Jib said, "an absolute lamb, and it's almost unbelievable that for a while none of the people at the Mahoras Mill would speak to her. And yet I'm perfectly certain none of them meant to be cruel."

"You like practically everybody, don't you?" Stanton said. "It's a knockout of a gift. I wish I had it the way you and Mrs. Stirling have."

For an instant Jib wanted to keep his praise unshriveled by the truth, but as she looked up at him she grinned and shook her head. "Around here I do; I like

156

the Kellys and Buzz and even all the human oddities that turn up at Cousin Honeys, but up at the Ridge I felt so sort of frozen I hated practically everybody."

Stanton leaned easily on his scythe. "I don't think that was you," he said, "or even them. It's simply that people can't like one another when the only thing that counts is social success. I've seen the same sort of freeze come over the nicest guys in the world during rush week at college. The people around here aren't saints any more than the ones on the Ridge, but we're free to like them because we have other things on our minds than just how we rate."

Jib laughed and filled a watering can at the outside tap by the tool shed. "You're right!" she said. "This minute a large part of my mind's on whether we're going to get the rain we need or not. Up at the Appersleys' the whole garden could have dried up and I wouldn't even have noticed it, I was so busy thinking about what other people thought of me."

A short time later Stan drove her up the hill and, as he had work to do, left her at the postbox. She was nearly at the door before she saw the four small rather peaked children sitting on the front steps. "Why, hello!" she said. "Who are you?"

For a minute four pairs of eyes considered her in silence, and finally the oldest, a girl of about ten, broke the silence. "I'm Sally Martin," she said. "Me and the other kids gotta see Mrs. Stirling."

Just at that moment Honey Stirling arrived, and, their shyness broken like the paper over a torpedo, the children exploded around her. It turned out that they came from the Methodist Orphanage, an old-fashioned turreted building that Jib had noticed on the far side of Oldtown, and that they needed costumes for a play they were to put on the following Saturday. "Costumes? Why, of course." Mrs. Stirling nodded as though it were the most natural request in the world. "Sally, you'll be lovely as a princess. Would you like to come up and help me bring the costume box down from the attic?"

The children greeted that with whoops of joy, and in no time at all the orderly living room was strewn with old clothes and bright swatches of material. Oliver Stirling looked in and, after locking up his own clothes closet, took himself off to the garden without a word.

At six o'clock the maelstrom seemed no nearer subsiding than it had a half hour ago, and Jib suggested that she start supper. "You're an angel." Cousin Honey smiled over the head of the smallest boy, whom she was pinning into a homemade clown costume. "This won't take long."

Jib was dubious, but in a surprisingly short time the costume box was gutted and the children trailed off, eating cookies and each hugging some borrowed raiment to his or her body.

Louisa Stirling came out to the kitchen to start supper, only to be interrupted twice by telephone calls and once by the personal appearance of an old lady who was sure that she had left her glasses at the town-hall office earlier in the day. But somehow the meal was accomplished, and at seven o'clock Louisa called out that supper was ready. Oliver appeared in his own good time, bearing an armful of roses which he insisted had to be fixed at once. Jib plunged them into deep water, planning to fix them later, and supper went on as peacefully as though it had been prepared by unseen genii.

After supper Oliver wanted to show Jib his early azalea mums, and by the time she reached the kitchen Cousin Honey had finished the dishes and was whistling away as she fixed the roses. "Let me do those," Jib said. "I should think you'd be half dead."

Cousin Honey laughed. "Don't be silly," she said. "I was born strong as a horse, and besides, Oliver does the hard things."

Jib looked out of the window to where Oliver was

158

peacefully reading a book while he waited for the coffee which he knew would be brought to him. The telephone rang behind him and a neighbor's dog trotted perilously close to the forcing bed, but he never looked up, and it was his wife who chased off the dog and answered the telephone. "I don't understand how you do it," Jib persisted when Cousin Honey came back for the coffee. "You know I think Cousin Oliver's wonderful, but you're the one who takes the brunt of things."

Cousin Honey was so surprised that she nearly dropped the coffee tray. "Are you joking?" she asked when she had righted it. "I'm no more a martyr than Oliver is."

"Oh, I didn't mean martyrdom exactly. I suppose every marriage is a matter of compromises—good ones, of course."

For a moment Louisa Stirling stood stock-still. When she finally spoke her words came slowly, as though she had examined each one of them to be sure of its truth. "I don't think you're right," she said quietly. "A marriage that's made up of noble compromises is sure to end up with one partner trying to change the other, and that's fatal. The real thing's more of a filling out, a sort of dovetailing. A good marriage makes one whole thing where there were only two incomplete ones before."

Jib would have asked more, but at that moment the doorbell rang and a moment later Cousin Honey called back that there was someone to see her. Jib hurried forward, everything else forgotten. Stanton. It must be. They had had such a good time during the afternoon that now he was coming to take her out for the evening. She paused for a second before the gilt mirror in the living room and almost collided with Buzz Winslow. "Oh, you," she said.

"Yeah. Look. The break I've been hunting for's actually come. Bennett Drayton, the man who runs the National Civic Freedom Council and who's just been investigated down in Washington, is in Oldtown, and nobody knows it but me. I just happened to stop in at the Oldtown Inn just after he registered. Old Mrs. Quail, who runs it, is such a dope she thought he was probably a rag salesman on a trip to Titanic. I've got to see him, and the best chance is tomorrow afternoon. He told Ma Quail he was going to sleep all morning and then hike up to Oldtown Falls in the afternoon. If I bike over there I can't miss him."

"Go ahead!" Jib snapped and hated herself because she sounded as cross and let down as she felt. "I don't see what that has to do with me."

"But it does," Buzz insisted. "I was going to spend the day with Stant Carter going over John Milkowski's farm. It'd make a good feature and now I can't go. Will you go with him instead?"

"Yes. Yes, of course I will, Buzz," Jib said and thanked her stars that Buzz was so in the grip of his own excitement that he did not notice hers. "Will Stant call for me here or what?"

"He'll be here at three," Buzz said and started off toward his bicycle. "And for Pete's sake, wear sneakers because you'll be walking all afternoon. Try not to miss a thing. I could use a thousand words."

For the rest of that evening and the following morning Jib's mind was much more on what she was going to wear, on what they would talk about, on every facet of being with Stanton than it was on Buzz's story. But when Stanton arrived, punctual to the minute, it was clear from the beginning that as far as he was concerned this was strictly a business trip. "Thanks loads for taking me," Jib said and got into the car, but Stanton only nodded and moved his notebook and the air map of Milkowski's farm to a safer place.

They drove as far as the turn below Oldtown in silence, and then Jib tried again. "I hope you don't mind taking me," she said. "It means a lot to Buzz." But Stanton kept right on being impersonal.

"Any favorable publicity's to the good," he said. "And quite a lot of people are reading Buzz's paper. Not enough, though. I thought we'd never land Milkowski."

"He's important, then. Mr. Milkowski, I mean?"

"Not in himself," Stanton said, and as he jerked on the brakes by a traffic light and then raced his motor Jib realized that he wasn't trying to be cold or mean but simply that he was so nervous over what was ahead of him that he couldn't put his mind on anything else. "But his land happens to be absolutely crying out for just the sort of help we can give, and besides, he has a good deal of influence among the other Polish farmers. If I can sell him on our plan it ought to help with any of the ones who haven't actually got a son or a daughter working for Bean. I have a hunch Milkowski's going to be the turning point."

John Milkowski was waiting for them when they arrived at his barn, and a few minutes later Jib and the two men began a long, careful walk over every acre of his farm. Stanton had been nervous on the way over, but he didn't show it now and listened attentively while Milkowski told him which field he thought of keeping in pasture and how much he needed for hay. Once or twice Stanton asked a question about the boundary of a field or made a suggestion for a rotation of crops, but for the most part he took notes and listened in silence to what the short, ruddy-faced Pole had to say.

At the bottom of a long, gradually sloping field John Milkowski stopped and, putting his foot up on a low stone wall, turned to Stanton. "Is good hay here," he said. "There"—he pointed to a farther portion of the field—"she stink. Too wet in spring. Hay rot."

Stanton nodded and began searching over the lower fields as though he had lost his watch. "What are you looking for?" Jib spoke for the first time since they had left the farm buildings. "A gold mine?"

Milkowski guffawed, but Stanton only grinned and

shook his head. "The springs that make this marshy," he said. "When we know where they are we'll be able to chart a drainage ditch that'll make this all grade-A meadowland. Right now they're hard to find because of the drought."

Jib walked a little distance from the two men and, when she came to a spot where some ground myrtle looked greener and more luxuriant than the neighboring grasses, leaned over. "Could this be a spring?" she asked, and Stanton and Milkowski hurried toward her.

"Yes. Good for you!" Stanton said, and Milkowski nodded approval.

"Your girl got good eyes," he told Stanton. "I work over this field for ten, twelve year and don't find so quick."

Stanton didn't answer and went on searching for other springs. He's only interested in his job, Jib told herself. He didn't care one way or the other when Milkowski called me his girl. She forced herself to pay attention to what the two men were doing. They found two other springs and then went back to the stone wall, which Stanton eventually said should be buried.

Milkowski scratched his head while he considered the idea. "One big field in place two leetle chopped-up fields is good," he said. "But expensive. I hear from Scott, the man who work for Bean, it cost a fortune to buy stone wall."

Stanton Carter's neck grew red under his sun tan, but his voice when he answered was completely under control. "Our district office will supply a man with a bulldozer at cost. He could dig a trench, roll the stones into it, and cover them again in one day easily. Westerdahl had it done, and Jenkins over at Wessex Falls."

"Maybe you right," Milkowski said finally. "But now come see other fields."

Once Stanton stopped to describe a new method of plowing for a steep grade where there were already signs of soil erosion. Another time, when Milkowski showed them a strip of land he said he had always wanted to fence in for pasturage, Stanton suggested a hedge of multiflora roses.

"A hedge of roses?" Jib spoke up. "Why, that sounds right for a garden."

"It's a lot more than that." Stanton answered Jib, but his powers of persuasion were all directed toward Milkowski. "I don't know, Mr. Milkowski, whether you've seen any of the ones they've put in over Redham way. If you haven't, I'd be glad to drive you over tomorrow. It really is a member of the rose family, but in a few years it'll make a good solid hedge to keep cattle out."

Once more Milkowski was uncertain. "Is expensive," he said. "Mr. Bean's man tell me the hedge cost——"

"The government gives out the rose plants free," Stanton cut in. "As many as you need or want. We could also get you up to three thousand pines if you decide you want to plant them along that hillside. If you want more than that number, you pay for every other one after the three thousand. I'd definitely recommend the multifloras, but I'd rather wait about the trees until Gallagher gives us a report on the soil."

They walked on again, and Jib followed after them, mentally beginning her article for Buzz. She had seen Stanton in action, and Mike Gallagher had shown her both a soil report and a detailed map of another farm carefully keyed and colored to guide the farmer in keeping to the Bureau's recommendations. She knew she had a pretty clear outline of the work involved, but what she wanted now was a catchy descriptive sentence of the whole procedure with which to begin her piece.

She caught up with the men on a small hillock at the far end of the farm. Milkowski looked back over the long valley and up toward his barns. "I begin understand what you do," he said excitedly. "Uncle Sam help farmer make his land give and keep rich for more giving.

163

Farmer sign paper to say he do what you say best way he can."

"That's it!" Stanton said, but Jib hardly heard him as the words Milkowski had just spoken clicked into place in her mind. This was a new kind of patriotism that had nothing to do with jingoism or brass bands. With a little polishing, that idea could be worked up into just the sort of catchy but accurate opening that Buzz needed.

By the end of another hour Jib was very thirsty and acutely conscious that she had had only a sandwich lunch. She was out of sight of the men, who had forged ahead of her still enthusiastically discussing soil problems. Finally she stopped mentally struggling with her article for Buzz and gave herself up to enjoying the welcome coolness that was spreading over the bottom lands. It had been hot and dry all day, but now, as the river mist fingered its way along the valley, the air was moist and fresh on her warm cheeks.

She walked on in the general direction of the barns until a small lane leading off into the woodlands caught her eye. She hadn't paid any attention to roads when Stanton had driven her over, but now something familiar and appealing about the little lane on her right held her attention. The faint, grassed-over ruts might have been made years ago, but new hay festooned the trees on both sides and she guessed that Milkowski used the trail as a short cut. She climbed up on a pile of rock to get her bearings, and when she saw Quentin's Cobble, looking dark and formidable in the near foreground, she knew where she was for the first time. The deserted little lane, which looked like nothing more than a farm trail, was actually one of the oldest roads in the county and prominently marked, on the old Geodetic Survey maps which her father cherished, as Queen's Saunter. She and her father had discovered it together years ago, and ever since then they had ridden over it as a special treat the week before she went back to school. Until this moment she had not had the faintest idea that it bordered Milkowski's land.

She hurried back uphill and, as soon as she was within speaking distance of the two men, told Stanton what she had found. "I always loved that road," she finished. "But I didn't know it ran near here. We always went in from the Ridge end."

Stanton looked at her with an expression she couldn't fathom and then, after telling Jib that the Milkowskis wanted them to stay for supper, asked John Milkowski if he could help with the milking. "Is done," Milkowski said. "Wife's father milk before he go home. I do other chores and we all eat."

"Can I help you with those?" Stanton asked, but Milkowski was adamant in refusing, and a moment later he went off to the barn.

"Is it all right?" Jib asked as soon as Milkowski was out of hearing. "Will he sign up with you?"

"Sure to!" Stanton was jubilant. "It's in the bag. I'm to bring him the contract tomorrow. And Jib, Jib honey, I noticed that little road, the Queen's Saunter, myself! Why couldn't we rent some nags someday next week and ride there?"

"It'd be wonderful!" Jib had hardly spoken before they both heard a slight rustling sound in the long grass behind them. They turned and saw an old man, whom they guessed might be Milkowski's father-in-law, trudging away toward the road. He was a very small man in faded blue work clothes, and in his right hand he carried a tin pail and in his left a child's basket filled with apples.

"Good evening." The words came to both their lips, but the little old man neither heard nor saw them, and they stood in silence until the bent, diminutive figure disappeared through the apple trees into the lonely twilight.

"I—I wish he had a dog," Jib said softly. "He looked so

old and so lonely. Like the little old man in a songbook of Mummy's."

"*Der Erste Lieder Buch!*" Stanton said and now he took her hand. "I had it, too, when I was a little kid."

A few minutes later Mrs. Milkowski had supper ready, and Jib found herself at table between the two men. Milkowski served out the food and then began eating while Jib and Stanton tried unsuccessfully to prevail on Mrs. Milkowski to join them. "Is better here," she said, one foot firmly planted over the kitchen sill and the other in the musty-smelling dining room which was obviously being used only for this occasion. "If anyone want milk, butter, pork, I get him quick."

"But do let me help," Jib protested, but Mrs. Milkowski pushed her down with a firm, plump hand.

"Married woman, maybe. Bride-to-be, no. For little while she is treated like queen. Is good."

"But I'm not engaged," Jib said, and then added rather lamely, "to anyone."

Mrs. Milkowski gave a hearty gold-toothed laugh and her husband stopped eating long enough to chuckle, but Stanton Carter buttered his bread with exaggerated care and his eyes avoided Jib's. "You see, he wouldn't take me as a gift," Jib said, but her crack hung flat and tasteless on the air and she was glad when a moment later Milkowski asked Stanton some further questions about the intricacies of terracing.

It was after nine when they left, and both the Milkowskis followed them to the car.

"I'll bring the report back tomorrow just as soon as Gallagher's made his soil tests," Stanton said, and Milkowski nodded.

"Fine," he said as they drove off. "And bring your girl. My wife and I see she is good girl."

"They seem to be throwing me at your head." Jib was still suffering from the aftertaste of her own remark at supper. "I'm sorry if it upsets you."

Stanton stopped the car with a jerk, and for one instant as he turned toward her she thought he was furious. The next second his tension broke and they came together as swiftly and inevitably as two streams surging down a mountainside.

"Jib. Jib, my darling." Stanton's broken whisper melted in Jib's ears with the singing chorus of her own blood.

A car roared toward them, and as the driver pressed on his horn the spell was broken. Stanton stiffened instantly and, without even looking back at Jib, switched on the ignition and drove toward the Stirlings'.

Jib was too stunned by the change in him to speak and sat feeling cold and shriveled on her own side of the seat. It was only as he drew up by the garden gate that she touched his sleeve. "Stanton," she whispered. "Stanton, what is the trouble?"

For an instant she thought he was going to tell her, and then he sprang out of the car and opened the gate for her without saying a word. She moved past him as numb and bewildered as though he had slapped her and let herself into the silent house. If he had followed, if he came in and explained? But she knew even before she turned around on the threshold that he was not behind her. She stood very still, and a moment later she heard the sound of his motor, hard, rhythmic, and inhuman, as he drove away.

17. LISTEN, THE WIND!

It was a long, long time before Jib fell asleep. No matter what else had happened, she knew that her relationship with Stanton Carter would never be on the same happy-go-lucky plane again. That at least was as clear as though they had been wandering carefree down a woodland trail and had arrived at an unexpected fork where they had to make a decision. One branch of the fork dwindled off into nothingness and the other branch led on, up and up, to the highest summit of the mountains. It'll be all right, Jib told herself over and over again. Tomorrow Stant'll come over and explain. Everything will be better than before. We'll take the fork that leads up into the mountains.

But she did not hear from Stanton Carter the next day or the next. At the end of the week she could not stand it any longer and that evening, when she found herself alone at the Stirlings', telephoned Cobble Top.

Mike Gallagher answered and said that Stanton had not come home. "I'll get him to call you as soon as he gets in," Mike promised, but although Jib sat glued to the telephone for the rest of the evening, it never rang and she went to bed feeling cheapened and betrayed.

She dreaded the thought of working on her article about Milkowski's farm, which was all tied up in her mind with her last day with Stanton, and she was relieved when the days passed and Buzz never mentioned it. She thought of making it up to him by getting more Mahoras Mill news, but when she took her lunch over to the mill yard the women were evasive and absent-minded and it was hard to pin them down to local gossip. "What's bitten everybody?" she asked when she had a moment alone with Ellen Perkins. "Do people still think I'm stooging for Millard Bean or what has happened?"

"It's not you, dearie." Embarrassment made Mrs. Perkins look thinner and more exhausted than ever. "I swear it isn't you. It's just more rumor, a lot of talk about unionizing that's gotten everybody stirred up again. When anything's decided I'll let you know first thing."

Jib had to be satisfied with that, and in the afternoon, for the first time in weeks, she bicycled over to see Buzz in his corncrib office. "Couldn't get much at the mill," she said. "A kitchen shower for Mrs. Perisotti's daughter and a card party at the Elks. Sorry I've been such a washout."

"Pretty soon I'll have to dig up a story about sharks in Mahoras Creek or shut up shop," Buzz said bitterly. "My last issue was a washout."

Jib, who had been too immersed in her own troubles even to look at the last *Chronicle*, realized guiltily that she had never asked him about his interview with Bennett Drayton.

"I didn't get it," Buzz said when she had spoken. "Drayton changed his mind about hiking to the falls and drove on up to the White Mountains instead. He's coming back this week end."

"But you'll get him then," Jib said. "Whyever not?"

"Because every other paper in the state will be after him. The *Berkshire Informer* found out about his trip when he hit Pittsfield, and since then even the New York papers have covered everything he's said or done. What I wanted was a scoop or a special interview, and now I haven't a chance."

"Next week I'll get some Ridge news," Jib said, relieved that he hadn't asked about her farm article. "And on Tuesday there's a Village Improvement shindig of some sort and Cousin Honey's sure to bring back some tips from that."

"Thanks," Buzz said, but he never looked up from the copy he was working on, and a few minutes later she left, feeling more depressed than ever.

Even the weather, which had been so glorious earlier in the summer, seemed against her now, and as one dry, relentlessly hot day followed another she felt that she was fighting a losing fight in the stable garden. She watered until her back ached, but the sprinkle only rolled off in dusty balls and a few minutes later the baked earth was hard and dry as ever. Six more cans, Jib told herself, and began playing a hopeless, superstitious little game. Six more cans and then Stant will turn up and help me.

She carried six more full cans and then another six, but still Stanton did not appear, either that day or the following ones. On Saturday, out of desperation, she bicycled over to Quentin Mills on the chance of seeing him in his office, but he was not there and she pushed her bicycle back along the crowded sidewalk in front of the A&P, the dime stores, and the chain drugstore, loathing the place, the Saturday marketers, and above all herself.

During the night both the wind and the temperature

rose, and even before Jib was fully awake she could hear the sere rustling of the ivy leaves and the louder rattle of the shutters blowing against the shingled walls. She had spent a good part of the night going over and over what had happened between Stanton and herself and, like a squirrel on a wheel, had arrived nowhere. A few weeks ago she would have been openly rebellious, as she had been about the country-club dance, and would have managed to have it out with him somehow. Now that she hadn't seen him for days, she was so eager for any crumbs of his time and friendship that she was ready to accept them on any terms.

She felt frustrated and ashamed as she dressed and brushed her hair, and when she went downstairs the hot wind seemed as nagging and inescapable as a wrenched muscle. Cousin Honey, on the other hand, seemed totally unaffected by the weather. "Going to church with me, darling?" she asked when Jib came back from a dust-blown, unconsoling tour of the garden. "I'm going to the ten o'clock service."

Jib toyed with the idea of staying with Cousin Oliver, but he had been more than usually silent at breakfast and now he went into his study and shut the door with ostentatious care. Rather than face an hour of her own company, she decided to go along.

They drove down to the ivy-covered Episcopal church and, holding onto their hats, crossed the ancient grave-yard. Jib was wondering if the wind would uproot the moss-covered gravestones when she saw the Misses Winslow and Buzz, looking preternaturally brushed and neat, waiting at the church door. "Have you picked up any Ridge news that's worth using?" Buzz asked, and any sympathy Jib had felt for him a few days ago dried up like rain in a desert. "If it's halfway decent, I could use it."

"No," Jib said. "I haven't a thing——"

"Better hop to it this afternoon, then," Buzz said. "I'll call you up about it this evening."

A dozen sharp protests fought for precedence in Jib's mind, but the choir had cued up in the sacristy and before she could say a word he darted after his aunts up to the front pew. "This way, dear," Cousin Honey whispered, and willy-nilly Jib found herself kneeling beside her cousin in a back pew.

She was too cross with Buzz, the weather, herself to concentrate on praying, and she straighted up while Louisa Stirling, her face relaxed and peaceful, knelt beside her. Louisa had been her friendly and very voluble self right up to the door of the church, but now she was as absorbed and still as a nun. It's an act, Jib thought, or maybe just manners, like her being nice to everybody. But even as the thought crossed her mind she knew it was not true. Louisa Stirling was not changed but merely tuned in to the very wellsprings of her being. ". . . above all, for thine inestimable love . . ." Jib heard the familiar voice beside her repeat the General Thanksgiving and bowed her head.

"Oh, God, let me believe in you like that," she prayed. "Then maybe I can learn to live without Stant or Cobble Top or anything. Give me faith and hope and lots more courage."

For a moment she was soothed, but then as the service went on her restlessness returned, so that even Cousin Honey noticed it. "Do you feel all right, darling?" she whispered. "Or would you like me to drive you home?"

Jib shook her head and struggled to concentrate, but even when she managed to take her mind off her own problems she was only aware of the flaws and crudities in the service which seemed to escape her cousin as though they did not exist. The sermon was dull, and when the old clergyman leaned foward in his pulpit the wood creaked so that a small boy snickered and a pewful of old maids looked annoyed.

When it came to the offertory Millard Bean and Simon Planter, the old man who had turned Jib down as a gardener, passed the plate. Jib tried to avoid looking at Millard Bean, but as he waited for the wriggling family of children just ahead of them to disgorge their nickels and pennies she couldn't help seeing the sanctimonious expression on his lined, lecherous face and her gorge rose. It's all humbug, she thought. Except for a few people like Cousin Honey, who's a saint, it's all phony.

Helen Benton, the girl who had been at Cobble Top the night Stant had taken Jib there, sang the solo, but Jib was so busy tormenting herself with recollections of that lovely and apparently not to be repeated evening that she never heard a note. She was glad when the service was finally over and Cousin Honey, for once eschewing all the good-natured visiting she usually indulged in after church, bundled her off to the car. "Are you sure you feel all right, Jib?" she asked as they drove home. "Sure you haven't a headache?"

"I feel fine," Jib said, which was technically true, although at the moment she thought a broken leg would be preferable to the furies that raged inside of her. "Perhaps I just need some exercise."

"Well, you're not to help with dinner, that's clear," Cousin Honey said firmly. "It really is hot, and one person in the kitchen will be plenty. I want to have something specially good, because old Mrs. Oakley's coming and the poor old soul does suffer from the heat."

They had reached the house by this time and as they walked through the living room Oliver Stirling waved to them from the garden. "If you're sure you feel all right go out and help him, there's a good girl," Cousin Honey said. "I can see he's half wild trying to stake up all his flowers before the wind ruins them."

Without much wanting to Jib did as Cousin Honey had suggested. What was it Stan had said once about following your own plans or you'd end up following other people's? Well, he was more than right. At the moment, as Jib pulled her cotton shirt and shorts on, she felt as rudderless as a fallen leaf.

Oliver was working in the furnacelike blast of the wind when she joined him. The heat was relentless and his face and arms gleamed with sweat. "Hold up that dahlia while I tie it, would you?" he asked. "The wind's sure to change by evening, but by that time, if I don't tie them up, they'll all be gone."

For a moment or two they worked in silence, and then as they moved on to another bed Oliver Stirling asked about church. "It was all right if you like it, I guess," Jib said, but she could not keep the bitterness out of her voice. "For saints like Cousin Honey, I suppose it means something, but for old Bean and a lot of others it's just an act."

Oliver Stirling tied up the last of the dahlias and then tried to light his pipe. When the fourth match in succession blew out he put it back into his pocket and motioned to Jib to join him at the bed behind the woodshed where there was at least some shelter. He began to weed, and Jib dropped down on her hands and knees to help, certain that she couldn't be any hotter no matter what she did. For a few minutes they worked resolutely on the tiny bits of chickweed and yard grass that seemed to come up almost overnight, and then Oliver spoke. "You're right about Honey," he said. "But for the rest of us, I don't imagine that God ever resents an honest doubt. Each person has to find his or her own way of reaching Him, but I don't believe that we have the right to suspect the other fellow's method. You know that sonnet of Wordsworth's that ends up, 'God being with thee though we know it not'?"

Jib, who did know, nodded and for the first time all morning really concentrated on something once removed away from herself. There was a quotation, a description that she had read somewhere that fitted in with what

174

Oliver had just said. For a moment it eluded her, and then as she followed him back across the drying grass it came back vividly.

"Did you ever read a book called *Each to the Other*, by Christopher La Farge?" she asked. "There's a bit in the beginning where the grandfather tells the little boy not to worry about the dandelions in other people's lawns because they may like them there, which sort of means the same thing."

Oliver finally managed to light his pipe. "Not bad," he said. "Perhaps you'd take the book out of the library and show me that. It's depressingly easy to get one-tracked in one's reading."

"I will," Jib said, and she would have gone on to the house, but Oliver Stirling put out one long arm and touched her shoulder.

"Your nickname suits you, my dear," he said, and because he was so seldom complimentary or even personal, Jib blushed with pleasure. "You do remind one of a very gallant little sail."

He said nothing more, nor did Jib answer, but she was so enheartened by his unexpected little speech that she went upstairs and spent the hour and a half before dinnertime in finishing up the farm article which she had put off for so long.

Mrs. Oakley had already arrived by the time Jib came downstairs again, and a moment later Cousin Honey led the way into the dining room. The food, as usual, was excellent, but Mrs. Oakley only pecked at it while she complained endlessly about the heat. Only once, during the dessert, when something was said about two people whom Jib didn't know, who were getting a divorce, Mrs. Oakley perked up and her lips puckered, as eager for gossip as a hen for grain.

"The Citizens League is putting on a lecture in the library this afternoon." Cousin Honey changed the subject before she could be sucked down in the bog of the other woman's maliciousness. "I think I ought to go. Poor Guy Blaisdell didn't want to take the chairmanship in the first place, and he's had the most dreadful time getting speakers. Roger Bundy from Pittsfield, who was going to speak, is ill, and I don't know who they'll get."

"Bother Guy Blaisdell." Mrs. Oakley was as cross as a child deprived of a toy. "Who wants to think of civics when the thermometer's over ninety. Now as I was saying, Honey, they do say that the reason why the Whitfields separated——"

"Are you going to the lecture, Jibbie?" Cousin Honey sounded slightly desperate as they went back into the drawing room and Mrs. Oakley continued to pursue her subject.

"I don't think——" Jib began, and then Mrs. Oakley interrupted her and she changed her mind.

"Of course she's not going, Honey. The trouble with you is that, never having had any children of your own, you don't understand young people. Now when my Adelaide was Jessica's age she wouldn't have dreamed of going!"

"I'd like to go very much," Jib said quickly, and for the second time in a short while Oliver patted her shoulder approvingly.

"Well done," he said quietly, and then, more loudly· "And now, Mrs. Oakley, I really must insist on driving you home myself. I know the village taxi on a day like this would be nothing more or less than an instrument of torture."

Mrs. Oakley had had no intention of leaving for hours, but in the face of Oliver's implacable courtesy there was nothing she could do but accept his offer. "Peace! Men are wonderful!" Cousin Honey said when they had finally driven off. "And some women are fools enough not to want to be clinging vines. I couldn't have gotten rid of her for a week."

Jib laughed, but as she helped carry the dishes out

to the kitchen her mind flashed back to Carley's drug-store when Stant Carter had handled Stella Drelincourt. It was all very well to revel in being a clinging vine, but what if the support you had chosen didn't want to be leaned on, then what?

18. PINKIE!

WHEN Mrs. Stirling and Jib arrived at the Oldtown Public
Library there was a surprisingly large number of people
there ahead of them. "Why, how wonderful!" Mrs. Stirling said as they walked up from the parking lot. "A
splendid audience. Whom do you suppose Guy found to
speak?"

Before Jib could answer she was cut off by the neighbors and friends of all ages who invariably swarmed
around Cousin Honey at any village gathering. Jib
stopped to speak to the Kellys and one or two of the
people whom she knew at the Mahoras Mill, and by the
time she went into the lecture room Cousin Honey was
already seated between Miss Winslow and an old lady
who had appeared at the Stirlings' house a few days ago
to borrow a recipe for spongecake. There was no chance
of dislodging them, and Jib sat down in a chair near a
window where there was at least some faint hope of

178

air. A moment later Buzz Winslow dropped into the last empty chair beside her.

"You!" she said. "I thought you were mimeographing this afternoon."

Buzz paused long enough to wipe his hot face and his glasses. "Drayton's speaking!" he said. "I wouldn't miss it if I have to work all night."

At that moment Guy Blaisdell stood up on the platform, looking more ill at ease than ever in a heavy suit and tight-fitting collar. "Ladies and—er—gentlemen," he began, "due to—er—illness, Mr. Roger Bundy of Pittsfield is unable to be with us, but I am—er—privileged to announce that Mr. Bennett Drayton, formerly executive head of the Civic Freedom Council, has consented to be—er—our speaker of this afternoon."

"What a break for you, Buzz," Jib whispered while Blaisdell struggled on with his introduction.

"I am—er—not certain what members of the press are present, but it is my duty—I mean my pleasure—to ask that in accordance with Mr. Drayton's expressed wishes this entire meeting will be considered—er—completely off the record."

Buzz, who had been sitting forward like a cat at a mouse-hole, slumped back discontentedly. "Hang it all. It's those darned investigations down in Washington. They've made Drayton edgy as a moose!"

"Sh—sh!" A woman near them shook her head disapprovingly, and Buzz, who had started to sidle out, slid back into his chair with a grunt of disgust.

Jib grinned, and then as Guy Blaisdell sat down with an audible sigh of relief she looked at Bennett Drayton with real interest. She had heard of him as a fearless defender of the underdog and half expected a modern-dress St. George or a latter-day Lincoln. The slight, carefully dressed man who was moving to the front of the platform looked more like a scholarly businessman or a college professor about to address a class. "No one re-

179

grets Mr. Bundy's absence as much as I do!" he began, and his voice and smile, the careful timing of his words, were typical of the professional lecturer. "As I am unfamiliar with the usual procedure at your meetings, I throw myself entirely in the hands of your good chairman, Mr. Blaisdell. He understood that I came up to your beautiful country-side totally unprepared to speak, and so has generously given me carte blanche as to subject. As I have not had time even to make any rough notes, I am going to confine myself to the subject which has been the major interest of my adult life and rehearse for you briefly the history of labor unions in this country."

For the first time since the outer doors had shut there was something like silence in the hall. At the word "unions" Buzz Winslow moved back to the edge of his chair, and Jib saw that the three gum-chewing girls directly ahead of them held their jaws rigid in mid-chew. "As many of you know, the Knights of Labor, founded in 1869 and reaching its heyday in approximately 1880, was the precursor of our present-day——"

Drayton's clear, carefully modulated voice went on and on, and Jib found that despite his logic and his obvious knowledge it was hard to pay attention. If Bennett Drayton had chosen a conversational bombshell for his subject, he was certainly contenting himself with treating its safer and duller aspects. She looked around her and saw that the rest of the audience seemed to have the same reaction. The three girls were chewing rhythmically, and one or two of the older people had begun to nod sleepily.

Drayton paused once for a drink of water, and there was a stir at the back of the room. "I should like to ask Mr. Drayton where and how he assembled his so-called historical facts?" a man's voice said, and Jib turned and saw that Michael Parker, the man whom Tommy Genovese had driven up to the Ridge, stood only a few rows behind her.

"They are available to anyone——" Drayton began, but Michael Parker cut him short.

"The Devil quotes Scripture to suit his purposes," he said, and his deep, curiously dramatic voice echoed through the hall. "And the capitalist historians for a capitalist society have not been lacking in a similar expertness. But those of us—and I would include the vast majority of people in this hall—who have always worked for our daily bread know that the working-man learns about the conditions and difficulties of labor through his own job! What I should like to know, Mr. Bennett Drayton, is where you started working and where, since you have been delving into ancient history, your father worked?"

"Got him there," Jib heard an unfamiliar voice behind her whisper, and then Bennett Drayton leaned forward. "That is hardly in point," he said. "As I was saying——"

"It is my understanding that at the beginning of this lecture we were guaranteed our constitutional right of free speech!" Michael Parker interrupted. "Therefore I should like to read a short excerpt from the *Daily Worker* which gives accurately Mr. Drayton's background. He was born in Lenox—a privileged community, my friends, not unlike Quentin Ridge—the son of a gentleman well known for his reactionary——"

"That isn't true or fair," Buzz whispered. "Why doesn't Blaisdell break it up?"

Jib, thinking of Blaisdell's inarticulateness in his own office, was not surprised when he half rose and then slumped back into his chair. Drayton, who had obviously been waiting for him to intercede, leaned forward and struggled to make himself heard. "My first job at the age of twenty-two was as a social worker in the slums of New York City."

"Which is more remote from work in a mill than New York is from Quentin!" Michael Parker boomed. "We have New Yorkers here, Mr. Drayton, summer people

181

who fill the mansions on Quentin Ridge, but you will not find them at this meeting. They are at the country club, those New Yorkers, consorting with their economic bedfellows, the owners of the Mahoras, the vaster Titanic, and the other Quentin Mills."

The remark was completely irrelevant, but the toothless old man in a neat Sunday suit next to Jib nodded his head approvingly. "Never did take much stock in 'Yorkers,'" he muttered, and Jib saw that more and more of the people in the audience were turning toward Michael Parker with expressions that ranged from surprise to unmixed approval.

He's getting them, she thought. It doesn't make any difference what he says. Why can't Blaisdell do something?

At that moment Blaisdell did get to his feet, but Michael Parker had taken advantage of a strategic spot in the middle of the center aisle, and his voice, alternately persuading and then aggressively challenging, rang on unchecked.

Once Drayton tried to make himself heard, but Michael Parker, who seemed to feed and grow on the power of his own voice, drowned him out.

At that moment someone pounded a cane against the floor in the middle of the room. "Aunt Hat!" Buzz breathed, and Jib saw Miss Winslow rise to her feet.

"Mr. Chairman," she asked, "may I have the floor?"

Blaisdell nodded, purple with relief. For an instant Miss Winslow stood upright and simply gazed at her audience, looking exactly what she was—an old-time school-teacher who was used to obedience. The next second she turned on Parker. "Young man," she snapped, "what is your name and where do you come from?"

"Parker, Michael Parker. I come from Chicago. What has that——"

"Ah, I thought so!" Miss Winslow shook her finger at him as though he had been a naughty first-grader.

182

"You're a stranger here, Mr. Parker, and so perhaps you don't know that in Oldtown—in fact, in all of the Quentins—we believe in fair play.

"Those of us who are interested in current events know that within recent months Mr. Bennett Drayton has been harried—I use the word advisedly—by a congressional committee that chose to besmirch his reputation on the grounds that he is the avowed enemy of exactly the reactionary forces with which Mr. Parker has attempted to associate him."

Parker tried to interrupt, but there was a loud boo from the back of the room and old Tommy Genovese called out, "Mees Winslow gotta da floor."

Miss Winslow beamed over her pince-nez glasses. "I see that you agree with me that it is absurd and unjust to call a man black and white at the same time. And now, Mr. Drayton, I'm sure we'll all be very happy to hear anything you may care to tell us."

Drayton bowed to the first real applause he had received that afternoon, and Jib and Buzz Winslow rocked in their seats with joy. "Aunt Hat did it!" Buzz breathed. "She's the only person here who could."

Bennett Drayton had been clear and concise before, but now he was excited and his emotion transferred itself to his audience. "I am deeply grateful to Miss Winslow," he said, "and, in an oblique fashion, glad that Mr. Michael Parker has unintentionally given us such a clear example of the party which he serves. I have never met Mr. Parker before, but I have heard of him and his work, and I will be willing to wager everything that I hold most dear that his purpose in coming to this community is to see to it that any unions which you people see fit to form are Communist-controlled."

"Fascist!" Parker started from his seat. At the same instant Miss Winslow rose from hers and frowned reprovingly in Parker's direction. The audience tittered and, as Miss Winslow shook a long finger at Parker and

183

then nodded complacently to Drayton to continue, rocked with laughter. Michael Parker reddened as he sank back in his seat, and then a few moments later he left the hall.

"The gentleman's methods were the traditional techniques of tyranny," Bennett Drayton went on. "First he would impugn the motives of honest men and then he would create schisms where no schisms exist. It is true that I was born in Lenox, in the parsonage which burned down years ago. My father was the Methodist pastor there, and despite Mr. Parker's allegations, I think you will agree with me that Methodist ministers without private means are not usually classed as economic Bourbons!" After that Drayton returned to his original subject, but now he made the history of the labor movement the stirring story of struggling men and women instead of a recital of facts. He had dropped the world-weary manner of the experienced speaker, and with every word, every syllable the passionate love of justice which had shaped his career became more apparent. "Despotism," he said once, "and mind you, I mean the despotism of the extreme right quite as much as the despotism of the extreme left, is invariably a lust for power fattening upon selfishness and fear."

"Bean," Buzz murmured to himself. "Fits him to a T."

Jib nodded, thinking of Stanton Carter's struggle against Bean and all he stood for. A few moments later Drayton brought his talk to a close that swept the roomful of people to their feet. "This country will survive," he said, "and our children's children will live in a world of hope and justice only if we realize our enemies for what they really are. What we must fight above all is the sloth and stupidity within ourselves. Only if each of us will accept the responsibilities as well as the privileges of citizenship can we be sure that Abraham Lincoln will not have lived in vain and that government of the people, by the people, and for the people shall not perish from this earth."

Jib was so moved that she followed Buzz out of doors like a sleepwalker and was almost as surprised by the blinding heat and the crowd as though she had just woken from an especially stirring dream. Buzz, on the other hand, was all business and was eeling his way up to the place where Mr. Drayton stood surrounded by polite, slightly overawed Oldtowners. "There goes McKenna of the *Pittsfield Star*," he said suddenly, and they both watched as the reporter approached Mr. Drayton.

"Sorry, no story," Drayton said firmly. "Not a word."

"That rips it," Buzz said gloomily. "I'll just have to fill in with whatever local truck I can get and start mimeographing. See you later."

Jib nodded, still with her eyes on Drayton, as Buzz backed away. Drayton's carefully studied manner had returned to him, and several ladies who approached him gushingly turned away discomforted. It was at that moment that Cousin Honey emerged from the library, waved to Jib, and then trotted up to Bennett Drayton.

"Pinkie!" she called out. "What a lovely surprise!"

"Honey!" For the second time in one afternoon the man behind the mask emerged and he pushed past the gasping townspeople and kissed Louisa Stirling on both cheeks. "I'd actually forgotten that you lived here. How's Noll?"

"Spendid. Better than we ever thought he could be again when we left Washington."

Just then Jib was cut off by the crowd, but a few moments later she joined Cousin Honey on the way to the car. "Wasn't Pinkie wonderful?" Cousin Honey was obviously unaware of the sensation she herself had just caused on the steps of the library. "We knew him down in Washington. Noll will be thrilled that he and Guy Blaisdell are coming for tea."

185

Jib, who had been laughing to herself at the faces of the bystanders during Cousin Honey's and Drayton's reunion, was suddenly inspired. "He's coming today?" she asked, and Mrs. Stirling nodded as she turned on the ignition.

"Yes, isn't it wonderful? But I'll have to hurry. I haven't a thing ready, and they're coming in twenty minutes."

"Cousin Honey!" Once more idea and action fused simultaneously in Jib's mind. "Could we ask Buzz? He's dying to meet Mr. Drayton. Even if he can't use a word about this afternoon, if he could just hear him talk about something else and print that, it would be a terrific scoop."

"Why, of course," Cousin Honey said, and then as they passed the clock by the firehouse she frowned. "Nearly four already, and you may have trouble in finding him. And you know Noll hates to be kept waiting for tea——"

They had had to stop because of the other cars pulling away from the parking lot behind the library, and Jib reached for the door. "I'll find him," she said. "And we'll walk up, so you won't have to wait."

"Well, if you're sure you don't mind. But it's frightfully hot——"

Jib was already out of the car, and as the Ford in front of Mrs. Stirling moved on she had to keep up with the line. "We'll be as quick as we can!" Jib called out, and then she turned and ran across the blistering sidewalk to Carley's drugstore.

Buzz might have biked straight to the parish hall, which was at the other end of town, or he might have stopped in at Carley's drugstore, which was on his regular beat for local news. The soda fountain was crowded, and as Jib hurried past she was afraid she had missed him. She was just going to turn away when she caught a glimpse of him at the back of the store talking to Mr. Carley.

She moved on again, and then for the first time in

186

days she saw Stanton Carter. He was seated at a table only a few feet away from her with Mike Gallagher, Stella Drelincourt, and a girl whom she didn't know. Jib's heart seemed to turn to water, but as Stanton turned toward her she stiffened and ran on to Buzz. "Buzz," she began, and it seemed queer that she could still walk and talk when Stanton and Stella were right behind her. "Come on out of here. I've got the story of the ages."

For what seemed like an eternity Buzz only stared, and then the next instant he turned and went out so quickly that she had trouble keeping up with him. Stanton was on his feet now, and she knew he had seen her, but she avoided his eyes and dashed after Buzz as though her life depended on it. "It's Drayton," she said when they were finally outside. "Cousin Honey knew him in Washington and he's coming for tea. You can come up right now and meet him."

"Boy!" Buzz's face went white. "I'll never forget this, Jib Bolton, not ever."

"Well, we've got to get there first," Jib said. "It's easily three miles, and in this heat it'll take us forever. Where's your bike?"

"Home," Buzz said. "I came down with the aunts because I was going to work at the church. We'll just have to hoof it."

They started across the street and heard the sharp honking of a horn directly behind them. Jib turned and saw Fatsy Hammond's full-moon face peering at them through his cracked windshield. Jib put out her hand, and when Fatsy stopped she ran over to him, pulling Buzz behind her as though he had been one of the twins. "Hey, Fatsy," she panted, "if you're going to the Ridge, would you drop us off at the Four Corners? We're in an awful hurry to get to my cousin's."

"Sure." The fat boy swung open his door. "That's right on my way. Hop aboard."

They got in, and it was only as they pulled away from

the center of town that Jib saw that Stanton Carter had left Carley's and was looking up and down the deserted Sunday sidewalk as though he were searching for someone.

"Please let me o——" Jib began, but now Buzz's fingers dug into her arm.

"Not now, Jib," he pleaded. "We've got to see Drayton. It'll just make the paper."

Jib hesitated, and by the time she had found her voice again Fatsy had taken the turn at Beaver Street, Stanton was out of sight, and they were speeding along into the open country.

19. THE STORM IS UP

"Never see you around the pool any more," Fatsy Hammond said to Jib as he drove up toward the Oldtown hills. "What's the matter? Did you and the Apps have a fight?"

"No. No, of course not." Jib managed to answer him, but her mind and heart were still on Stanton Carter. After days and weeks of not hearing from him, to find him in the drugstore with Stella Drelincourt, of all people, was almost unbearable. He had left Stella, it was true, and come out on the sidewalk looking for her, Jib was sure of that, but why, why had he been with Stella in the first place?

"So they had a knockdown, drag-out argument right in the men's locker room." It was not Fatsy's gossipy voice so much as a sharp poke from Buzz's elbow that snapped Jib back to the immediate present.

"Mr. App had a few too many and he called old Bean

189

several kinds of plain and fancy stinker, and Bean just got quieter and uglier looking by the minute. Golly, I wouldn't have had the nerve to argue with him, and I guess Mrs. App felt the same way. My mom was around when Mrs. App first heard about the fight, and Mom said she was sure Mrs. App was going to faint. The first thing she thought about, of course, was the Mahoras Mill insurance. Mr. App's had so much bad luck with his claims that it seems that if he lost the Mahoras account the Mutual Indemnity would take his agency away. The funny part of it is that according to my dad, old Bean saw to it that the Titanic accounts were switched but let Mr. App keep the Mahoras. Old Bean was pretty decent about it, I guess, and that just made Mr. App madder than ever. It all happened just about the time you left the Ridge."

"Was it the day my *Chronicle* came out with the story about the 'Pigs in the Powder Room'?" Buzz asked

"Why, yeah. Guess it was. Say, that was sharp. You haven't had anything nearly as good since. Too much Oldtown and Quentin Mills news, if you ask me."

Usually Buzz was sparky about anything to do with his paper, but at the moment he was remarkably self-controlled. "That's where most of the people live who buy the paper," he said. They had just reached the place where the road to the Ridge branched off from the narrower road that led past the Stirlings'.

"Sure you don't want me to take you all the way up?" Fatsy asked. "Wouldn't take long, and there isn't a thing happening at the club. Practically everybody's off cruising or out West or something."

"No, thanks a lot, but this is swell." Buzz spoke up before Jib could answer, and a minute later Fatsy drove off, one plump arm waving nonchalantly as he went.

"Well, we shook him!" Buzz said and turned on Jib, his face pink with excitement. "Do you realize it must have been Mr. App who sent that twenty-five dollars marked 'Compliments of A Friend'? I've been itching to know who it was ever since it arrived."

"It probably was," Jib said vaguely. "I think he likes to be kind but he's sort of forgotten how."

"Kind!" Buzz snorted. "Don't be dumb. The whole point is that money turned up just after his fight with Bean and our pig story. Jeepers, the whole reason why I bustled you out of Hammond's car was because I was afraid you'd give it away."

"I wasn't even thinking about it," Jib said, and as she followed Buzz up the hill it occurred to her that the Ridge, the country club, and anything that happened there seemed more remote than her family in California. For days the only important, the only concrete thing in life, had been Stanton.

"It's hotter than ever, now that the wind's gone down," Buzz said once. "If we don't have a storm soon everything's going to blow up."

Jib paid no attention to him. Suspicion gnawed at her heart like a rat at cheese. What was it that Stanton had said ages ago? "There's nothing silly about loving any man, woman, or thing." Well, perhaps he had fallen in love with Stella, was engaged to her even, and had come out of Carley's to tell her his news.

They had reached the Stirlings' by this time, and Jib went into the kitchen while Buzz wandered off toward the garden where they could see the three men sitting under the cherry tree.

"Where's Buzz?" Cousin Honey asked the moment she caught sight of Jib. "It wasn't a good idea asking him up for this afternoon. Something very serious has happened."

"To Mr. Drayton?"

"No." Cousin Honey paused halfway between sink and stove and her usually tranquil face looked hot and

191

worried. "He did come with you, didn't he? Has Oliver seen him?"

"Why, yes. No." Jib was finally aware that something was seriously wrong. "What has happened?"

Cousin Honey did not stop to answer but hurried into the dining room. "Oliver. Oliver!" she called, and as Jib followed her she saw Buzz leaning against the pollard oak where none of the men could see him. Cousin Honey must have seen him at the same moment, and when she spoke to him her voice was high-pitched and angry for the first time since Jib had known her. "Buzz!" she snapped. "Buzz Winslow, come out from behind that tree!"

"Can I help you with anything, Mrs. Stirling?" Buzz's smile was elaborately casual, and Jib guessed that he must have heard something supremely worth hearing.

"Yes. No." Cousin Honey was obviously rattled, but the effect on the three men was even more astonishing. Blaisdell's face turned a blotchy red, Drayton looked irritated, and Cousin Oliver, who usually moved so slowly and deliberately, sprang to his feet. "Brewster," he said, and for the first time in weeks Jib remembered Mrs. Clarkson's describing him as an iceberg, "I should like to talk to you in the study."

For one ghastly moment Jib could feel Buzz's answer hang in the balance. Was he going to be flip and fresh or try and wheedle out of something the way he often did with the great-aunts? To her surprise, Buzz turned on his heel and looked straight at Oliver Stirling. "Yes, sir," he said quietly. "Do you want me now?"

While they were gone the two men carried out the tea-things and Cousin Honey poured. She seemed more worried than ever and never said a word other than to ask how people took their tea. Blaisdell was no help at a party, and once when Bennett Drayton made some remark about the garden his conversational offering wilted as quickly as a cabbage leaf in a broiling sun.

For a few minutes after Oliver and Buzz returned the atmosphere lightened. Buzz was unusually quiet, but Oliver Stirling looked natural and when he sat down next to his wife she cheered up perceptibly. Blaisdell left early, and Oliver Stirling asked Drayton searching and intelligent questions about the afternoon's lecture.

"If Parker stays around town he's potential news for you, Buzz," he said once and then, turning to Drayton, added, "Young Winslow here's a first-rate reporter. Someday we're all going to be proud to say we knew him when."

Buzz's face and neck, even his ears, turned a fiery red, and as he put down his teacup he looked so wretched that Jib felt sorry for him. "I guess I'd better be going," he muttered. "Storm's coming and I have to walk home."

Not a word had been said about his interview with Drayton, and when Jib followed him to the gate and asked about it he looked near tears. "No dice," he said and began to make patterns in the dusty road with his feet. "Mr. Stirling squelched that."

"Oh well, you've got something else," Jib said. "You told me you always kept one or two articles ahead."

"Yeah, sure," Buzz said bitterly. "I can use the piece Aunt Loopy wrote about the local graveyards. It's learned as heck and about as exciting as lukewarm beans."

For the first time in hours Jib thought about the article she had finished earlier in the day. "Listen, Buzz, wait a sec," she said. "I've just the thing for you. The piece I started ages ago when I went over to Milkowski's farm with Stanton. I've been wondering why you didn't ask me for it."

Buzz kicked out angrily at a small stone. "That'd be a big help," he said sarcastically. "Isn't it bad enough having articles that are dull without having ones that are plain moldy?"

For an instant Jib was too angry to speak. She had slaved over that article, when it hurt her even to think of it, and on the hottest day of the year, and here was Buzz Winslow, fifteen, and looking twelve, daring to say it was moldy before he had even read it. "You've got a nerve!" she blazed. "Milkowski must have signed up with the Bureau at least ten days ago now, and as nobody else has touched it it's practically a scoop."

Buzz stopped kicking and looked up at her curiously. "Say, I thought Carter was a friend of yours," he said. "Doesn't he tell you anything? Milkowski kept the contract nearly a week and then refused to sign. Mike Gallagher told me that himself."

"He turned it down?" she said, but when Buzz nodded she did not see him. "You mean Milkowski didn't sign?"

"Yes," Buzz said. "That's why I didn't ask you for it, you chump. Well, at least we were spared having the *Chronicle* pull a boner."

Jib stepped forward and shook Buzz Winslow with all her strength. "I'm not thinking of the *Chronicle*," she said. "I'm thinking of Stanton Carter, you fool. He was simply living to sign up that farm!"

Buzz brushed himself off with an injured expression. "You don't have to maul *me*," he said. "I didn't have anything to do with it."

Jib never heard him. Her mind and heart seemed to have exploded inside of her like conflicting rockets. He's in love with Stella, her mind said. It has nothing to do with you. But all the while Stanton's face as she had seen it at Milkowski's spun before her. He had looked so gay, so eager, so transparently hopeful. "I tell you, I didn't change Milkowski's mind for him!" Buzz spoke again. "You don't have to lose your temper at me!"

Jib took a deep breath, and in that second she knew that no matter how Stanton felt she loved him so terribly that if there was any way on earth in which she could help him she would do it. "Who did change his mind?" she said, and now she spoke very quietly. "Who did it and why?" Even before she had finished her sentance she knew the answer. "It's Bean, of course. Milkowski kept talking about Bean's foreman the whole time the day we were over there. What can we do about it, Buzz? What can we do?"

Buzz pulled his lucky piece out of his pocket before he answered. "We might bike over to Milkowski's to-morrow afternoon," he said. "Even if we can't convince him, we can try, and there might be a story——"

Jib did not let him finish. "You're right! I wish we could go sooner, but I just promised Blaisdell I'd be at work tomorrow morning. I'll take along a sandwich and meet you at the stable at noon. We'll *make* Milkowski sign."

Buzz considered Jib through shrewd eyes. "I'll go," he bargained. "But only on condition that you go over to the mill during the lunch hour and find out what people are talking about. Things are blowing up around there."

Jib hesitated, but she was caught and knew it. Oliver Stirling believed too strongly in noninterference to dream of going, and Louisa would not stir a step without his approval. Buzz was old beyond his years, and she knew his keen, completely impersonal intelligence would be useful with Milkowski. She needed his help, but she realized that unless she did what he had just asked he would feel no qualms about refusing to go with her. She looked over at him, standing at the side of the road flipping up his lucky piece and expertly catching it. "Have it your own way!" she said. "I'll meet you at half-past one."

She walked slowly through the garden, so concerned with plans for the next day that she was totally unaware of the hush, the sense of suspended animation that im-mediately precedes a storm. By the time she wandered back to the house Bennett Drayton had gone and the tea things had been carried away. She let herself in and saw Cousin Honey and Oliver Stirling standing arm in arm by the open window so deep in conversation that they never noticed her.

"I'm frightened, Noll," Louisa Stirling said. "And black discouraged. First Guy's being so inadequate, and then that man Parker, and finally Buzz's eavesdropping on things he oughtn't to have heard. I hoped when you came back to the garden with him he hadn't heard much, and now you say he has."

"It won't matter," Oliver said and, still unconscious of Jib's presence, he kissed his wife's lips. "Every man has his honor, you know, love, as well as his price. Buzz's honor is his newspaperman's code. He won't use a word ahead of time."

"Even if he doesn't, it's still all going to be a mess," Louisa said. "People fighting and arguing and not knowing what to do, and then half of the town hating us for starting something new."

"There are much worse things than unpopularity, Honey," Oliver said, and he touched her cheek as though he longed to give her his own courage and hope. "It will work out in the end."

"I hope you're right, Noll." Louisa's voice was more hopeful as she turned toward him. "You usually are, darling."

Jib tiptoed silently up the stairs. She was still worried about Stanton and worried about the next day, but in spite of all her concerns the words that Cousin Honey had spoken long days ago in the kitchen were, for the first time, manifestly clear. "A good marriage isn't compromises. It's a filling out, a dovetailing. Making one whole strong thing out of two incomplete ones."

Jib sighed as she reached the top of the stairs, and at that moment the storm broke and she dashed forward to shut down the windows.

20. COME BE MY LOVE

THE NEXT morning Jib pulled at the cat brier and the sumac that choked the farther part of Blaisdell's land as though they had spitefully blocked her progress. Milkowski must be convinced. He has influence with other Polish farmers . . . He'll be the turning point . . . Over and over again Stant's voice rang in her ears, and she jerked at the weeds until her arms ached and her hands were scratched and sore. At quarter of twelve she stopped work and, without bothering to look back at what she had done or make plans for the next day, hurried over to the Kellys' to wash up before going to the mill.

Claire Kelly let her in as usual, but for once she did not ask Jib what she had been doing or stop to tell her some little thing that Jamie had done or said. Jib, wholly concerned with the afternoon ahead of her, did not notice anything out of the ordinary until, as she turned

197

to reach for a towel, she saw Claire surreptitiously wipe her eyes with one hand while she fed the baby with the other. "Claire! What's the matter? Don't you feel well?"

"Perfectly." Claire struggled to smile, but her face looked peaked and her eyes were watery. "I—I couldn't be better."

Jib was beside her in an instant, her arm around the older girl's shoulder. "What has happened?" she asked. "I know something's wrong."

Her sympathy was the last straw, and Claire's head went down on her arm and she cried like a child. "It's the mill," she got out. "Up for sale."

"The mill for sale!" Jib spoke in a startled whistle. "Since when?"

"Yesterday. Bean was waiting here for Red when we came back from the meeting, and apparently he told Guy Blaisdell just before it. Guy put up the notices in the mill this morning, but of course nobody's going to believe that he hasn't known it for ages. He's just frantic, and so's Red!"

Jib's mind flashed back to the meeting the afternoon before and Guy Blaisdell's face. So that was what had happened. It wasn't simply Blaisdell's normal shyness, but worry and fear, that had made him so supremely inadequate as moderator. "Blaisdell and Mr. Drayton came over to see Cousin Oliver after the meeting," she said. "Was it about that?"

Claire dried her eyes on Jamie's bib. "Mr. Stirling's thought from the beginning that one reason why Bean more or less forced Guy into taking over the management was that he knew it wouldn't work and that would give him a good excuse to sell. It seems he likes to be highhanded but he always wants what sounds like a good public-spirited reason."

Jib, thinking of Mr. Bean's fulsome and meretricious patriotism at his own dinner table, nodded her head. "What does Cousin Noll suggest?"

"A workers' co-operative. He's been interested in them for years, but I guess yesterday was the first time Guy was willing to listen to him. Like a lot of shy, self-contained people, he can be terribly stubborn. Anyway, what Mr. Stirling wants is to see the mill co-operatively owned with Red as manager and Guy doing nothing but machinery. It'd be wonderful, and I know it'd work if they could ever get started, but there are so many difficulties."

"What difficulties? Why?" Jib demanded. "I don't see why it wouldn't be a natural."

Claire Kelly smiled wanly at Jib's enthusiasm and shook her head. "It isn't so easy, according to Red. I don't understand it all, but it seems Bean's dead set against co-ops and has publicly stated he won't hire anyone in his other mills who goes in with the plan, and then there's some man in the mill who's been going around telling the other men that if they'll just organize into a union every other paper mill in the country will go on a sympathy strike and Bean and the other owners will have to come around. I don't begin to understand it all, and last night and this morning Red and Guy were so upset I couldn't ask much."

Jib would have stayed longer, but the noon whistle had already blown and she knew if she was going to keep her promise to Buzz she would have to leave for the mill. After saying good-by to Claire she picked up her packet of sandwiches and left, but by the time she had reached the mill yard she had forgotten all about eating. There were more people outside than she had ever seen there before, and all of them talking in small excited groups that visibly contracted and cold-shouldered her as she came up. She caught sight of Ellen Perkins and hurried toward her. "I've heard about the mill," she began. "I'm so terribly sorry."

Mrs. Perkins looked tenser and more tight-lipped than

199

ever. "Yes," she said stonily. "Yes, everybody's heard now."

You don't know. You can't know what it's like. Jib's heart felt leaden and she turned away to where Kurt Cramer was haranguing a group of men. One or two of the workmen shifted uneasily as she joined them, but Cramer was too caught up with what he was saying to notice her. "The Party'll take care of you," he said. "They are powerful enough and they are the only agency on earth with your interests at heart. What do Kelly and Guy Blaisdell care for the likes of us? They belong to management heart and soul!"

"They work for a living same as you and me," a man near Jib muttered. "Their bread and butter comes from this mill."

Cramer, his voice cracking and straining, shouted him down. "This is war!" he roared. "We've got to fight 'em and win!"

"How about some of the old-timers?" another man asked. "Pop Gantry and old Manchowis and Mrs. Perisotti up in sorting? If this was a co-op they'd still have jobs. They wouldn't have a chance outside of Oldtown. Red Kelly says——"

"Kelly!" Cramer sneered. "John Michael Kelly, with his fine education and his gift of the gab. He wants to be manager, you fool. He and Blaisdell didn't take you into their confidence, did they? Oh no, they went up to talk to fancy-pants liberals like Drayton and Oliver Stirling and God knows who all, but they didn't tell you about the sale!"

"They didn't know about it!" Jib burst out, and the men turned and stared at her. "Neither of 'em knew a thing about it until yesterday afternoon, and they didn't have a chance to get you all together until this morning."

"Yeah, that's right, that's what I think." The man who had pleaded for the old-timers looked at Jib and she reddened, suddenly aware that a dozen pairs of eyes were all focused on her. One or two of the other men nodded or spoke their agreement, while still others drifted back toward the factory. Jib started to turn away herself, when for the first time she happened to look Kurt Cramer straight in the face. "Hello," she began uncertainly, but Cramer only spat on the ground and then stalked off.

At that moment the one o'clock whistle sounded and Jib went back across the footbridge to meet Buzz. He was there ahead of her, perched on the seat of his bicycle, his thin legs balancing him on either side. "So you've heard the news," he said and grinned like a Cheshire cat behind his glasses. "Biggest story that's hit Oldtown since 1776, and boy, tomorrow I'm coming out with a *Chronicle* that's going to carry more facts about it than all of the big papers put together. What'd you dig up?"

Jib, still thinking of Claire, Ellen Perkins, Cramer, and the whole gamut of hopes and fears that she had sensed at the mill, turned on him furiously. "Nothing," she said. "And I won't get anything. Don't you ever think of anything but your paper? Have you blood in your veins or is it really ink?"

Buzz shrugged. "Ink," he said. "But at least I keep my promises. Yesterday I overheard enough about the mill to justify an 'extra,' but I promised Mr. Stirling I wouldn't write a line until the whole thing came out and I haven't. And I don't get carried away by one thing after another, the way you do, either. Right now my mind's still working on how we can help Stant Carter up at Milkowski's, while you've gone so emotional over the mill you've forgotten it and last night nothing else in the world mattered!"

An angry answer came to Jib's lips, but Buzz had already rolled off on his wheel and there was nothing to do but follow him. They rode in silence for the better part of two miles, and then when they had to dismount to push up the long hill near Milkowski's, Buzz spoke. "I don't suppose you've even thought of finding out any more reasons why Milkowski won't sign?"

Jib shook her head, too miffed to speak. "Well, I did. Went around to see Mike Gallagher first thing this morning. He'd been up here yesterday, but as soon as Milkowski knew he came from the Bureau he shut up like a clam. Said you never knew where government interference would lead to and let it go at that. Bean's own phrase, you see. He must have been in on it."

"I guessed that much," Jib said loftily as they remounted. "What we have to do is think of something Stant missed in order to convince Milkowski the whole thing's to his advantage."

That was easier said than done, and all the appealing speeches which Jib had rehearsed ahead of time left her mind as they turned into the barnyard. She had seen it so clearly, safe in bed last night at Cousin Honey's, herself, poised and charming in her most becoming dress, effortlessly persuading Milkowski while he beamed at her from over his corncob pipe. Now, in the reality, she was hot, dirty, and disheveled, and Milkowski, appearing before they had expected to see him, looked as cross as his own watchdog.

"We came to talk to you about the Government Soil Conservation Plan," Jib said, and her voice sounded flat and hopeless in her own ears.

"Too much talk, talk, talk," Milkowski said and turned back toward his barn as Buzz entered into the conversation.

"You don't happen to know if Mr. Millard Bean is selling his cattle, do you?" Buzz asked, and Jib blinked in amazement.

"No. Why?" Milkowski stopped short, and Buzz shrugged.

"Just thought he might be, that's all. He's selling the Mahoras Mill, you know, and I thought perhaps he was moving out lock, stock, and barrel. Of course a lot of mills have gone south, and I believe there's some talk about the Titanic and the other Milltown factories pulling out."

Milkowski took a step closer. "Mahoras Mill in Oldtown she *sold*?"

"Not sold yet. Up for sale, but work stops in two weeks."

"And mill hands? What they gonna do?"

Buzz lifted expressive hands. "That's their lookout, I'm afraid. Of course a few of 'em might get work in other mills outside of Oldtown, of course. I guess the best bet's the workers taking over Mahoras as a co-op, but Jib Bolton, here, knows a lot more about that than I do. She was over there this morning. Seems they just posted notices about the closing-down this morning. Bean makes up his mind to sell and that's that."

Milkowski turned to Jib and peppered her with questions, and then in a few moments Buzz pulled at her elbow. "We ought to be moving," he said in the same offhand voice he had used from the beginning. "We're wasting too much of Mr. Milkowski's time."

"But we haven't—that is, we didn't——" Jib spluttered, but Buzz's fingers dug into her until it hurt.

"Well, so long, Mr. Milkowski," he said and, still keeping his hold on Jib's arm, piloted her toward their bicycles.

"What is this all about?" Jib demanded when they were out of earshot. "Did we or did we not come up here to try and find a way to fix things for Stanton?"

"We did!" Buzz said and laughed so hard that his front wheel wobbled dangerously. "Milkowski's sister-in-law, Mrs. Gereg's, one of the old hands at Mahoras, you dope! Do you remember a while ago when I asked for a list of names of all the people who worked there? Well, I went over it name by name with Aunt Loopy to find out what she knew about any of them, and that was one of her minor items. I'll bet you dollars to doughnuts that when Mrs. Gereg's out of a job Milkowski'll be ready to sign up just to spite Bean. And now, for Pete's sake, let's step on it. I've got about a thousand things to do today, and besides, I'm famished. Did I tell you the aunts were expecting you for supper? They said they'd tell the Stirlings."

Jib did not catch up with him until they had reached the Misses Winslow's house and he had gone into the corncrib. "Buzz," she said as she followed him in, "if you're right about Milkowski, it's the best thing that's ever happened and Stant Carter's going to be terribly grateful and so am I. I'm sorry I didn't do anything for you at the mill this morning."

Buzz looked at her over his glasses. "It's as bad as that, is it?" he asked, but before Jib could protest he was off on another track. "Well, if you really mean what you say, perhaps you'd help me with tomorrow's issue right now, and then after supper we can mimeograph. The church is on your way home and we'd have a couple of hours before dark."

Jib could think of a hundred things she'd rather do than mimeograph, but Buzz's earlier shaft about her shifting emotions had sunk deep. Her feelings at the country-club pool, about Stella, and even about Ellen Perkins' troubles, had all been subject to swift change which she had to admit had had nothing to do with anything except her own mood.

"Mike knew we were going to Milkowski's," Buzz said and grinned like a superior gargoyle. "So if you were thinking of a long phone call to Carter, you can skip it. Unless you want to hear the sound of his voice, of course."

"I'll be glad to help you," Jib said coldly. "What is it you want me to do?"

Buzz was a hard taskmaster, and by the time Jib had helped him, writing and rewriting, and then after supper had struggled with him over the mimeograph machine, she was very tired. It had been a long, full day, and when she came to the last long hill up to the Stirlings' her legs ached so that she dismounted and walked along slowly, pushing the bike ahead of her. It was nearly dark and the air was cool and clean after last night's storm. At the side of the road a squirrel swished off over a stone wall and an early katydid prophesied frost. Jib did not notice either of them. She had kept her promise to Buzz, and with his help she had been able to do more for Stanton Carter than she had dared hope, and still she was discouraged clear through to her bones. The moment Stanton had taken her into his arms beyond Milkowski's farm had been the peak, the zenith of her life so far, but then he had turned away from her and she had not seen him again until yesterday afternoon in the drugstore with Stella. Jib plodded on, step after tired step. She could see Stanton's face when he heard the good news, every aspect, every feature alive and eager. But to whom would he turn to share his happiness? Was it Stella or someone else whom Jib did not know?

At that moment a tall figure slid out from the bushes and stood in front of Jib!

She sucked in her breath with fear and her heart thundered. Then she recognized Kurt Cramer and, relaxing a little, began to move on. He moved forward menacingly, and it came to her, with a new, more sweeping wave of terror, that he had been waiting for her to pass and meant to stop her. "What do you want?" she asked. "I— I'm in a hurry to go home."

"Not so fash. Not yet," he said thickly, and as he moved closer and she smelled his breath she realized he was drunk. "Not till I tell you all the harm you've done."

Jib swallowed, trying to fight down the panic that mushroomed inside of her. Don't argue. Don't look at him, her mind issued orders to her frightened heart. "Oh, I hope I haven't done any harm," she said out loud. "I wouldn't do that for anything."

"Oh, I hope not. Oh, I wouldn't!" Cramer mocked and held fast to her bicycle. "But you've done it, damn you. This morning in the mill. Those men were lishening. To me! The way Parker said they would. And then you came in with your little bleat about Blaisdell and Kelly, and this afternoon I couldn't get them to listen!"

His angry words fell like hailstones while Jib looked about her. It was a long way to the Stirlings' and quite as far back to any other house. I'll have to keep him talking, she decided, and then, when he isn't expecting it, run! He seemed to read her thoughts, for now his free hand clamped down on her wrist. "Oh, no, you don't," he began. "Oh no——" and then they both heard the car roaring up toward them from the valley.

For an instant they both stood frozen, and then Jib jerked free and began to shout for help. She heard Cramer swear. Heard the squeal of brakes. Then, as the driver pulled to a stop, Cramer dropped her bicycle and made for the woods. For an instant he stood in the full glare of the headlights, and as Jib saw his white, frightened face framed by the car lights she knew where she had seen him the first time!

"Jib! Jib darling, are you hurt? For God's sake, what happened?"

Jib turned and the next moment she was in Stanton Carter's arms. "Oh, Stant," she whispered. "Oh, Stant, I was so frightened."

Stanton stroked her shoulder as though she were a little child and then he straightened up. "Exactly what did happen, Jib?" he asked. "That man, who was he? Are you sure he didn't hurt you?"

"Yes," Jib said. "It was Kurt Cramer. He works at the Mahoras mill. But the first time I saw him, Stant, was the night Bean's cattle were let out. He did it. I'm sure of that, and he thought I was going to tell. That's why he was so scared the first time I saw him at the mill."

Stanton hurried a little way down the road, and then

they both heard the sound of an engine as Cramer pulled out from the side lane where he had left his car. Stanton muttered and started back up the hill. "I'll settle with him tomorrow," he said. "And he'll be in luck if I don't kill him. Jib, you're sure he didn't touch you?"

"Positive," Jib said as Stanton came up beside her.

"Lord, what a break that I came when I did! Mike, the poor chump, had only just told me what you and Buzz Winslow were trying to do, and I jumped into the car to come over to thank you. If you knew how I've been trying, struggling, fighting myself not to come over every day for the past——"

"If *I* knew," Jib said and her voice was soft with wonder. "If I knew, Stant, and I thought you—I thought you and Stella——"

Stanton spun her around so that she faced the car lights. "You thought what?" he said grimly. "Tell me."

She told him, and for a long moment Stanton Carter was completely silent. "I went into the drugstore with Mike when we were taking his sister to the train," he said finally. "La Drelincourt was out of admirers for the moment and came and sat down with us. I saw you and ran after you, but you didn't wait."

"I know," Jib muttered. "I was a fool, Stant."

"Don't say that," he said. "What I'm thinking about is that you thought—well, what you did think, and still went to all that trouble with Buzz Winslow to help me. It certainly wasn't his idea."

Jib looked up at him and then turned away, blinking from the bright light. "If you really love someone, you want to help them," she said unsteadily. "Even if you think they've stopped loving you."

Stanton Carter took her in his arms and held her as though he never meant to let her go. "Jib. Jib darling, I love you so," he whispered. "I've loved you even before I knew you. Fell in love with the picture at Cobble Top, and then the real Jib was a hundred thousand times better. I wanted to ask you to marry me practically the first time we really saw one another, but you're so young, Jib, such a little kid, I swore I wasn't going to bother you yet awhile. I wanted to give you time to grow up."

"I've done it," Jib said. "Oh, Stant, each day without you has been so long that I've aged years and years in just a few weeks."

21. NEW-MINTED WORLD

"WE'LL have to leave," Stanton said a while later. "The Stirlings will be frantic if they don't know where you are."

Jib said nothing, but helped him to balance her bicycle on the bumper of his car. As he made it secure she moved out of his way and turned to look back at the valley. At that moment the moon rose above the dark tops of the trees, brightened the bayberry bushes, and turned the white pebbles in the middle of the road into silver pennies. The warm wind lifted the hair on her forehead and in the distance an owl hooted softly. Jib stood motionless, suddenly so aware of the beauty around her that it pressed on her heart like pain.

Stanton came up beside her and they stood in silence watching the moonlight wash over the valley. "It's never been so beautiful before," Stanton said finally. "Every sight, every sound, the smells even are more wonderful because of us."

Jib quivered and lifted her face to his. "I don't want to leave," she said when he had kissed her. "I want to stay here forever."

Stanton sighed, and then a few moments later led her gently back to the car. "I feel the same way," he said. "If I weren't so incredibly grateful to the Stirlings for bringing you here, we'd stay longer." He started the car, and then as he looked down at Jib his deep-set eyes were dark with love. "Nobody can take this away from us, my darling. Those minutes on the hill—and they're more than some people have in a lifetime—are ours for good."

With that Jib had to be satisfied, and a few moments later they reached the Stirlings' house. "What—what—are we going to do now?" she whispered as he unlatched the white wooden gate. "Tell them?"

"Right away!" Stanton said, and she thrilled to the ring in his voice and the strong grip of his hand. "And as soon as it's humanly possible we're going to tell your family and make plans for getting married."

They had hardly opened the front door before Louisa Stirling flew toward them. "Jib. Jib darling! Where have you bee——" Then she saw their tightly clasped hands and the look on their faces.

"Cousin Honey, it's true! Stanton loves me. And I do so love him!"

Louisa reached one hand out toward the wall and then in the same instant she rallied. "Noll. Noll! Come here at once. Oh, Jib darling, Stanton, I'm so delighted for you both!"

She hugged them separately and together, in a flurry of happy excitement, but it was a matter of long-drawn-out moments before Oliver Stirling joined them in the hall. "Oliver, they're engaged. They want to get married."

For what seemed like hours Oliver Stirling smoked his pipe without speaking. "I think you're both too young," he said, and his quiet words were wet sand on a little forest fire of excitement. "What do Jib's parents feel about it?"

"They don't know. They couldn't have. It's just happened!" Jib hurried over to him and put her arms around his neck, but he gently removed them and turned to Stanton Carter.

"What have you to say?" he said. "I'd like to hear it."

Stanton's shoulders were back and his deep voice was as level as Oliver's. "I'm twenty-eight, sir, and I was afraid I was too old for Jib, but she doesn't seem to think so. That's a very personal decision, isn't it, sir?"

Oliver nodded. "And your work? Things are going better than they were?"

Stanton reddened, but his eyes never left Oliver Stirling's. "Worse, if anything. But the Bureau needs men and I'm sure of a job. I can support a wife."

"Oh, Oliver, be human! The children were so happy when they came in." But for once Oliver Stirling ignored his wife and, with an expression that was neither friendly nor unfriendly, continued to look at Stanton.

"I can't reach Jib's parents at once, Mr. Stirling," Stanton went on, "and that's why I'm so anxious to talk to you this evening. When I drove up the hill toward this house Jib was being bothered by a man called Cramer. I want your consent, sir, to my going down tomorrow, as Jib's fiancé, to make certain that he never does it again."

"Kurt Cramer!" Louisa Stirling's hand flew to her throat. "Jib sweetheart, what did happen?"

For once Jib had no desire whatever for drama, and described exactly what had taken place in terse, unembellished sentences. "He was drunk, I think, and furious because when he was talking to the men at the mill this morning I interrupted to say that Blaisdell and Red Kelly hadn't known about the sale ahead of time. He was telling them a lot of stuff that Parker, the man who nearly broke up the library meeting, had told him to say, and it seems after I butted in they wouldn't listen to him. He was furious, and I guess he was waiting on the road to get even with me. I was scared for a minute, and then Stant came along."

She turned back to Stanton, and it was several minutes before they realized that they were no longer the Stirling's main interest. "This is extremely important," Oliver said. "Not only to the four of us, but to every man and woman who works at the Mahoras Mill. You see, the thing that's likely to stop the Mahoras from going on as a co-operative isn't so much finances—there's more money around than you might think—as it is lack of faith. The people who work there are divided. Some of the ones who are perfectly sure of jobs with Titanic or any of the other big mills are perfectly ready to follow along with Bean. Then there are others who have been listening to this man Parker and think if they have a Communist-dominated union everything will work out in their favor. Parker's much too clever ever to appear at the mill himself, and Blaisdell's never been able to find out who was his agent. I don't suppose for a moment he even thought of Cramer."

"He wouldn't, because I asked him to give Kurt a job." Cousin Honey sounded miserable. "I vouched for him personally. I was a fool, I suppose, but he used to be such a pathetic little boy. He's never really had a chance, and I felt so sure if he only had a good job he'd straighten out."

"But it's all so crazy," Jib said. "I can't prove it, but I'm almost certain that Kurt Cramer was the one who let Mr. Bean's cattle out the night of the dance at the country club. They hate each other like poison, and yet they're working for the same thing!"

"Which is power," Oliver said grimly. "And the unfortunate ordinary citizen who happens to need a job is totally unimportant to either of them. If it's acceptable

212

to you, Carter, I think I'd like to go with you tomorrow when you interview Cramer."

Stanton hesitated, and Oliver Stirling spoke again and for the first time since they had come into the room he was smiling. "I concede your rights in the matter," he said, and his formal, old-fashioned speech was even more reassuring to Jib than Cousin Honey's immediate enthusiasm. "But what Cramer does in connection with the mill is important, and besides, my boy, I think it would be unfortunate to begin your engagement with a murder on your hands."

It was settled that way, and the next morning Stanton called for Mr. Stirling while Mrs. Stirling dropped Jib at the stable on her way to her office. Usually Jib did her heaviest work at once, while she herself was feeling rested and the ground was soft from dew, but this morning she caught a glimpse of Claire Kelly inside the house and went right in to tell her the news. "It's still a secret," she ended up. "We wired to Mum and Dad last night, but we're going to try and not tell people until they can come on and meet Stant."

"I'd like to tell Red," Claire said. "If you're sure you wouldn't mind. It would be so wonderful to have some good news for him when everything in the mill is in such a muddle."

"Of course that's all right," Jib said, and a few minutes later she started to work. She had a great deal of weeding to do, but the work left her mind all too free, and the shadow of fear that had sprung up inside her when Stanton had first announced his intentions of going down to see Kurt Cramer grew like a thunderhead. Oliver's going too, she tried to reassure herself, and Cousin Honey isn't worried. But that thought was cold comfort. Cousin Honey had known Cramer as a small child and still thought of him as a pitiful boy who was incapable of real evil.

Oliver and Stanton are both sensible men, Jib told herself, and Stant's wonderfully strong. But even so she could not rid herself of fear, and worked with her back to the river facing the driveway, hoping against hope that at any moment Stanton would reappear. There was no sign of him, and except for the milk truck there were no arrivals behind the stable until Buzz rolled in on his bicycle at quarter of twelve.

"Congratulations!" he called out even before he dismounted. "I've been betting on Carter!"

"How did you find out?" Jib's voice was sharp. "Nobody but the Stirlings knew, and then this morning I told Claire."

"And Stanton told Mike Gallagher, and he told me when I went over to find out when they're planning to approach Milkowski again. Mike told me he was going there this afternoon, and he's practically sure we've fixed it. Satisfied?"

"Yes," Jib said, and at that moment she saw Stanton's car turn into the driveway and ran toward it, every other thought forgotten. "Stant! Oh, Stanton, what happened? I've been so worried!"

Stant stepped out of the car looking sheepish. "We didn't even find him," he said. "He'd given Blaisdell his old address, the place where he lived when he was a kid, and when we went there the new people had never heard of him. Then we started combing every bar and diner in Quentin Mills, and finally we found a man who thought he knew a boardinghouse in Oldtown where two Joes who sounded like our descriptions lived. We went there and both of 'em had left. It seems Cramer borrowed Parker's car last night, probably without Parker's O.K., because at all events they had a terrific fight and Parker cleared out then and there. Cramer left early, and the last Mrs. Wessel—that's the woman who runs the place—saw of him, he was hotfooting it toward the Oldtown station at about six o'clock."

Buzz was beside them by this time and bristling with

questions. "Did you ask the stationmaster where he was going? Or are you sure he didn't take another car? Did you see old Tommy Genovese? He's usually around at that time in the morning, and he might have seen them. It's easy enough to find out if Cramer's left town, but why is it so important?"

They told him what had happened the evening before, and Buzz whistled. "Boy, what a gyp!" he said. "It might make a marvelous story, and I can't use it because I haven't enough facts. We'll have to find that guy."

Stanton shook his head. "I don't think we will," he said, "and as long as he stays away from the three Quentins, I promised Mr. Stirling I wouldn't try and find him. Any influence he may have exerted at the mill is gone, and he certainly can't annoy Jib from long distance. Mr. Stirling's in hopes that now he's had this scare he'll buck up and turn over a new leaf."

"Mr. Stirling?" Buzz said. "You mean Mrs. Stirling. She's the one who believed in him."

"Both," Stanton said, and although the word was for Buzz, the look in his eyes was for Jib alone. "You know how they work things."

22. GIVE MY LOVE GOOD MORROW

FOR THE next ten days happiness spun around Jib like a silver-stranded cocoon. Her parents had telephoned long distance from California, and although at first they had sounded more dubious than she would have wished, by the time Cousin Honey was finished with them they were at least ready to agree that when Dad came East in September to report to the home office Mother would come with him and they would both stay at the Stirlings' for a few days, during which time the engagement could be announced.

"I don't see why they can't let us do it at once," Jib said. "Practically everybody in all three Quentins knows it anyway. When I went into the drugstore yesterday Mr. Carley came over and kissed me, and Stant says that Mr. Milkowski stopped by at his office the other day just to congratulate him. You'd think Mum and Dad would understand."

"Wait until they see Stanton," Cousin Honey suggested, "and after that you won't have a bit of trouble. I know, because I went through exactly the same thing when Oliver and I were engaged. You see, we'd met in New York, and when I told my parents we were engaged they were certain I'd fallen in love with an Englishman who thought all Americans millionaires and wanted to marry me for a fortune I didn't have. I remember the first time Noll came up here it was August, but when I went down to the station to meet him I was shaking with cold fear. But of course as soon as the family saw him and talked with him everything was perfectly all right."

Jib hugged her and then finished putting away the dishes. "You're right. When they know Stant it'll be easy. They'll probably want to marry me off at once, for fear he'll change his mind."

"I doubt that," Honey Stirling said dryly. "But they'll be contented about you the way I am. Nobody could be in the same room with Stanton Carter without realizing he's an exceptionally fine person."

Jib smiled to herself as Cousin Honey disappeared to take Oliver's coffee out to the garden. She was warmed by what Honey had just said, not alone for the praise of Stanton, but by the sudden picture her words had conjured up in Jib's own mind of her cousin as an engaged girl. Gradually, during Jib's visit at the Stirlings', she had become more and more aware of the love that existed between them. But that was the quiet, experienced understanding of middle age, whereas now she could almost see, and feel at one with, the breathless, emotional girl who had gone down to meet her English lover at the Oldtown station.

"Jibbie, your dress came," Cousin Honey's voice called back. "I put it on the hall table upstairs."

Jib hurried out and, taking the parcel into her own room, cut the string. Cousin Honey had promised a party to announce the engagement when her family came

East, but before that there was to be a big afternoon carnival on the Oldtown common for the benefit of the Community Chest. It was the only event of the year that drew all three Quentins together, and Jib, thrilled and excited at the prospect of going with Stanton, had spent a good part of her summer savings on a new dress. She tried it on, and every soft fold of aquamarine silk fitted as though it had been made for her. "Now winds blow soft, lark rise aloft," Jib sang as she pirouetted in front of the mirror. "And give my love good morrow. Give my love good morrow!"

For the next week the morrows were good indeed. One perfect day followed another, and nowhere was Jib more aware of the unexpectedly golden weather than in the garden behind Blaisdell's converted stable. After the July drought Oldtown had had all the rain it needed, and by the middle weeks of August, Jib's planting flourished beyond her wildest hopes.

At first the place had been a wilderness, and long after Jib had been working daily her efforts at best looked raw and bare and at worst only served to emphasize the overgrown spots she had not had time to touch. But now the whole area seemed pulled together in triumphant flowering. The swaying white cosmos and lemon-yellow marigolds nodded, as Jib had dreamed they would, above the lower blue lobelias she had transplanted from the Stirlings'. Her azalea mums flourished beneath August lilies, and at the far side of the old driveway the tall altheas which she had cleaned out and cultivated during her first week at work burst forth in late splendor with dazzling white flowers.

On the third Saturday in August, Jib thought the garden had reached it absolute peak and called Claire Kelly out to see it. Claire put the baby in his pen and followed Jib down to the river, where wild coneflowers and jewel-weed had made a second transformation. "It's all beautiful, Jib," Claire said and twisted a bit of sweet clover through her strong musician's fingers. "I never thought you'd make it happen so soon."

"It wasn't making it happen as much as letting it happen," Jib said. "Once the weeds and sumac and cat brier were cut back, the good things that had either seeded themselves or been planted here really began to flourish. Did I tell you Stant and I found a whole clump of crown imperials behind the dump? Wait until you see those next spring."

Claire didn't answer, and Jib looked up at her, instantly ashamed of her own tactlessness. If the mill changed hands, who could tell where the Kellys would be living next spring? Claire was looking downstream, where long pennants of smoke from the mill chimneys flickered by above the wall of pine trees. "I wonder if it wasn't better in the old days," she said, "when the man who owned the mill lived here and bossed everything. Even though he was rich and everyone else was poor, at least people knew where they were. I'd rather live in a hut and eat porridge than go on like this."

"I know," Jib said, and her heart ached for the girl beside her. "But I doubt if it was really simpler in the old days. I used to think that when my great-grandfather lived in Oldtown everything in his life must have been absolutely black or white, but from what Cousin Honey says, I guess he was as puzzled about things as we are."

"You're probably right," Claire said, "and there's no use worrying. Next week, if Red doesn't have to work in the evening, I want you and Stanton Carter to come to dinner. No matter how things turn out at the mill, we'll have that to celebrate."

"Wonderful," Jib said, but when Claire went back into the house she was no longer as happily absorbed in the garden as she had been before. The fate of the mill would be decided by a vote of all the workers on the following Monday. For the past ten days Cousin Oliver, Kelly, and two of the machinists had met daily, discussing ways and means of convincing the rest of the mill community to take on the Mahoras as a co-operative. Early in the week Blaisdell had suggested that they invite Bennett Drayton back to address a mass meeting of the workers and their families, but the next day, forty-eight hours after Buzz's *Chronicle* carrying his own account of the pending sale had appeared, both the *Berkshire Bugle* and the *Inquirer* had come out featuring violently prejudiced accounts of Drayton's life and activities. The papers had avoided any actual untruths but had cleverly used some of Drayton's most radical speeches, many of them made as long as twenty years ago, and had lifted them out of context so that the impression made on all but the most careful and well-informed reader was that Drayton was a dangerous and irresponsible revolutionary.

"But they can't think that," Jib had said when Oliver had shown her the papers. "At least none of the people who heard him at the library."

"As usual, the people who needed most to hear him weren't there. Most of the audience was made up of people like Honey and Miss Winslow, who went because they wanted to support the Citizens League."

"But there were quite a few others, Noll," Louisa Stirling put in. "People from Quentin Mills and a few right from here in Oldtown that I'd never seen at a League meeting before."

"Kramer and Parker urged them to go," Oliver Stirling answered. "And Parker's sole purpose was to paint Drayton as a reactionary just as surely as, though less successfully than, these Bean-controlled papers have tarred him as a radical. Both sides are completely uninterested in the truth, which is that Drayton is neither."

"But Mr. Drayton convinced people at the library," Jib had said. "Couldn't he do it again?"

That time both Stirlings had shaken their heads. "There isn't a chance," Oliver had said. "About generalities, maybe, but about their own bread and butter, no. Our only chances of success are a person-to-person campaign, which we are trying, or a modern miracle."

Right now, as Jib put away her rake and clippers, there was no way of knowing which way the decision would go. Once again, urged on by Buzz, she had taken her sandwiches over to the mill, but except for a few little personal items she had gathered no news and the almost universal wariness and distrust that she had seen on every face had made her feel like an outcast. "I can't do it," she told Buzz when he bicycled over to see her just as she was leaving for the day. "Perhaps if I sneaked around and listened when they didn't know I was there, I could get something, but I wasn't made to be an eavesdropper."

For the first time since Jib had known Buzz he picked up an insult where none had been intended. "Who said anything about eavesdropping?" he demanded, and his face flamed with anger.

"I didn't mean anything personal," Jib said. "I know how you feel about your newspaper, and I know you wouldn't do anything you felt was dishonest."

"You don't know how I feel about anything," Buzz said furiously, and the next minute he rolled off, leaving Jib confused and hurt, with her meager little notes still in her hand.

Later on, when Stanton called for her at the Stirlings' to take her to Cobble Top, she told him about it and he put his hand over hers. "Poor Buzz," he said. "You've been awfully tough on him, you know. He shouldn't have heard about us from Mike. He's been in love with you as long as I have."

"You're crazy," Jib said. "Buzz never really loved anything except his papers. He's only liked me because I was useful. I'm not even in the same category as his great-aunts."

"Try and convince me," Stanton said and kissed her.

They did not speak of Buzz again, but his red, distressed face kept reappearing in Jib's mind throughout supper and she was unaware that Stanton, too, seemed to be worried about something and that it was Mike Gallagher who did most of the talking.

They were not alone again until just before dusk, when they stood out on the porch a few minutes before Stanton was to drive Jib home. Jib moved to the railing, thinking of the day she had looked out over this same view while Mrs. Clarkson waited impatiently in the car. She had felt lost and unhappy then, and the familiar hills had only underlined her nostalgia. Now, as she looked out to where the purple mounds rippled off to nothingness, the hills, like the house behind her, were all a part of her own entranced vision of the future. "Think of next summer, Stant. The garden we'll have, and all the work you've done around the pool more beautiful than ever."

Stanton Carter never stirred and she put her arm through his. "And this winter, Stant. I've never spent a winter here, and I've dreamed of doing it ever since I was a baby. Snow and purple shadows and the two of us coming back here together." She turned to him, her face radiant with happiness, but there was no answering light in his eyes as he looked at her.

"What's the matter, darling? Mike said he wanted to board in Oldtown."

"It's not Mike," Stanton said, and his voice sounded as though each word hurt. "We may not be able to live here ourselves."

"But whyever not? The family will be thrilled. They've never had a chance to rent it before in the winter, and I know we could keep warm."

"It isn't that," Stanton said. "You see, I'm going to ask for a transfer. I'm no use here, darling. Not because I don't try, but because Bean can't stand me. I know he says it's government interference he's against, and he doubtless is, but his personal loathing for me is the final stumbling block. If the Bureau sent down another man, somebody brand new, I'm positive he and Mike could do a better job."

"Stant!" Jib breathed, but he went right on talking.

"It's too important to just wait around for Bean to get friendly or to die. And it's simply his wanting to get even with me for cheeking him that first day in front of some of his own men that's really kept him working to undermine everything we do. I learned that from Milkowski and a lot of the others. It hasn't been any easy decision. I love this countryside the way you do, and going to a new district'll mean we'll have to put off getting married until I can find us a place to live, and then we may both hate it. It's asking you to give up such a whale of a lot."

"And you," Jib said, and her heart yearned over him, "you hate leaving as much as I do, and what's more, you're ready to swallow your pride—and it's honest, justified pride at that—simply because you feel the work is more important than you are."

"Jib darling. Darling!" he said and took her in his arms. "As long as you can understand and not love me any less, nothing else is going to matter."

"When did you make up your mind?"

"Just now. Being with you gives me the courage to be what I am, I guess, but I first started thinking about it that day Oliver Stirling and I went to look for Cramer. Stirling's amazing, Jib, the way he makes you understand things half of which he never mentions. We never even spoke about the Bureau that morning, but I knew then that just working for a salary, even if it was our keep, wasn't enough. It's hard to put it into words but if I let the job down it wouldn't be right for either of us. Does that make sense, Jib, or am I just being a selfish stiff-necked fool?"

"You're being wonderful," Jib said quietly. "And I love

and adore and just plain respect you more than anybody on earth."

Just then Mike rejoined them, and a few minutes later they drove off.

"When will you tell him—your district boss, I mean—about your transfer?" Jib asked as they drove up the hill toward the Stirlings'.

"Saturday," Stant said. "It's the only day Hackley is in Massachusetts, and next week he leaves on his vacation."

For an instant Jib struggled inside of herself. Saturday was the day of the party, the day for which she had bought the new dress. Oh, Stanton, put it off, she thought, even if you waited another month it wouldn't be so bad. But she didn't say a word out loud, and it was Stanton who spoke.

"That's the day of the town party," he said. "I'll miss the beginning of it, but I'll be there for most of it if I have to hitchhike on a rocket ship!"

"Stanton, I'm so glad!" Jib clapped her hands like a pleased child. "I know it's silly, kid stuff, but I do so want us to go to a party of all three towns together just once."

"And you weren't going to say anything." Stanton grinned down at her. "And that's definitely bad. I want to marry a spitfire, not a martyr. I'd hate someone who wailed or complained, but you'd never do that. So don't change, love, but be yourself, always."

"You too," Jib said, and as he kissed her good night she could feel the strong triumphant beating of his heart. "In our marriage we're taking each other as is."

"A spitfire and a stuffed shirt," Stanton Carter said. "For keeps."

23. JUDGMENT ROCK

THE NEXT morning Jib woke up after a night of confused dreaming in which old school friends, a mason who had once worked for her father at Cobble Top, and Millard Bean met and mingled crazily. She lay still, blinking at the bright morning light that flooded through the shining panes and fell on the flowered wallpaper. Her dreams floated back to nothingness, and she pushed off the covers and padded across the cold floor toward the clothes closet. She paused for an instant at the window, and as she looked out over the familiar hills Stanton's decision, with all its implications, came back to her. She sighed involuntarily, as though a weight had been returned to her shoulders, and went on to the shower.

Last night she had been so aware of Stanton and of their being together that she had accepted his leaving the Quentins as an established fact. Now as she dried and dressed herself her instinctive eagerness for action reasserted itself and she struggled to think of some scheme which might circumvent his having to leave. As she began to brush her hair she thought she did see a possibility and wondered why it had not occurred to her before. Although Stanton had done everything in his power to make his work a success, there was one approach that had not dawned on either of them, and that was that she, Jib Bolton, should personally appeal to Millard Bean.

She hurried downstairs to find that Cousin Honey had already left for church with friends and that Oliver was just about to drive over to confer with Blaisdell, Kelly and some of the other men from the Mahoras Mill. Jib went with him as far as the gate and then walked back to the kitchen, where Cousin Honey had left breakfast for her. She ate mechanically, so absorbed with her own thoughts that the coffee, rolls, and country sausage were without substance or flavor. "You made the most colossal hit." Mrs. Clarkson's words, spoken so many weeks ago, returned to her now with a foretaste of triumph, and she saw herself gracefully thanking Mr. Bean at the end of a completely successful interview.

"I never really understood the situation before," Bean said in her mind. "I am genuinely grateful to you for pointing it out." The next instant Jib thought of Bean's face, cynical, sardonic, and sensuous by turns, and remembered the repellent touch of his dry, scaly hands. I can't do it, she thought, and shivered. Stanton wouldn't want me to go without telling him. But Stanton was off with Mike for the day, visiting an experimental farm on the other side of the county, and since he had pledged her to secrecy she couldn't even bicycle down to talk over her plan with Claire Kelly.

She went through the routine of straightening up the kitchen and making her bed and then went out to the garden, but for once there was nothing there that needed to be done. By the time the Stirlings returned home for Sunday dinner enforced delay and idleness had worked on Jib like a tight lid on a boiling pot and any action seemed better than none.

I won't toady to Bean, she told herself, and immediately another inner voice countered with, But you're not asking for favors; all you want from Bean is fair play. Surely you can make that plain if you're not a fool and a coward.

While Cousin Honey served up the ice cream Oliver announced that as Bennett Drayton was calling to take him down to the mill that afternoon he would have no need of the car. "Neither will I," Cousin Honey said. "I'm going to stay home and catch up on my mending, and then I might take a walk."

Her offhand words struck Jib like a long-awaited omen and she immediately asked if she might borrow the car. "Of course, darling," Cousin Honey said. "But aren't you going off with Stanton? There's a ball game down in the village at half-past three."

"Stanton had to go over to Fencliffe, but he's coming here for tea," Jib said, and at that instant an image of herself telling Stanton that everything was arranged in his favor grew and brightened in her mind. "I'd like to borrow the car—to pay a call up on the Ridge."

"Well, have a good time, dear." Cousin Honey, content with the sudden happiness in Jib's face, turned away to answer the telephone.

But once Jib drove the rattling old car up the Ridge hill the momentary sensation of triumph which she had experienced as she had thought of telling Stanton that he need not transfer gave way to nervousness. She drove up to the clubhouse, but the parking lot was solid with cars and she had to leave the car farther down the road and walk onto the club grounds past the entrance to the swimming pool. The usual crowd was there, and Jib asked if anyone had seen Millard Bean. Fatsy Hammond and Amory Holt shook their heads, and Mibsie Tarrant looked up and giggled. "Dating a rather elderly boy friend, aren't you? You don't suppose he's walked out on you?"

Fatsy roared and Jib walked on to the clubhouse, acutely aware of more laughter that met some further sally of Mibsie's which she couldn't hear. What does it matter? she scolded herself. What if they are laughing at you? You belong to Stanton Carter and they can't touch you. But no matter what she told herself, the brief encounter had snapped her back to the insecurity she had felt in this place in June, and by the time she reached the club steward's desk her voice shook as she asked for Mr. Bean.

"Sorry, miss, he's not here today," the man told her. "I think you'd better ask at his own house."

Jib thanked him and, going out by a back door, eventually reached the Stirlings' shabby car without having to pass the swimming pool. She drove quickly to Bean's house, and when she rang the bell the maid whom she had helped with the young goat and the pigs opened the door. "Why, good afternoon, miss." The woman's elderly Irish face smiled down on her. "I am glad to see you again."

The woman's genuine friendliness was encouraging, and Jib asked for Mr. Bean. "Ach, what a pity," the maid said. "He left about ten minutes ago for Quentin's Cobble. Would you come in and rest yourself, miss? We expect him back before five."

Jib shook her head and turned away, torn between disappointment and relief, when the maid stopped her. "If it's anything special, miss, you could meet him over at the Cobble, you know. If you drive onto that Milkowski's farm and take the short cut you'd be there in no time. Mary Mullins, who used to be chambermaid here, and I did it once and sure it was a beautiful walk."

"Thanks a lot. That's just what I will do," Jib said, and she hurried back to the car with new resolve. Surely meeting Bean out of doors on neutral ground would be easier than approaching him either in his own house or at the club. She drove past Milkowski's farm buildings, which were sheathed in Sunday quiet, and did not leave the car until she came to the place where she had first recognized the beginning of Queen's Saunter. She could see the Cobble ahead of her now and hurried toward it with a pounding heart. In five more minutes she would be there, in five more minutes she would be face to face with Millard Bean. Well, it was no worse than taking nasty medicine. One horrible gulp and then it would be over. She walked quickly, with her head down, concentrating on her footing over the rough, little-used trail. She didn't stop until she came to the druid's circle of boulders at the very base of the Cobble. She looked up now, and her breath came in a shallow, excited gasp. She had gazed over at the distant Cobble all during her childhood, but now that she stood within its shadows the massive majesty of silent stone moved her as it had years ago when she had first ridden over here with her father. "The Indians called the peak of it Judgment Rock," Dad had said. "And the story goes that there were three young braves who were tried for treason on the top of it. Not a bad idea, when you come to think of it. For a people who were aware of nature it would have been almost impossible to lie in a place that's as beautifully austere as that."

Jib's fingers worked nervously and she bit her lips, loathing the errand ahead of her. She knew that no matter how much justice she had on her side the only approach to Bean that could possibly succeed would be an insincere mixture of flattery and coyness. She took a few more steps and then stopped short, her hand at her throat.

"I know very well indeed what I'm doing!" Millard Bean's voice, amplified and echoing by the circle of boulders, thundered in her ears. "I always do know!"

For a moment there was silence, and then Jib heard another voice which she did not recognize. "No offense meant, I'm sure," a man said. "Cramer was drunk, of course, and probably didn't know what he was saying. I just thought I'd be doing you and Mr. Appersley a favor by mentioning it."

"I do favors. I don't ask for them." Bean's voice was electric with sarcasm. "And sometimes I take them back at compound interest."

Jib turned and began to steal back the way she had come. I'll never ask him, never, she thought, and at that moment she heard heavy footsteps behind her. She plunged off the trail and, cowering behind some underbrush, saw Jason Scott, Bean's farm foreman, walk past her. The man's face was red with anger and the twigs crackled underneath his feet. Jib crouched in silence, waiting for Bean to follow him, and after minutes that seemed like hours she began to run through the woods.

She did not stop until she was over the stone wall that bounded Milkowski's hayfield, and then, feeling that she was safe, threw herself panting onto the ground. She was breathless and exhausted, but above everything else she was aware of relief. I didn't ask him, she thought. Thank God I didn't ask him. She lay still for a long time, and gradually the peace of the cool grass and the lengthening shadows stole over her. I'll never tell Stanton, she decided. He'd be disgusted I even thought of it. She stood up, feeling stiff and shaky, as though the emotions which she had experienced had weakened her like an illness. What a workout! she thought, and then as she stretched she caught sight of the Cobble still silent and aloof in the near distance. Judgment Rock is right, she thought and kissed her fingers wryly in the direction of the peak. You win again.

She walked slowly back to the car, and it wasn't until she was on the hill road beyond Milkowski's that she was aware of the fire siren above the sound of her engine. For an instant the sound only penetrated to the periphery of her mind, and then, as it wailed out, again and again, she stopped the car and stood up on the running board to see. Probably just a fire drill, she thought, but at that moment she gazed down into the valley and saw the black umbrella of smoke that had already formed over the Mahoras Mill.

24. THIS BUBBLE, REPUTATION

BY THE time Jib reached the mill half the town seemed to be there, and more and more people poured out from the ball game down the road and eddied toward the mill like a many-colored tide.

"Jib!" She wheeled at the sound of her name and, seeing Stanton, started to turn toward him, but he waved her back. "Get back!" he roared. "Get those people back. The firemen haven't room!"

She could see he was right and, pulling two excited children by the hand, hauled them away from the mill. She had just reached a safe place when she caught sight of Cousin Honey running toward her down the road. "Jib! Jib! Have you seen Oliver? *He was in the mill!*"

Jib shook her head, and as she gazed over at the smoke-filled building panic gripped her by the throat. "No. No. I haven't! she began and started back into the crowd when both she and Mrs. Stirling saw Oliver running toward them.

"It's all right, my darling. It's really all right." Oliver Stirling gently disengaged his wife's arms. "We were outside almost as soon as it started. Buzz warned us!"

The crowd was still surging toward the mill when a fireman stamped back toward one of the engines. "It's under control!" he shouted. "We have it under control. But KEEP BACK!"

For an instant the shifting mass of people stood still, and then as the town policeman and another fireman emerged from the back of the mill carrying a man's limp body between them the line wavered and would have stampeded forward again if Stanton Carter and two other men had not shoved and bullied the vanguard back out of the way.

"He's hurt!"

"He's suffocated!"

"What happened to him?"

Question, hypothesis, and false rumor spread and billowed up from the crowd, and then as the two men carried the body nearer to where Jib was standing she saw that it was Kurt Cramer. "It's Kurt!" she whispered, and at the same instant a woman's voice, keening and hysterical, rose up from the very center of the crowd. "He's killed. He's killed. The poor boy's dead, I tell you!"

Andy O'Brien, the town policeman, turned and shook his fist, and his Irish voice lashed out at the crowd with rough authority. "Faith and he is not killed!" he roared. "Though I'm not saying he didn't deserve it, the louse! 'Twas him set the fire, and didn't we catch him red-handed and he fell and knocked himself goofy when he tried to run from us?"

The crowd turned, following Andy and the fireman like sheep. Jib turned with it, but before she had taken a step Oliver Stirling reached out one long arm and grabbed Buzz Winslow's collar just as Buzz tried to

233

wriggle past them toward the mill. "Let go!" Buzz pleaded. "Please, Mr. Stirling. I can't miss anything now."

"You won't. It's practically over," Oliver Stirling said, and as Jib saw that some of the firemen were already pulling extra hoses from the mill she realized that he had not exaggerated. "What I want to know is how did you happen to be around here in time to warn Drayton and the rest of us and then turn in the fire alarm?"

"Because I've been watching for Cramer!" Buzz answered, and his changing voice cracked with triumph. "Ever since the day, Jib, that you and Stanton told me about his threatening you. I knew if he ever came back it would make the story of the ages, and by golly, it has."

"When did you find him?" Stanton, who had joined Jib and the Stirlings by this time, asked Buzz. "Did you just happen to see him sneak into the factory?"

Buzz snorted. "Of course not," he said. "I've been watching out for him for days. I met every train and I had a regular beat of people I asked every day if they'd seen him. All the little kids who deliver the *Chronicle* were on the lookout too. Well, for days nothing happened and I really was getting discouraged, and then this morning he pulled in on the late freight. I saw him slide out of a boxcar and go straight for the parking lot in back of Cassidy's garage, where he helped himself to his sister's car. I thought I'd lost him, but just after lunch I ran into old Tommy Genovese and he said he'd seen him go into Pielan's bar. I went after him, of course, but they threw me out for being underage, but not before I'd caught a glimpse of Cramer drinking like a fish and telling anybody who would listen just how he was going to knock hell out of Bean."

"That's what Scott heard," Jib put in, but nobody but Stanton listened to her, and Buzz went on with his story.

"Well, I waited outside Pielan's until I thought I'd go nuts, and then finally Cramer came out. He was drunk and mean-looking, so I decided that wasn't the time to ask any questions and I just followed him without being seen. I was scared to death he was going to drive again, but he didn't. He just walked along until he came to Blaisdell's land, where Jib's been working, and then for a while I couldn't make out what he was doing. I trailed him down to the river by the footbridge where Jib worked last, but even then I didn't get the idea. He seemed to be gathering up leaves and moss and stuff and leaving it in a little trail all the way to the wooden end of the mill. For a while I thought he was just crazy, and then when I saw him jimmy open one of the bottom windows, slide in, and open the back door I was sure he wasn't. I crawled up as close as I dared, and there was Cramer yanking out rags from the new bales and adding those to the trail he'd made right up to the door. For a couple of minutes I didn't dare move, and then when he leaned over and began to fumble with a match I ran like blazes. I jerked the alarm as soon as I reached it and then beat it back to Mr. Blaisdell's office to warn all of you."

"Buzz! Oh, Buzz!" Louisa Stirling took her husband's arm. "If you hadn't been there——"

"Or if the wind had been different!" Buzz said. "It's been shifting all day, and that's what Cramer didn't count on. You see, it veered to the east just as I rounded the building. Andy O'Brien, who had come up to see about the parking at the game, heard me yell, but Cramer didn't. He must have waited for the wind to shift again, because he was still there when you and Andy and the others jumped him."

"He had the fire started," Oliver Stirling said, "but by the time the engines reached here, there wasn't a great deal left but smoke. But there was enough of that to cause a near panic."

"But the trail?" Mrs. Stirling asked. "The line of leaves

and things leading back to Blaisdell's stable? Was he trying to burn that down too?"

"No," Stanton Carter said, and his face was harder than Jib had ever seen it. "I doubt if he had that in mind."

"Of course not," Buzz said. "You'll understand it perfectly if you'll go back and look. His trail leads back exactly to where Jib was burning brush yesterday, and if the wind had been right it would have looked as though it had happened because of embers, and carelessness. I don't believe he had any of it planned when he turned in here. From what Tommy Genovese said, he began making wild threats about what he was going to do back at Pielan's right after his first drink. Then when people wouldn't believe him he nearly went crazy and said he could hurt Bean and get away with it. Pielan and the others thought it was all hot air, of course, and maybe it would have stayed just that if he hadn't wandered in here and gotten inspired with burning down Bean's mill and pinning the blame on Jib."

"But there were witnesses who actually heard him making threats?" Oliver Stirling asked.

"Plenty," Buzz said, "but he's always been a wild talker when he's had a drink, and nobody believed him, which was what probably drove him to really trying it. Why, even Jason Scott, Bean's farmer, was there when they threw me out. Boy, I bet he's wishing he'd tipped off old Bean ahead of time."

"But he did!" Jib burst out, and then she told him about her trip to the base of the Cobble and what she had inadvertently overhead. They had moved to the land behind the mill now, where Cramer's trail still lay as Buzz had described it. Bennett Drayton and two or three of the mill workers had joined them, and they listened intently to every word that Jib had to say. "I still don't understand it," she finished. "I was thinking about something else and I didn't want to hear them, but I couldn't help it. Scott said something about somebody—I guess it was Cramer—making threats, and Bean laughed, and then when Scott said he'd only been trying to do Mr. Bean and Mr. Appersley a favor, Bean was furious."

"You're sure he mentioned Mr. Appersley? When were you there? When did Scott leave?" Buzz turned on Jib and began worrying questions like a bull pup after a bone. "And what did Bean do then?"

"It was about half-past three when I heard them," Jib said. "Scott left at once, but I don't know when Bean did. I waited at the corner of Milkowski's land until around four. The only two trails leading away from the Cobble cross there, but I didn't see a soul."

Buzz turned from Jib to the circle of men and then, pushing his hand through his hair so that it stood up like a shoebrush, leaned forward. "Bean believed that Cramer meant what he said! He must have believed it or he wouldn't have gotten so angry with Scott. And he didn't do anything about an alarm, although at the base of the Cobble he could have seen the first whiff of smoke and he could have reached his own house or Milkowski's in ten minutes. Why didn't he do anything? Why? Why?"

"Could it have been the insurance?" Louisa Stirling said. "I've always heard the mill was heavily insured."

The circle of men shook their heads, and then Jib spoke again. "After Scott said that he'd only wanted to help Bean and Mr. Appersley, Bean said something about doing favors and sometimes taking them back at compound interest. What do you suppose he meant?"

"Bean's there now." The machinist who had joined them last jerked his thumb toward the other side of the mill. "When I left he was standing on the front steps giving a pep talk about how this sort of thing was what you could expect when you hire communist labor."

"I think I'd like to hear him," Bennett Drayton said dryly, and without another word the others turned and went with him to the front of the mill. Only Buzz did not follow, but waited until they were out of sight and then tore off in the direction of Blaisdell's stable.

The fire engines had gone by this time, and part of the crowd had returned to the ball game, but there were a great many people left, and among then Jib recognized most of the men and women who worked at the Mahoras Mill. All of them were listening to Millard Bean. He stood on the steps of the mill, and every once in a while he gestured dramatically toward the building behind him. "There is damage here and waste," he said, "and it might have been incalculably greater if it had not been for the gallant action of our Volunteer Fire Company which, as all of you will remember, was originally financed by contributions from the Titanic and affiliated mills——"

"He's making hay, all right," Stanton Carter said, and as Jib glanced at the faces around her she knew he was right.

This was an example, a horrible example—Bean emphasized his point over and over again—of what all Quentonians could expect if they tolerated communist agitators in their midst. "I, too, have made mistakes!" Bean was the very picture of magnanimity as he postured on the steps. "And I willingly accept my share of blame. As you good people know, it has always been part and parcel of the liberal policies of all Bean enterprises to allow a free hand to responsible employees. Last spring, when I appointed Guy Blaisdell to the post of manager of this mill——"

"He did it because he knew he'd be a flop," Stanton muttered, but Jib was too intent on Bean to hear him.

"—I did so fully determined to let him exercise his own judgment in the hiring of mill personnel. How he abused my trust in employing Kurt Cramer, whom he knew I had once dismissed from my own farm, you have all seen. But what concerns us now is not the mistakes of the past but the decisions of the future. The very people, amiable but misguided citizens of this town and known to you all, who urged Blaisdell to employ Cramer are now urging you to form a co-operative under their so-called expert guidance. Now, my friends, I ask you if such parlor practitioners, such self-styled experts are to be trusted with your time, money, and well-being? I have no desire to boast, but I think you will all agree that I and the men most closely associated with me deeply respect property, not for our own selfish purposes, but purely and simply as an ultimate responsibility, a trust for the citizens of this commonwealth!"

As Bean paused Louisa Stirling took a deep-shuddering breath and Jib felt Oliver Stirling's hand on her own shoulder stiffen. For one sickening second Jib stood rigid, and then in two quick steps she was on the steps facing Millard Bean. "Mr. Bean," she said, and the man stared at her as though she were out of her mind, "before you go on I'd like to ask you one question. If you are so careful about property, why didn't you do anything about this fire when you were told it might happen? I was there, Mr. Bean, when Jason Scott warned you!"

"This is absurd. Fantastic!" Bean exploded. "The girl is demented."

At that moment Oliver Stirling joined Jib on the steps and turned toward the crowd. "There is more to this than at first seems apparent," Stirling said. "Millard Bean was forewarned that Cramer had publicly made threats against him at a time when he, Bean, was standing at the foot of Quentin's Cobble where he would have seen the very first vestige of smoke rise from this mill."

Bean attempted to ignore the two beside him on the steps and beamed down upon the crowd. "My good friends," he pontificated, "if a man in my position listened to every vicious threat, every drunken boast——"

"But in this case you weren't sorry when the threat eventuated!" Oliver Stirling cut him short. "You weren't sorry to see that fire! We all know John Appersley. Many of us know what your taking the Titanic accounts away from him meant. And it doesn't take an insurance expert to guess that if one of the other major properties covered by Appersley was destroyed, the Mutual Indemnity Company would not be long in seeking another agent. You were glad to see that mill burning because it spelled ruin for a man whom you hate."

Bean's face changed color but his voice was under control. "This is calumny, slander," he said. "I am not a young man or a well man, but as soon as was humanly possible I came down to help put out that fire. I was ready and eager to fight it with the best of you."

For a second Oliver Stirling was ominously silent and Jib trembled. The matter of timing was vital, and Bean was making the most of it. She could hear the relief, the growing triumph in his tone. "As usual, I put the interests of the community above my own personal well-being."

"That doesn't fit in with the facts, Mr. Bean!" A gruff young voice that spiraled to a falsetto challenged him from the edge of the crowd. "You're lying and I can prove it. You were heard talking to Scott at around half-past three; the fire broke out around four. You must have heard the alarm, and if you had gone straight home for your car you would have reached there at four-fifteen at the latest, but according to your own servant, you did not reach there until quarter of five, when you were told of the fire and made a great show about rushing down here. Your story won't stand up, Mr. Bean."

"Buzz!" Oliver breathed. "God bless the boy, he had the wit to telephone."

"I came down at once!" Bean burst out. "As soon as I knew Scott was right."

"Ah, then you admit you saw him!" Oliver Stirling
240

pounced on his words. "You admit being at the Cobble where you must have seen the fire!"

Bean's last vestige of self-control shattered. "I repeat this is calumny," he raged. "If you people are stupid enough to believe it——"

"We do!" "Boy, yes." "You bet we believe it, Mr. Bean." The angry shouts hit Millard Bean like blows in the stomach. He wavered and then plunged down the steps and hurried to his car while catcalls and boos spattered after him like hot bullets.

"This bubble, reputation," Oliver said as Buzz joined them. "Between you and Jib you've pricked it. Do you know what it means?"

"It means people hate Bean's guts," Buzz said placidly. "They always have, but today they showed it."

"It's a great deal more than that!" Oliver said, and his usually calm face looked feverish with excitement as he led the way back to Cousin Honey, Drayton, and Stanton Carter. "It means that nobody who works in this mill will entrust it either to Bean or his like, or to Cramer and the gangsters he thought he was serving. From now on they'll rely on themselves. Tomorrow will be the proof, of course, but I'm willing to bet everything I hold most dear they'll vote for a co-operative."

"And that's another story I'm going to scoop," Buzz said. "There's no reason why the *Chronicle* can't come in on the ground floor this time, is there, Mr. Drayton?"

Bennett Drayton laughed and shook his head and then he turned to Oliver. "This whole story is good for a great deal more than local coverage," he said. "I can't write it up after the attacks on me, or people would put it down to personal pique. But you ought to do it, Oliver, for both the New York and Boston papers."

Oliver Stirling took his time about answering. He lit his pipe, and as he looked over the dwindling crowd his usual reserved, almost indifferent expression had returned. "You should do it. It's really important!" Drayton urged.

"Ah yes, quite," Stirling said, and his eye caught Jib's. "So much so that it should be done by a journalist. Would you care to do it, Buzz? Mr. Drayton and I would be glad to help you, and it might not be a bad way to get your first big circulation by-line."

For an instant there was absolute silence, and when Buzz spoke his voice sounded hollow. "Would I?" he got out. "Yes, sir!"

As Jib looked at Buzz's entranced face she couldn't think of anything but his happiness, and then Stanton touched her elbow. "Come on, darling," he said. "This afternoon has been colossal and you've been the star turn in it, but now I want to have you to myself. Mr. Stirling'll bring home their car."

Jib followed him over to his car and then she looked up at him and laughed. "So that was the answer to Buzz's troubles," she said. "He wasn't upset about me, us. He was just working himself dizzy trying to catch up with Cramer."

"Then all I can say is I'm sorry for him," Stanton said, and as he took her into his arms nothing else seemed very important.

A little while later he started the car and drove slowly up the hill toward the Stirlings'. As they came to the old ford Jib had a good view of the Cobble and saw that the afternoon sun had turned Judgment Rock to a deep, glistening red. "Stanton, look at that," she urged. "Have you ever seen anything so perfectly beautiful?"

"That's it," Stanton said and pulled on the brakes. "That's my conscience caught up in stone. Every time I thought I could stay on here even if another man would do a better job, I'd look at that from Cobble Top and then I knew I couldn't."

"Stant, oh, Stanton, is that true?"

"Why, yes, honey, sure. It may sound silly, but when you love a piece of country and every——"

Jib's arms were around his neck and her face was ecstatic. "Stanton," she whispered, "Stanton darling, you couldn't have told me anything in the world that could make me happier. Listen to what happened to me. I didn't mean to tell you, I didn't think even you could understand, but you do, you will."

Stanton held her very close while she told him what had happened to her earlier in the afternoon in the shadow of Judgment Rock. By the time she had finished his strong young face was broken with tenderness. "I love you for going," he said. "And I love you more for holding back, and I love you most of all for telling me."

"It's the Rock," Jib said finally. "No matter who owns it, from now on it belongs to both of us."

25. THE BIG WHEEL TURNS BY FAITH

OLIVER STIRLING was an accurate prophet. On Monday
the workers at the Mahoras Mill voted for the co-
operative, and a few days later a full account, signed
by Brewster Winslow II, appeared in the New York and
Boston papers. Claire Kelly's face looked like someone
newly admitted to paradise, and Guy Blaisdell, once
more working with the tools and machinery he loved,
greeted Jib with boyish enthusiasm when he passed her
on his way home to luncheon. "Those asters," he said,
pointing to the mignon dahlias which were Oliver Stirling's handsomest contribution to the garden. "They're
terrific, aren't they? I didn't know any two men, let
alone one girl, could make this place look so pretty."

Jib grinned and went on with her work, humming to
herself a Negro spiritual that had been running through
her mind all day like an enchanted and unseen chorus.
"The Little Wheel Runs by the Grace of God and the

244

Big Wheel Runs by Faith. The Big Wheel Runs by Faith!" Jib sang aloud, her spirits rising to that pinnacle of happiness that can be reached only in the midst of general rejoicing.

Later that day, when she walked down to the parish hall to join Buzz, she was aware of a look of relief and good will on the faces of nearly everyone she met on the village street.

"It's like Armistice Day after the first World War," Cousin Honey said that night at supper. "Even the people in Quentin Mills have taken a new lease on life. Do you suppose it can last?"

"I doubt it," Oliver Stirling said, "but I'm not certain that that matters. I think with John Kelly running the Mahoras as a co-operative it's going to be a success, and that has a way of being contagious. I think it's entirely possible that within a few years you'll find most of the big plants in Quentin Mills are also workers' co-ops."

"I hope so," Cousin Honey said, but Jib's mind was on Stanton and she did not hear her. "Whatever do you suppose John Appersley will do about Millard Bean?"

"Nothing, I imagine. It's all pretty tenuous grounds on which to sue. Millard Bean's pretty generally discredited, and I rather guess that as far as John's concerned that's enough. He's not a vindictive chap."

A few months, even days ago, Jib would have plunged into the conversation. How about Stanton? There's no need for him to apply for a transfer now, is there, Cousin Noll? The questions formed in her mind but she did not speak them. Stanton had made his decision and he would have to go through with it in his own way. "You can't always help the people you love most"—was it weeks or years ago that Mum had written that?—"sometimes you have to go on loving them and believing in them and let them fight out their own conclusions."

After supper Jib tried to read a book, but it was no use. It was Thursday now, and Saturday was such a short way off. Mr. Hackley can't decide to exchange Stant, she thought, he can't, he can't. But the very intensity of her desire made her uncertain, and by the time Saturday afternoon arrived and it was time to dress for the carnival her fingers were icy and she shook with nervousness. Cousin Honey had left earlier with a neighbor, and when Jib drove down with Oliver the party on the village common was already in full swing. Oliver, who was judging the flower show, left her at the entrance, and she went in through a bunting-draped gate to be immediately approached by Billy Haines, who was selling lollipops. A moment later Miss Lucinda Winslow, who was selling chances on a refrigerator, came up to her, ticket book in hand. "Brewster has told us about your young man," she said. "Under pledge of secrecy, of course. Brewster has the highest regard for Mr. Carter, and Sister and I are so happy for you both."

Jib thanked her and, catching sight of Claire Kelly, started to join her, but before she had passed the fortuneteller's tent old Mrs. Oakley and two other friends of Cousin Honey's stopped her to offer their congratulations. "You can't keep a secret in a village," Claire said when Jib finally reached her. "I hope you've warned your people."

"They won't mind, and I love every minute of it," Jib said, and she was so warmed by the heady wine of congratulations and friendliness that she actually beamed on old Simon Planter, who had turned down her offer of work the same day as Mrs. Oakley.

"I am most happy, and, if I may say so, most relieved," the old gentleman said primly. "I must say the idea of a young woman—a young lady—engaged in out-of-door labor has always been slightly repugnant to me."

The last time they met, Jib would have argued or been resolutely silent, only to shadowbox his opinions in her own mind. Now she only smiled and turned away, quietly secure in the knowledge that Stanton approved of her working and wanted her go on with it wherever they were living. But where would that be? That was the issue that clouded everything else in Jib's mind, and she listened to Mibsie Tarrant's and Bet Barnes's gushing enthusiasms about her engagement without hearing half of what they said. Public approval and popularity were pleasant, even intoxicating, Jib realized, but, compared to what happened to Stanton, no more important than tinsel in a dream.

"Is this a carnival or your private reception?" Claire asked when the girls from the Ridge moved on. "There are two ladies over there who've been trying to get close enough to speak to you for five minutes."

Jib looked across the crowded midway and saw Mrs. Appersely and Mrs. Clarkson tripping toward her on fantastically high heels. "Why didn't you tell us?" Mrs. Appersley demanded. "Fay came back from Newport yesterday and she heard it at the railroad station."

For a moment Jib was submerged in the familiar wave of expensive perfume, and then Mrs. Clarkson released her, gesturing with one lacquered finger. "You're a naughty child not to have written me at once," she said, "when I was really responsible for your summer. Of course I've written your mother everything I've been able to find out, but, my dear, I can't imagine what she's going to think."

"We let her know about the engagement right away," Jib said. "She and Dad are coming East to meet Stanton next week."

Mrs. Clarkson might have pursued the subject further, but Mrs. Appersley had other fish to fry. "That beast Bean!" she murmured. "My darling child! Of course I've seen through him from the first and I always said he was completely insignificant, but I must say I was amazed, simply amazed, that you and that precious little Winslow boy were the ones who finally gave him his come-uppance."

Jib, inwardly wondering how Buzz would react to such a Little Lord Fauntleroy description, introduced Claire, and a few moments later that group broke up and Jib found herself surrounded by Mike Gallagher, Helen Benton, and a group of Helen's friends from the normal school. "Stant hasn't turned up yet, has he?" Mike asked, and when Jib shook her head he spoke more quietly. "I wish he hadn't gone, Jib. I tried to argue him out of it, but you know how he is. Hackley's perfectly capable of accepting his application for a transfer without even going into the reasons behind it."

"Stant had to go," Jib said, but deep in her heart she knew it was one thing to accept Stanton's reasoning when she was in his arms and quite another to give up Old-town and Cobble Top, to postpone their marriage and eventually to live in a strange place which, as Stanton himself had said, they might both loathe.

It was nearly seven o'clock by this time, and the crowd which had overflowed the common at five was beginning to thin out. The bunting sagged and the ground was covered with little scraps of paper and confetti which a few of the more loyal members of the steering committee were trying to rake up. "Aren't you ready to go home, my dear?" Oliver Stirling, looking cool and immaculate in his white linen suit, reappeared at Jib's elbow. "Even Honey's ready to call it a day."

"I can't," Jib said. "I promised Stanton I'd meet him here," and then she looked up at Oliver Stirling's face and laughed. "How did you manage it?" she asked. "You hate shindigs like this and yet you still look fresh as a daisy and everybody else is wilted."

"I escaped," Oliver admitted. "I judged the flowers and then, realizing that an umpire is never popular, I went home and made myself a drink and read. Old Genovese came by just in time to give me a lift down here so I could walk back with Honey in the cool of the evening. What I call a well-planned afternoon."

"You're terrible and wonderful," Jib began and then, hearing her own name, wheeled from him.

"Jib. Oh, Jib!" Stanton Carter ran toward her, his arms outstretched, totally unaware of the interest he was exciting among the small boys and women whom he passed. "We're staying, darling. We don't have to move!"

He caught her up and, lifting her off her feet, whirled her halfway across the common before he set her down again. "Stant, Stanton, are you *sure*?" Jib gasped.

"Absolutely. Positive! Hackley wouldn't even discuss it. He wants us to stay, Jib!"

They had reached the edge of the common by this time, and the sharp tinkle of a bicycle bell warned them off the road. Buzz looked over at them and grinned as he dismounted from his wheel. "What's the excitement?" he asked. "Did you win the Ford coupé in the raffle or have you both gotten a raise?"

"Neither," Jib sputtered. "But, Buzz, listen. Stant isn't going to be transferred! We thought he might be because of Bean and all, but he isn't, and we're going to stay here and live at Cobble Top. Bean doesn't matter a bit any more."

Buzz looked at her pityingly over his glasses. "Are you the last two people in town to understand that? But listen, something really big's just broken. Bean put his farm on the market at four o'clock this afternoon. I've been over at De Voe's real-estate office in Quentin Mills all afternoon getting the facts, and that was why I was late getting here. Anything exciting happen?"

"Yes. No. Nothing. Everything!" Jib was much too excited to make sense, and Buzz looked disgusted.

"Aw, you're hopeless," he said. "I'll have to depend on young Bill Baines and Aunt Loopy for any real dope. You're both so blind with stardust you wouldn't see an elephant until he stepped on you."

"Buzz is probably right," Jib said when he had left

them. "What a day, what a place! So much has happened I feel dizzy."

Stanton looked down at her and grinned. "When Miss Loopy Winslow writes the definitive history of the three Quentins she's going to have to devote a considerable amount of space to this August. A near sabotage at the Mahoras Mill, the decline and fall of Millard Bean, the establishment of the first Oldtown co-operative, and, as a star-spangled finale, the unannounced but entirely official engagement of Miss Jessica Bolton to Stanton Jefferson Carter, formerly of Balmoral, Virginia, sir, and now of Cobble Top, Quentin."

"It's incredible," Jib said slowly. "We've seen and felt and been a part of such an awful lot. I didn't know so much could happen in a small country town."

By this time they had reached the dirt road behind the common where Stanton had parked his car. He opened the door for Jib and then they both saw the Stirlings, supremely unconscious of being observed, walking arm in arm up the long hill toward their own house.

For a moment both Jib and Stanton stood quite still and then she looked up at him. "Next to getting engaged to you," she said softly, "knowing them has been the greatest thing of all."

Stanton looked after the Stirlings and nodded. "You're absolutely right," he said. "Two marvelously good and totally unalike people who have been deeply in love with one another for over twenty-five years are important. But even Miss Loopy won't mention that."